SEAT 97

Wrong place, wrong time:
the mystery of a very public murder

TONY BASSETT

THE BOOK FOLKS

Published by The Book Folks

London, 2023

This book is a work of fiction. Names, characters, businesses, organizations, places and events are either the product of the author's imagination or are used fictitiously. Any resemblance to actual persons, living or dead, events or locales is entirely coincidental. The spelling is British English.

ISBN 978-1-80462-077-9

www.thebookfolks.com

SEAT 97 is a thrilling standalone mystery by Tony Bassett. Details about the author's other crime fiction titles can be found at the back of this book.

Chapter 1

The assassin slid his sleek, silver Porsche Boxster into the narrow Victorian mews and switched off his Miles Davis CD. He reached into the glovebox and pulled out his favourite toy – a rare 92S Beretta.

'This should be child's play,' he muttered as he cut the engine.

He checked his watch. It was just before 7 p.m. and still light. Sunset wasn't for a while yet. Time to get ready, he thought as he put on a pair of black leather gloves and screwed the silencer into place.

He loaded ten rounds in the magazine and put the safety catch on. Then he climbed out, opened the front boot and concealed the gun beneath the spanners and wrenches in his plumber's bag.

The car was parked between two rows of charming, two-storey houses. It was just a brief walk from there to the concert hall, where he would carry out his mission.

He smiled to himself because, a short distance away at the far end of the terraced street, lay the Kensington Road. Afterwards, he could join the fast-flowing traffic and disappear into the anonymity of the London night.

Slipping off his blazer and trousers as discreetly as possible, he slid his legs into light-grey overalls and buttoned them at the front.

As he fastened his tunic, his eyes rested briefly on the purple wisteria clambering up the wall of the white-washed house opposite. Red geraniums, crowded into two wooden tubs, added colour to the street, which lay in the shadow of the high-rise Royal College of Art building.

He glanced around. The cobbled lane was deserted.

After collecting his tool bag, he put on a grey, peaked cap, locked the car and set off at a brisk pace towards the Royal Albert Hall's southern entrance.

His brow was already glistening with perspiration. He ventured past the glass entrance doors and came to the stage door on his left. He waited there for an opportune moment, which came a few minutes later.

Some men wedged the two wooden doors open and began carrying in some camera equipment from a lorry. Then a minibus drew up, packed with chattering musicians.

A pert young woman with blonde hair was perched behind a reception desk on the left, protected by a glass screen, as he slipped through the doors.

'Yes. Can I help?'

The workman set down his bag. 'A leak in the toilets.'

Her face was blank. 'First I've heard of it.'

He frowned. 'Well, I got a call two hours ago.'

She shrugged. 'I'll have to call the manager. Where did you say the leak was?'

'Disabled toilet, behind Block L in the stalls.'

She dialled a number on her phone as two men shuffled in, wheeling a trolley laden with sandwiches and desserts, all wrapped in cellophane.

'Oh thanks, lads,' he joked. 'I'll take my supper in the champagne bar.' The two men ignored him.

'Special order from Miss Kay's dressing room,' one of the trolley men announced. Recognising their lapel badges, she waved them through the turnstile before her call was answered.

'Is Graham there?' she asked. 'Do you know where he is?'

Two other men with badges plodded into the reception area, carrying flowers. She beckoned them through as well while the musicians began filing in.

'Can you ask him to call me?' she asked, swivelling to face the wall.

By the time she turned back, the assassin had slipped through the barrier along with the flowers.

'What the hell?' she cried as he disappeared from view.

* * *

While the receptionist desperately continued calling the deputy manager, ticket holders in the auditorium were beginning to take their seats.

Nick Colton, a journalist on *The Post* newspaper, and his wife Greta had arrived early to avoid any last-minute rush.

They were sitting near the back of the stalls but nonetheless had a clear view of the stage.

A few minutes after they took their seats in Block L, a stout man clutching a ticket could be seen stepping gingerly down the aisle, peering at the end of every row. He was in his mid-forties with receding greyish hair held back in a ponytail, and was wearing gold-rimmed glasses.

'Oh, the view's just as good from here,' the man said, while nodding at the couple and smiling.

The stranger gazed around the vast arena until his eyes finally settled on the stage.

'Yes, this will be fantastic.' He peeled off his jacket, placing it on the empty aisle seat beside him, and settled himself down beside Colton.

'I've just switched seats,' he informed the couple.

Greta, a slim, olive-skinned brunette, leaned forward and smiled at the man. 'Oh really?'

'Yes, I was sitting over on the other side of the hall a few minutes ago. Then this young couple arrived. They said they'd made a late booking and failed to get two seats together. The woman had J51 while I had J50. She asked would I mind swapping tickets so they could sit together. I felt sorry for them. You pay all this money and want to sit together, don't you, if you're a couple?'

Colton frowned. 'So, this seat you've taken here, L97, was originally the boyfriend's seat?' he asked.

'That's right. The view is just as good though. It's also near the bar and toilets.' He showed him his ticket, which stated, 'Door 8. Stalls L. Row 7. Seat 97.''

Colton, who'd just celebrated his thirty-eighth birthday, tutted. 'I think he should buy you a drink in the interval for doing that.'

Greta, two years his junior, bent forward again. 'Is that the couple you mean?'

A blonde woman in a black dress several blocks of seats away was waving her hand in gratitude. Beside her was a ginger-haired man with wire-framed glasses in a blue shirt and jeans.

The man squinted across at the couple. 'Yes. That's them.'

As he waved back, Colton noticed a Cartier watch on the man's wrist.

More and more fans of the American soul singer Loretta Kay were drifting in. It was now just after seven o'clock. The show was due to start in less than an hour.

'I'm glad we came early,' Greta remarked. 'It's good to miss the crowds.'

Colton, who was slim with short, dark hair and a studious look, grinned. 'When we were in the bar a few minutes ago, I overheard someone say that Loretta's concerts rarely begin on time, so we may have a long wait.'

He gazed round. One by one, or in pairs, ticket holders were arriving and filling nearby seats.

'You a big fan?' Colton asked the newcomer. He gazed intently at the man's chocolate brown eyes which lay at the centre of a slightly podgy face.

'You could say that. I've travelled all over the world to see her. She was sensational when I saw her at a concert in Atlantic City last year. Afterwards she signed her autobiography for me.'

Greta peered across. 'What did she write?'

'Oh just, "To David, my number one fan. All my love now and always, Loretta Kay." I've got all her albums. Do you know that, over the years, I've seen her in America, Germany and Britain? If she sees me, she always remembers my name.'

Colton smiled. 'It's great to have an interest like that.'

'She's a living legend,' he continued. 'She may be in her late sixties now, but she's note perfect.'

'What's your favourite song of hers?' asked Greta.

'It's probably *End of The Dance*.' He sighed. 'Unfortunately, my wife's not a fan.'

'That's a pity,' Greta replied, gazing over her left shoulder to watch for any new arrivals.

As she did so, she caught a glimpse of a man through a gap in the tall, red velvet curtains that hung near the exit behind them. Tall and bearded, he was wearing grey overalls with a peaked cap and seemed out of place among the well-dressed music fans searching for seats. He was just a few feet away and staring towards her. Embarrassed, she quickly averted her gaze.

'What's your wife's choice in music?' Colton asked.

David never replied. At that moment, the couple were startled by the muffled sound of a gunshot behind them. It was followed by two more in quick succession.

Concertgoers nearby screamed. Some leaped from their seats. Security staff in the gangways raced around like rookie sailors in a cyclone. Two of them ventured bravely in the direction of the noise.

Greta shrieked and sat trembling in her light-green dress. Colton gazed about him in shock. Loretta Kay's most loyal fan slumped forward in his seat with the grace of a toppled statue. As his head struck the seat in front, blood began to drip from his skull. His dislodged glasses slipped down his face and dropped to the floor. He emitted a croaking noise.

Colton bent down anxiously and listened. The man was trying to speak. The faint words sounded like, 'Please help me.' But nothing more passed his lips.

'My God!' he whispered to Greta as other concertgoers stared in their direction. 'I think he's dead.'

Chapter 2

'Dio mio!' cried Greta as blood trickled down seat L97 and formed a pool on the blush-coloured carpet. Colton stretched his right arm round the man's chest and gently returned him to his seat. The man's head rolled back, his eyes open and lifeless. His arms lay still.

Raised voices echoed round the auditorium. Some of the audience raised their hands in horror. Some remained rigid in their seats, transfixed by shock.

Greta was so frightened she was nearly sick, and crouched down on the carpet. Her husband handed her a white handkerchief. Then, as she seemed to recover, he helped her to stand and wrapped his arms around her. He hugged her while, together, they stared down at David's body.

For a moment, Colton felt himself standing as still and expressionless as the statue of the Prince Consort outside. He'd written much over the years about violent death in his newspaper, but he'd never witnessed it in real life before.

Even when his mother had died suddenly, he'd recoiled at the suggestion he might view the body.

The cold reality of the present tragedy dawned on him. Other concert fans were rushing to the dead man's side.

He stared into Greta's appalled face.

'What the hell happened?'

'Nick, there was a man in a grey uniform and cap looking through the curtains behind us. He was staring at us. I'm sure he pointed something. It could have been a gun.' She gasped and began sobbing.

As a Fleet Street reporter, his first thought was, 'This is a cracking good story. I better ring the bloody news desk.' Then he had another thought.

He released his embrace and stepped round the body before reaching the aisle.

'Back in a minute,' he shouted as well-meaning audience members, unaware the man's life had ebbed away, rushed to see if they could stem the blood.

'Nick, where are you going?'

'To find the man you saw.'

He ran along the walkway, passing several access doors that led to the stalls, until he reached the main south exit.

'A grey uniform and cap,' he repeated to himself.

He dashed outside onto the stone concourse and caught a glimpse of a man in grey. He was running away from the hall clasping a tool bag.

As he sprinted along the pavement, Colton guessed the singer known in the press as the 'Sovereign of Soul' would be unable to perform that evening.

But he was not concerned about their evening being ruined. He was intent on following the man.

His quarry remained in sight as he hurried past the south-western side of the hall and passed the Imperial College Union building on his left. He observed the man was wearing distinctive, black work-boots with red laces. He pursued him past a row of five-storey mansion blocks in Kensington Gore until, finally, they arrived in a mews.

The man in grey, apparently unaware he was being followed, opened the front boot of his car and placed his bag inside. Then he jumped into the driver's seat.

Colton darted to the passenger window and tapped on the glass. The driver had piercing blue eyes and a short, dark, goatee beard. He'd removed his cap to reveal a mop of black hair.

The journalist could see the driver was in no mood to answer questions. He started the car and the engine purred into life. Colton slipped his phone from the breast pocket of his grey shirt and hunted for the camera button.

But, before he could snatch an image of the driver, the car had careered away up the lane. He managed to take just a single shot of the speeding Porsche before noting down its registration.

Then, as he stood alone on the cobbled street between two tubs of red geraniums, he drafted the first few sentences of a news report and then called his newspaper, *The Post*.

'News desk,' growled the voice of the night news editor.

'It's Nick. Nick Colton.'

'Hello, mate. You were on days. Haven't you got a home to go to?'

'You're right, I was working earlier. Listen, I'm at the Albert Hall. A guy in the audience has been shot.'

'Yes, there's something on Twitter about it. I've sent Luke Foster down. He should be there in forty minutes. Can you link up with him?'

'Yes, no problem. But listen. I was right there when it happened. The guy was sitting next to me, for God's sake.' His breathing was erratic. The dark reality of the gruesome crime was swirling through his mind.

'You all right, mate?' the desk man asked.

'Yes, I'll be OK, but the shock's still with me.'

'I'm not surprised. You sure you're all right?'

'Yes. I can file some copy straight away, if you like.'

'Good man.'

Within minutes, the call had been transferred to one of the staff, who listened carefully and typed as Colton slowly dictated. His report began,

> *This reporter witnessed a brutal murder last night when a concertgoer was shot dead in the seat next to mine at London's Royal Albert Hall. I chased the killer into the street after the brazen attack and watched as he drove away in a silver Porsche.*

He stated the victim's name was David, was in his forties, lived in London and he was an avid fan of the singer Loretta Kay.

He also described how the suspect was wearing grey overalls. Then he sent his image of the car to the picture desk.

When he returned to the hall's south entrance, Colton discovered a police cordon had been set up. Two harassed policewomen were having to cope with a huge crowd of disgruntled Loretta Kay fans. He'd been working on newspapers for fifteen years, but he'd never seen such a smartly dressed rabble, he thought.

He guessed immediately that, as he'd feared, the sell-out concert had been abandoned.

'I've paid a hundred and thirty pounds for tickets,' one man shouted across the cordon.

'They'll start paying out refunds tomorrow,' a policewoman called back.

Colton pushed his way through the throng and waved his ticket in front of the younger constable, who had short, blonde hair and a harassed expression. 'Can you let me through? I've got a ticket. I only slipped out for a moment.'

He added in a low voice, 'I know about the incident. I was right there when it happened.'

'You were? Why didn't you say so? Let me see your ticket. All right. Go to the stalls and look for Block L. One of our detectives will need to speak to you. Just show them the ticket.'

She raised the tape and he ducked underneath.

The entrance to their block was by now cordoned off. A policeman was standing in front of the doors. Colton made his way instead towards the entrance to Block J, but found a melee of concertgoers blocking the corridor.

Chaos reigned. Stewards in red jackets were appealing for ticket holders to be patient. For a while, he was unable to make his way through. Then he reached the doorway and spotted Greta's green dress.

'Not so fast, sunshine,' said a burly policeman who was standing at the entrance alongside a policewoman. 'You can't go in there.'

Colton grimaced. 'I was sitting next to the guy who was shot. I've just been away for ten minutes.'

'What's your name, sir?'

'Nick Colton.'

'Would you wait there, sir?'

The constable ventured into the auditorium and approached a man in his mid-forties with untidy, dark hair who was speaking to Greta. The pair were standing some distance away from the corpse, which was still lying outstretched in seat L97. A forensic team in white clothing were huddled round it.

Greta's companion was dressed in a crumpled grey suit. His purple tie was hanging loosely round his neck. He moved away from Greta briefly to exchange words with the constable. Then he beckoned the journalist inside and beamed at him.

'Mr Colton?' he asked. 'DCI Haynes. I'm in charge of the investigation.'

'Pleased to meet you,' he replied, shaking the chief inspector's hand. 'Has my wife filled you in on what we saw?'

'Yes, you were sitting next to her when this terrible incident happened?'

'That's right. I'd been chatting to the victim.'

Haynes spoke with a pronounced London accent and gave the air of being an experienced, long-serving policeman.

'So I understand,' he said. 'Look, I've got a few things to ask you.'

Greta was sitting at the end of one of the rows of seats as Colton stepped towards her. She leaped up and hugged her husband, her face alive with questions. 'What happened? Did you see the man? You all right?'

'Yeah, I saw him. He jumped into a car and drove off. I've got the number, but it probably won't help. Probably stolen.' He paused before adding, 'Poor David's still there in his seat.'

'After you went, people came over and tried to help,' said Greta. 'One was a doctor. He tried his best, but without any luck and David was – how do you say? – declared dead.'

'Now, Mr Colton,' said the chief inspector as he joined them. 'Your good lady's been telling me you got into conversation with the deceased. Is that right?' He took a small, black notebook from his trouser pocket and a pen from his shirt pocket.

'Yes,' said Colton. 'Only a few of the seats had been filled at seven o'clock when he came over and sat right next to me. I suppose it seemed only natural that we should get into conversation.'

Colton's slim face adopted a sterner tone as he leaned against the end seat. He began explaining what happened whilst the detective assiduously jotted all the details down.

'Was anyone else sitting in your row?' Haynes asked.

'There was a couple at the far end of the row, but I didn't pay them much attention.'

'Anyone sitting in front or behind?'

'No. No one.'

'Mrs Colton noticed a man in grey overalls in the doorway.'

'Yes.'

'You didn't see him yourself?'

'No. I was engrossed in conversation with David. To be honest, I feel lucky in a way.'

Haynes's face looked blank. 'Lucky?'

'Yes. A foot or two further over and that would have been me lying sprawled out with a bullet in my head.'

'I see what you mean. Do you have any enemies then, Mr Colton?'

'I expect so.' Then the stark truth of what he'd just said sank home. Maybe the bullet had been intended for him.

Chapter 3

Detective Chief Inspector Harry Haynes was shaking his head. 'Why should this gangster who fired his gun in a crowded arena have been targeting you, Mr Colton?'

Greta interrupted. 'Nick's a journalist.'

'Oh, I see. Who do you work for, Mr Colton?'

'I'm a crime reporter at *The Post*.'

'*The Post*, eh? I expect you make a lot of enemies in your line of work.'

'A few. Some people harbour a lifelong grudge if you simply spell their name wrong. Look, Chief Inspector, did Greta explain why I went outside?'

'Yes, she did.'

'Sorry, excuse me,' the reporter said, moving a short distance away from the pair. With his phone clasped to his ear, he answered, 'Colton?'

'Why the hell didn't you come back to the desk after filing?' demanded the enraged night news editor.

'Sorry, mate. It's manic down here.'

'Where did you get that line about the Porsche? The cops are playing it down. They also deny they're searching for a man in grey overalls. Are you sure about all this stuff you filed?'

'Yes, definitely. My wife saw him.'

'With a gun?'

'Well, it looked like a gun to her.'

'You see, that's the problem we've got. It looked like a gun to her. Anyway, Luke's hunting for you, so get your skates on.' Then he hung up.

Chief Inspector Haynes was watching him intently as he walked back. 'What kind of Porsche was it?'

'A Boxster, I think, but I'm not well up on cars. He put his tool bag in the front boot and drove off. He completely ignored my attempts to attract his attention, but I've got the registration. If you give me your book, I'll write it down for you.'

Haynes handed over his notebook. Colton jotted the number down and handed it back.

'Seems like the car was originally registered in Kent, judging by the first two letters,' he told the detective. 'Probably stolen.'

'You may well be right, Mr Colton.'

Greta stood up, pale and weary. 'Do you mind if I go to the ladies?' she asked the chief inspector.

'No problem. The constable at the door will show you where it is.'

She sidled away, glancing briefly at her husband as she went.

'Now your wife's left us, I have to say I'm not sure if her account of the man she saw is valid. I'm afraid people imagine all kinds of things at a moment of great stress. Over the past hour, we've received reports of all manner of people who were acting suspiciously when the gun went off.'

Colton shrugged as the detective continued, 'We don't want to create a picture in the public mind of the man you followed being the prime suspect when the real killer's someone else entirely. We must keep an open mind.'

The journalist stroked his chin. 'Won't the guy running away have been caught on CCTV?'

'It's possible. We'll have people going through the footage.'

'What other suspects have you got?'

Haynes shook his head. 'I can't tell you that, obviously, particularly since you're a journalist. And I should mention right away that I'd be extremely annoyed if any piece of the information I've given you over the past few minutes should appear in your newspaper.'

Colton's eyes twinkled mischievously. 'You haven't told me anything yet, Chief Inspector. I've been the one recounting what I know.'

'Fair enough,' the chief inspector said. 'So long as that's understood. I don't want to prejudice our investigation. Look, thank you for your information about the man you followed. It may turn out to be helpful. And if he was responsible for the death, you obviously acted very bravely in pursuing him. He could have turned the gun on you. Thank you also for the car number. You never know, it might lead us somewhere.'

Colton was pensive. 'What about the change of seats? Is it possible the bullet was meant for the guy who was originally booked to sit in seat L97?'

The chief inspector shook his head. 'I don't think that's necessarily significant. That sort of thing goes on all the time – switching tickets and seats.'

The journalist realized Haynes, who had such a relaxed style, knew more than he was letting on. Perhaps his team already knew the identity of the gunman. Perhaps they had already identified the victim. Perhaps it was no surprise to him that David had ended his days in a pool of blood.

He studied the detective's eyes, searching for any signs of what Haynes was thinking. 'So, you don't think the gunman's real target was the man in Block J who swapped seats? You don't think he shot the wrong man?'

Haynes shook his head again. 'I doubt very much whether the guy – or woman – who carried out the shooting made a mistake. I've investigated countless murders in the capital.

'This is just another nasty attack. Whoever it was, I doubt very much whether they followed seat numbers. I believe the killer approached the task by using his eyes – using the victim's appearance, not seat numbers. After all, he was firing at close range under the glare of the lights.'

Having made a note of Colton's address and phone number, Haynes added, 'You and your wife are key witnesses. So don't leave town.'

A murmur of voices floated up from the café bar as the couple left the auditorium. The corridor was eerily quiet before they went downstairs to the foyer and noticed there was still a crowd of people milling around behind the cordon outside.

Most of the soul fans had departed. They'd been replaced by a swarm of news reporters, photographers, and TV crews.

As the pair emerged in the warm air of the June evening, Colton felt a pat on the shoulder. He turned to be greeted by his colleague Luke Foster, who was grinning broadly.

'Bloody hell, Nick. You like to get close to the action.'

He smiled back. 'Too bloody close. But it makes a change for me to be first on the scene, doesn't it?'

'Yes, I've known you turn up on a job two hours late.'

He was pleased to meet up with his younger colleague.

'Have you met Greta?'

Foster, who was tall, smartly dressed in a grey suit and with short, spiky hair, glanced at her rather shyly. 'Don't think I've had the pleasure. This must be the beautiful Italian lady I've heard about. I'm Luke,' he said, shaking her hand.

Colton's smile faded. 'What's the score out here?'

'A woman from Press Bureau is around somewhere. She's going to give us an update. The desk want you to file a first-person piece for the final edition – you know, your shock at witnessing the shooting, how you and Greta identified the gunman, and how you pursued him.'

Greta frowned as she eyed the nearby crowd of reporters. 'You two can leave me out of this. Don't put me in the paper.'

Colton stretched out his hands in a calming gesture. 'It's all right, darling. I don't need to mention you. Listen, I'd better go and file something to keep the night news editor sweet.'

Greta and Foster stood chatting as Colton sat on the wall and typed his report into his phone. Moments after he had sent it across to his news desk, the press officer from Scotland Yard appeared from behind the barrier.

'I've just got a brief statement,' the woman announced solemnly as the two reporters joined their colleagues. 'The Metropolitan Police have been alerted that, at approximately a quarter past seven this evening, a man attending the Royal Albert Hall in Kensington for a concert was shot dead. Police and ambulance crews attended. The victim of the shooting was pronounced dead soon afterwards by a doctor.

'The victim was in his forties and is believed to be from London. We're not naming him until next of kin have been informed.

'The American soul singer Loretta Kay had been due to give the second of two performances at the venue, beginning at 8 p.m. On the advice of police, the general manager decided to cancel the evening's show. That's the end of the statement.'

Press reporters began firing questions. Did she have any information about the gunman? Had Loretta Kay made any comment? Could she confirm the man's first name was David? The press officer ignored all the questions.

Foster stretched forward in an effort to see the woman's face. 'Do police believe the incident may be gang-related?' he asked.

'That's one of several theories detectives are working on,' she replied. 'Well, that's it for the moment. Please call us for any further updates.' Then she disappeared into the building.

'Come on,' said Greta, tugging her husband's arm. 'We've spent enough time here. Let's get a drink.'

'Where are you thinking of?' asked Foster.

'We passed a pub called The Queen's Arms on the way here,' said Colton. 'It's in Queen's Gate Mews.'

'Sounds ideal,' said Foster. 'I'll call the desk and, if things have quietened down, I'll join you. I just think I ought to stay here for the moment – just in case.'

'That's great, Luke. Give me a bell if there's any problem with the piece I sent over,' said Colton.

Chapter 4

Exhausted after the arduous events of the night, the Coltons reached their small Victorian terraced house in south-east London just before midnight. Bought with a huge mortgage and a deposit supplied by Greta's father, the two-bedroom house in a quiet close had been their home for the past three years.

Colton stepped past the mauve asters and blue clematis flowers in their small front garden, and turned the key in the lock.

Greta's mother, Carlotta, had been peering through the bay window of their through-lounge after a night spent watching television.

'Tutto bene, Mamma?' asked Greta as they walked in from the narrow hallway.

'Don't worry. Everything is fine,' replied the stern-faced lady, who was wearing no make-up and had her dark hair drawn back and tied in a bun. 'How was the show?'

Greta gave her a hug. 'Didn't you watch the news, Mamma? The concert was stopped.'

'What? You go ten miles to see the show and they cancel? Your first night out in weeks.'

'Mamma, there was a shooting. A man was killed.'

'What happened?'

Colton fetched their babysitter's coat and scarf from the hall. 'Come on, Mrs Bellini. I'll tell you about it in the car. It's late. I'd better drive you back to Blackheath.'

After he'd returned from driving Carlotta home, Colton relaxed on their brown leather sofa and, while Greta made them both a mug of hot chocolate, he checked online news reports on his tablet.

Rival newspapers were speculating on the identity of the dead man. Two suggested he was a wealthy accountant or stockbroker. His own paper, *The Post*, carried his personal account of witnessing the shooting.

Greta interrupted his concentration. She placed their two drinks on the coffee table before snuggling next to him. He gave her a light peck on the cheek, and she responded with a long, lingering kiss.

'What a terrible night, Nick,' she sighed. 'I'll never forget seeing that man in the doorway. I'm sure his face will come back to haunt me in my dreams.'

He gazed down at the attractive face beneath the curly hair.

'Greta, the detective cast doubt on your story while you were in the ladies. Other witnesses have come forward, making other claims about who the gunman was.'

'Nick, you've got to believe me. I saw the man with my own eyes. I can still see him now – his cap, his beard and his staring eyes. You believe me, don't you?'

'Of course. I don't know why the detective doesn't believe you.'

'The whole incident was very frightening. The man who died… he was such a nice guy.' She was sobbing now. He reached for some tissues on the table and handed her one.

'One of the papers says that, according to local sources, the dead man's name was David Barron from North London,' he informed her.

'I feel so sorry for his wife,' she continued, wiping her eyes. 'Do you know, Nick, I'd been so looking forward to seeing Loretta Kay and her band? We so rarely go out and for the evening to be cut short in that way… I know you had to stay and do your job, but as soon as I left the Albert Hall and had that quick drink, I just wanted to get home.'

'I know,' he replied. 'What I don't understand is, why shoot a man in a public place like that? There were potential witnesses. The gunman had no guarantee of a quick escape. Why not shoot the victim on the way to or from the theatre? Or shoot him outside his home or business? It doesn't make sense.'

Greta stroked her chin. 'I've been thinking about that as well. I think the answer may be because they knew he'd be there. Maybe whoever it was didn't know his home or work address. If he came by car, maybe they didn't know what sort of car.'

He nodded. 'I see what you mean. He was a big fan of Loretta Kay. Maybe they found out from the booking office that he had a ticket, and a decision was made that that should be the place of execution… Or maybe it was done in public as a warning to others.'

'Oh God, Nick. I don't like thinking about it.'

She leaned forward and sipped her drink. 'Nick, what about the guy who took the dead man's ticket? What was it, J20?'

'The man with ginger hair who waved? His ticket was J50, if my memory's right.'

'Do you think the dead man was killed by mistake?' she asked.

'And that the man in Block J was the real target?' He sipped his drink. 'Yes, it's possible. But the police don't seem to have much faith in our story. That detective claimed people often swap tickets and reckons the gunman must have known how to recognise his intended victim. But it's possible he may have killed the wrong man. I certainly don't think the bullet was intended for me, although even that crossed my mind earlier on.'

Greta looked up at him and then lowered her eyes again. 'Maybe we should find that couple.'

'You and me? Greta, I've got a busy week ahead of me and the chances of finding them are so slim.'

'If the police don't believe us, maybe their investigation will stall.'

'I don't know, Greta. Perhaps we should leave it all to the police. Clemmie on the news desk wants to talk to me tomorrow. She might think that *The Post* can get some more mileage out of the story. If so, she could give me a free rein to pursue it. I might get sent back to the hall and do some digging.'

Greta drank some more of her chocolate. 'Is there anything more online about the shooting?'

He tapped away on his tablet. 'The piece here says Loretta Kay's apologised to fans. The organisers say they were forced to follow police advice and cancel. They hope to reschedule the concert. Staff at the hall are arranging refunds. Oh, and it seems our friend was a wealthy guy.'

'David?'

'Yes.'

'What sort of a business?'

'Some kind of financial guru.'

'Guru? What is this?'

'A money wizard. An accountant.'

'Papa always says big trouble follows big money.'

'Your papa's right.'

The hall door creaked open. A small boy in blue pyjamas clutching a teddy bear stood in the doorway.

'Mummy, were you crying?' he asked.

His mother put her drink down and rushed to him, giving him a reassuring hug.

'Yes, darling,' she told her seven-year-old son, ruffling his curly black hair. 'It's all right now. I was just crying over something sad.'

Colton turned and waved to his son. 'Riccardo, it's very late.'

'What was the sad thing that made you cry, Mummy?' the child asked.

'It doesn't matter,' his father insisted. 'Mummy's stopped crying now. Let's all get to bed.'

But that night Colton found it impossible to sleep. He hadn't mentioned to his wife that the image of the dead man's bloodied face kept looming in his mind like a scene from a horror movie. He glanced across at Greta. She was restless too. However, an hour before daybreak, exhaustion overcame them both and they fell into a deep slumber.

Chapter 5

The editorial offices of *The Post* newspaper were based in a tranquil waterside location in London's Docklands. Staff commonly spied families of ducks waddling across the cobbled street and slithering into the dark waters while boats jerked and jolted along the quayside.

Nick Colton felt tired as he made his way up the stairs to the first-floor newsroom. He'd gone to bed late and had had only three hours' sleep after the grim events of the night before. He'd been tempted to call in sick, but Greta had finally coaxed him into going in.

On his way into work on the train, he'd read the latest online accounts of the shooting. One newspaper, the *Daily Graphic*, carried a report headlined, 'Bogus workman clue to hall shooting.' It reported that a man dressed as a tradesman had tricked his way into the hall.

He stopped on the stairway of the ten-year-old building at Bargemaster Quay for a moment to watch the rippling water glinting in the sunlight in the dock below. Then, just after 10 a.m., he climbed to the landing, pushed his way through the double doors and entered the vast, open-plan office.

Several colleagues greeted him with cheers and friendly smiles as he made his way to his desk in the centre of the room and removed his jacket. There were also a few whispered remarks and some muffled laughter. After he'd placed his jacket on the back of his chair, burly photographer Tommy Mundon walked past with several cameras strapped around his shoulders.

'I hear they're turning part of the Albert Hall into a shooting gallery,' he quipped.

Colton stood up and gave the grinning forty-five-year-old, who was over six foot tall, a good-natured punch on the shoulder. 'You won't win a joke of the month contest with that,' he said.

Luke Foster, who sat three desks away, joked, 'The plumber got his lines crossed when they told him, "Shoot up the back of the hall and fix the toilet."'

A few colleagues laughed, but Colton himself was still shaken by the events of the previous night. He was unable to appreciate their gallows humour.

Within minutes, the laughter dissipated, and the room reverberated instead with the customary sounds of phone conversations and fingers tapping on keyboards.

Colton spent more than an hour carrying out research at Companies House by phone and online. He quickly discovered the late accountant's firm, Barron & Partners, was a thriving business which had been making a healthy profit over the past three years.

Then, just before midday, as he began scrolling through press agency news reports on his computer, he was interrupted by the silky, amiable tones of his fellow reporter, blonde-haired Katie McMillen. Her desk abutted his.

'It sounds horrible,' she remarked as she peered round the side of her computer. 'You know, what happened last night.' She wore bright red lipstick and appeared as dazzling as a Hawaiian sunrise in a red and green floral dress.

'It was,' he admitted.

'I loved your first-person piece. It was alarming but also very moving. Your poor wife must have been in pieces.'

'We both were,' he whispered.

'Sorry to break in,' announced a voice behind him. It was the news editor, Clemmie Jones.

'Nick, are you all right after last night?' she asked as McMillen returned to her desk.

'Yes, I'm fine. We're both fine. It was a little hair-raising.'

'I'm sure,' she said sympathetically. 'Do you need any time off?'

'No. There's no need for that. I want to keep working. It'll take my mind off it, if anything.'

'That's the spirit,' said Jones. 'Nick, could you come into my office? I need to brief you on something.'

Moments later, she was sitting behind her mahogany desk in a room partitioned off from the main newsroom. He was relaxing on a vinyl bench settee at the side of her office.

'Nick, I want to involve you in a story we've been working on for some time. It's being spearheaded by the investigations department, but there's a reason why your assistance is required. The editor says we need a good, solid, experienced reporter like you to make sure the whole thing's copper-bottomed.'

Colton smiled. 'I'd be glad to help if I can, Clemmie. The only thing is that–'

'You'd rather stick to covering crime?'

'No, it's not that. It's just that, since I was personally involved in the Albert Hall shooting, I'd like to carry on with that if I could. You know, interviewing the widow, family members – that sort of thing.'

'No problem. This investigation's more long-term. But we need someone to check out a few facts. It's going to be a major story and we have to make sure our lawyers are happy.'

He shrugged. 'All right, if it doesn't prevent me from following the Barron story, no problem.'

'Good, then I'll tell you a little about it. But this will have to remain totally hush-hush.'

'Of course.'

'You know of the Cabinet minister Oliver Polebrook?'

'Yes. Isn't he the minister for the Cabinet Office and Chancellor of the Duchy of Lancaster?'

'You're well informed, Nick. Yes, he is. Well, a young woman came to see us three months ago with information about him.'

'Asking for money, I expect.'

'Not at first. Anyway, as soon as I heard a little about it, I realized it wasn't a story for the news desk and I put her in touch with the investigations team.'

Colton leaned back on the couch so that his head rested on the partition wall. 'So, what's this intriguing information then?'

'She claims that, while a member of the Conservative Party in West London, the minister took advantage of her, seduced her and carried on a twelve-month affair with her.'

Colton frowned. 'He's married, isn't he?'

'Yes, with three teenage children. This could be a major political story, Nick, if all the facts are right. Stories like this have been known to end a politician's career or even bring down governments.'

'So why can't Chris Lane and his team at the investigations department deal with the story?'

'Well, don't let this go any further, but the editor's got misgivings about one of the two reporters assigned to the case. He specifically asked me to have a word with you as a trusted newsman. He wants you to check on part of the story to make sure we've got the facts straight and we're not going to open ourselves up to any libel action.'

He grinned. He was used to Clemmie Jones bestowing faint praise on members of her team to get her way.

'All right. I'll give it my best shot.'

'Great. That's what I like to hear. I'll give Chris a call and tell him you're on board. The main thing is he wants you to find the house in West London where the couple are meant to have conducted their dalliances…'

'Their romantic trysts.'

'Precisely. This woman – her name's Sadie Robinson and she's twenty-four years younger than the minister – has made certain claims about the house and its contents. You'll be required to go round there and take a careful note of what's there and file a memo. You know, just to make sure that that part of the story's kosher.'

'And there's no hurry for this? It'll fit around my other commitments?'

'That's right. So long as you let Chris have something in writing in the next ten days or so.'

'Doesn't sound too difficult. I'll liaise with Chris and probably do it sometime next week.'

'Excellent.'

* * *

As the morning wore on, Colton made a call to a police contact based in Islington. Peter Moore was a detective sergeant and key contact that he had been cultivating as an informant since they had first met in a Southwark pub years before. The pub was a regular CID haunt. The pair had struck up a conversation in the bar one evening which had led to friendship.

The thirty-nine-year-old Scotsman was now a close confidant and Colton always made sure to remember Peter at Christmas.

'I canna talk long, Nick,' said Moore as he answered the phone. 'You'll be inquiring about the Albert Hall shooting, no doubt.'

'That's right, Peter. Have they traced the car?'

'Not yet, despite the publicity.'

'Peter, can you do me a favour? Can you let me know if anything pops up on CCTV at the hall or on the mobile network?'

'You're asking a lot, you know that.'

'I've got a personal stake in finding out what happened. My wife and I were both right there.'

'I know. Must have had a deep effect. I'll do me best, Nick. Meanwhile, there's one snippet I can pass on. The dead guy was having marriage problems.'

Chapter 6

It took Nick Colton nearly two hours to reach the affluent London suburb of Totteridge later that morning. His office had furnished him with David Barron's home address, and he was keen to speak to his widow, Deborah.

He was always reluctant to call on a newly bereaved person, but took the view that, apart from the police, someone had to be the first to ask questions about a death. If there's a matter weighing on someone's mind, it's probably good therapy to talk about it.

And in the event of a death occasioned by crime, publicity about the deceased might even help resolve it and bring early closure. So, albeit with a heavy heart, he drove into the suburb.

The Barrons' home, Orchard House in Pine Tree Avenue, was a Grade II-listed seven-bedroom home close to a golf course. The house, based on an Arts and Crafts style of architecture, was nestled in landscaped grounds behind a red brick wall. A single-storey annexe, built in similar style, was set around thirty metres back from the main house.

Although only ten miles from the centre of London, he knew he was close to the open countryside of Hertfordshire as he entered the quiet, tree-lined street at just after two o'clock. He'd arranged to meet photographer Tommy Mundon near the house and quickly recognised the photographer's black BMW, which was parked a short distance from the Barrons' entrance.

Mundon got out and wandered over as Colton parked his car and wound down the driver's window.

'Are you trying to grow a beard, young Colton, or has your shaver run out of batteries?' asked Mundon.

'I'm growing a beard,' Colton admitted as he stroked his whiskery chin.

'I tell you what,' Mundon continued, 'you've got to have some moolah to live round here. I've had a decko over the wall. They've got a swimming pool and a tennis court.'

'Very nice, Tommy. I've heard, if you do a few more years on *The Post*, you'll be able to afford a place like this.'

Mundon sneered. 'If I did thirty years, this would be way out of my league. Anyway, shall we make ourselves known?'

Colton locked his aging blue Volvo XC90 car, and the pair walked up to the Barrons' black timber gates. They'd been expecting other press reporters and photographers to be outside, but they seemed to be alone. Colton pressed an intercom button on the wall. There was no response.

As he stood back and gazed around, a grey car approached. Its female driver wound down the passenger window and peered out. He recognised her as Leyla Hussein, a reporter on the rival *Daily Graphic*.

'She's not speaking,' she yelled.

Colton walked across. 'How do you know, Leyla?'

'All the world and his wife have been up here trying. The PA girl's been around since seven o'clock.'

Colton eyed the photographer. 'Shall we leave it a few minutes?' His companion nodded and climbed back into his BMW.

Leyla beamed at him. 'Do you fancy a chat in the car?' She parked behind the Volvo. Colton ambled across and got into the passenger seat.

He yawned. He was still recovering from his late night in Kensington. 'Been here long?'

Her dark hair tumbled across her shoulders as she turned to him and laughed. 'Too long,' she asserted. 'I tell you what, though. This sure makes a change from some of the run-down hovels I've had to doorstep recently.'

A few minutes passed as they chatted about common acquaintances. Then Colton decided to have another attempt at speaking to Deborah Barron.

He collected his notebook from his car and then tapped on Mundon's window. Mundon spent a few moments deciding which cameras to bring. He selected two and then they both stepped across the road and pressed the intercom. This time they were in luck. A sultry female voice inquired, 'What do you want? If you're press, I've already made it clear I'm not making any comment.'

'I'm so sorry to trouble you, Mrs Barron,' Colton began. 'I was by your husband's side when he died. I'd very much like to speak to you if I could. I know it's an awful time.'

There was a brief pause. 'You're press?'

'Yes, Nick Colton from *The Post*. I was in the seat next to your husband at the Royal Albert Hall.'

'All right. I can spare a few minutes.'

'I've got a photographer with me, Tommy Mundon. Is it OK if he comes along?'

Another pause. 'You can both come in. But I'm not ready to have my picture taken. Is that understood?'

'Yes, thank you.'

The gates creaked open. Mundon turned and made a cheeky gesture to Leyla, thumbing his nose and wiggling his fingers before the two men walked inside the grounds.

They found themselves at the foot of a short gravel drive leading to the door of the house. On both sides were well-kept lawns, mature flower beds and a variety of shrubs and trees. The pool and tennis courts lay to the left of the house. Parked in front of the annexe on the right stood two gleaming cars – a black Mercedes-Benz E-Class and a red Ferrari. They were met at the door by a young woman with short, dark, spiky hair in her mid-twenties.

'Mr Colton?' she said. 'I'm the housekeeper. Mrs Barron says she'll see you in the living room. Would you come this way?'

The pair followed the scent of the housekeeper's musky perfume as she led them through a magnificent hallway with a vaulted ceiling and past a sweeping, cantilevered staircase.

'You're lucky. The relatives left an hour ago,' the woman remarked. He detected a faint accent, but he couldn't work out where she hailed from.

They passed along a corridor containing Lake District landscape paintings and photographs of American soul singers until they reached the large, sumptuous living room.

Colton noticed white and brown sofas arranged beside a white neo-classical marble fireplace, overshadowed by a crystal chandelier. In front of French doors which led to the rear garden stood a Regency-style mahogany dining table and Chippendale chairs. Fresh flowers, some open and some in bud, had been arranged in vases around the room.

A slim, attractive woman in her late thirties with long, blonde hair rose from the white sofa and walked across the red patterned carpet towards them. She was clutching a handkerchief in her left hand.

'Deborah Barron,' she announced with a faint smile. She was dressed glamorously in a purple top and light-blue ripped jeans that lent the impression of a younger woman. Her eyes were red, a sign she had been crying.

As she shook their hands, Colton again apologised for intruding at a time of grief.

'Don't worry. It's on my mind non-stop. Listen, I've turned all the other press people away. But I was intrigued when I heard your name. I've read your piece in *The Post*. The housekeeper went out and bought it for me this morning. Your account of what happened was very touching.'

'Thank you, Mrs Barron.'

'Would you both like to sit down?' she asked, directing them to the brown leather sofa. Mundon placed his cameras on the carpet as they both made themselves comfortable.

She continued, 'It must have been very frightening for you and your wife.'

'Yes, it was.'

Mundon's gravelly voice broke the tension. 'He looks too young to get hitched, don't you think?'

She laughed. 'I don't know what's "too young" these days. Anyway, could we start with you telling me more about what happened?'

Colton frowned. 'Well, I put some of it in my report. What I didn't mention is that your husband was originally seated on a different row. Not L97 at all. His ticket was for J50.'

'Why's that important?'

'Well, what happened was that another concertgoer hadn't been able to get a seat next to his girlfriend, so he asked David to swap seats – which he did.'

She looked as if someone had thrown cold water in her face. 'So you think maybe the bullet was intended for this other person?'

'Could be.'

Deborah sat down on the white leather settee, weeping. She wiped her eyes with her handkerchief. She reminded Colton of a lost child.

They noticed a half-empty bottle of white wine beside a full glass on the coffee table along with an unopened box of hand-made Belgian chocolates.

'You said in your report that you didn't see the gunman, but your partner did. Is that right?'

'Yes. My wife, Greta, spotted a man in overalls in the doorway. She thought, at the time, that he was staring at her. Perhaps he was staring at David. After David was shot, she said, "I'm sure he pointed something. It could have been a gun."'

Mundon glanced at Colton. 'Sounds like a case of after-thought to me. You know, you hear a gunshot. You think you know the direction the bullet came from. Your mind starts playing tricks. Was it a gun he was holding in his hand? It must have been because there was a gunshot,' he said.

Colton shook his head. 'Greta's not the kind of person who makes things up. If she saw something, she saw something.'

Deborah leaned back in her seat. 'What happened after he was shot?'

'Well, he slumped forward, so I gently lifted him back into his seat. It was then that we noticed blood trickling from the back of his head.'

Tears were once more slipping down Deborah's cheeks.

'Were there any last words?'

'His last words were, "Please help me."'

Deborah broke down uncontrollably, sobbing with her head in her hands. The pair were dismayed to see her so distraught.

'Would you like me to fetch the housekeeper?' Mundon asked.

Wiping her eyes, she said, 'No. I'll be fine in a moment. Forgive me.'

She rushed out of the room, dabbing her face with her handkerchief as she went. This gave them the opportunity to study their surroundings.

Mundon peered at his colleague. 'I'll tell you what I've noticed. There's pictures of the Lake District and Scotland all round. There's pictures of soul and blues singers. But there's no pictures of her old man or the pair of them together.'

'I'd noticed that as well.'

Colton was intrigued by the sight of an open laptop that was perched on the glass-topped table next to her wine. While keeping one eye on the doorway, he stood up and took a step towards the silver device. It seemed as though she'd been in the process of reading an email before they arrived. But, from his position, he could only read the words, *'I'm so glad we met. We seemed to click instantly. So looking forward to seeing you again'.* Mundon snatched hold of his colleague's shirt and pulled him back.

'She could come back at any minute,' he hissed. Then, as they gazed through the French doors at the timber-decked terrace, sweeping lawn and lily pond, they heard Deborah returning.

'I'm sorry. Just had to tidy myself up a bit,' she explained as she resumed her place on the settee. 'Now, where were we?'

Colton frowned. 'I was just telling you about your husband's final moments.'

'Yes, of course. I think I've heard enough about that for now. I was intrigued to hear about how you followed the man. Did you get a good view of his face?'

Colton nodded as he opened his notebook and took out a pen. 'He was taller than me. He had piercing blue eyes and a short, dark goatee beard. He also had a shock of curly, black hair.'

'So you'd recognise him if you saw him again?'

'If he looked like that. But obviously there's a good chance his hair and beard were false. Could even have had help with his face from a prosthetics artist. You can hardly breeze into the Royal Albert Hall with murder in mind if there's a chance you'll be recognised later.'

'It's a good point you make.'

'But assuming it wasn't a disguise, Mrs Barron, does that description – along with the fact he was driving a silver Porsche – mean anything to you? I mean, do you know anyone who might resemble that person?'

'No, not at all.'

'And can you think of anyone who might have any kind of motive at all for wanting your husband dead?'

Deborah gave a weak smile. 'The detective who came round last night was asking exactly the same questions.'

'DCI Haynes?'

'Yes, that was his name. No. I can't think of any reason why anyone would want to harm my husband.'

Chapter 7

'Can you tell me a little about your husband, Mrs Barron?' Colton asked.

Deborah sighed. 'Yes, he was brought up in Highgate, studied at the LSE and spent his whole life working as an accountant. For the last twenty years he's had his own business, Barron & Partners in North London.'

He smiled. 'He was obviously quite successful.'

'Yes, I suppose he was. He was also extremely kind, generous and, as far as I knew, he didn't have an enemy in the world. My whole life's completely shattered, and I don't know what I'm going to do without him. We met at a London nightclub, and I knew at once he was the guy for me. We married in Barnet seven years ago.

'To begin with, he was a wonderful husband. I don't mind showing you this. It's one of the birthday cards he sent me a few years back.'

She stepped over to a Regency sideboard near the fireplace, rummaged in a drawer and returned seconds later with a card emblazoned in red roses.

She handed it to him. 'See what he's written inside.'

Colton admired the neat lettering in which someone had written 'Doubt thou the stars are fire; Doubt that the sun doth move; Doubt truth to be a liar; But never doubt I love.'

He glanced up. 'That's from Hamlet, isn't it?'

'That's right. He found some lines that he knew would appeal to me. That's an example of what he was like.'

Mundon peered over his colleague's shoulder. 'Very thoughtful guy.'

'Yes,' she said in a whisper.

Colton continued, 'I suspect he may have been older than you.'

'Of course. There's seven years between us. He'd been married before.'

'Any children?'

'He's got a son, Raymond, from his first marriage. We weren't blessed with children.'

'And business was going well? He hadn't fallen out with any clients?'

She shook her head. 'No, it was all going extremely well. He'd been talking about opening a fourth office.'

There was a pause as Colton jotted this down. Then he said, 'Mrs Barron, I'm sorry, but I need to ask one or two rather delicate questions.'

'All right,' she whispered. She'd seemed confident to begin with and had given an impression of resilience. But, after Colton's revelations, her defences had begun to crack and she appeared alone and vulnerable.

'I take it you weren't called to identify the body, Mrs Barron?'

'No. Thankfully, my brother Mickey volunteered to go to Horseferry Road to see the body.'

'Now the other thing is, and I hope you won't mind me asking, but were you happily married?'

Deborah appeared surprised. 'How do you mean?'

'I'd heard a rumour you might have become estranged?'

She tried to regain her composure. 'I don't know where you get your information, but it's true to say that, in recent months, David and I had been living separate lives. I don't know if you noticed the annexe? He's been living there. To be honest, I'd forgotten that he'd been due to go to the Loretta Kay concert. Please don't mention this, Mr Colton. It's not really relevant. It won't help the police catch my husband's killer.'

He appeared embarrassed. 'Of course, I don't want to cause you any further upset,' he said.

'The fact is we'd been getting on a lot better in recent weeks and he'd been talking about moving back into the main house. I loved my husband very much, Mr Colton, and my brother and I are talking about setting up some kind of foundation in his memory. We've only just lost David and things are at an early stage, but we may set up some kind of bursary to help young accountancy students. I don't think there's much more I can tell you.'

'A foundation's a very nice idea, Mrs Barron,' said Mundon.

Then Colton's eyes lit up. 'Mrs Barron, there's one more thing. Have Loretta Kay's people been in touch with you?'

'I'm sorry. I forgot to mention that. Yes, her management couriered over a very nice letter.'

'Do you mind if I read it?'

She reached to the far end of the coffee table where a white envelope was lying. She picked it up and handed it to Colton. The letter was written on Savoy Hotel notepaper.

> *Dear Mrs Barron,*
> *We were all shocked by the shameful incident at the Royal Albert Hall in which your husband was killed. David was one of my most loyal fans who has watched me perform all around the world. I know his love and admiration for my music has led him to visit Georgia, where I grew up. He has also attended concerts throughout the United States and last year I was fortunate enough to meet him after my concert in Atlantic City. It's devastating to lose a husband who was such an honest, sincere and kind-hearted person. You've got our deepest sympathy at this tragic time and my team and I are all thinking of you.*
> *Loretta xxx.*

Colton was accustomed to dealing with victims of grief and being confronted by tragedy, but even he was deeply moved by these poignant words. After folding the letter, he cast his eyes towards her.

'Do you think I could take a copy of this letter? It shows the kindness and compassion of one of the world's greatest singers.'

'Yes, of course.' Before she could change her mind, Colton brought out his mobile phone and photographed the letter.

Mundon waited for his colleague to resume his seat on the settee before saying, 'Look, Mrs Barron, I was just wondering if I could take a nice picture of you.'

She shook her head. 'Oh no. I think you can see I'm not in any fit state to be photographed at the moment.'

'Perhaps just a head and shoulders? It needn't take a minute.'

'No, I'm sorry.'

'In that case, have you got some nice pictures of you and David that we can borrow?'

'I'll see what I can do.' She left the room and returned a moment later clasping several photographs in frames. Mundon selected three – one of the Barrons on a sun-kissed beach; one of the couple at an awards ceremony; and one taken on their wedding day. She removed them from their frames and handed them to him.

'Where was the holiday photo taken?' he asked.

'Mallorca.'

'Oh yeah. Whereabouts?'

'Cala Mesquida.'

'Know it well. My old girl loves it there. Do you mind if we borrow these three?'

'Certainly. But be sure to let me have them back. I'll fetch something to wrap them in.'

A few minutes later she reappeared with a buff-coloured envelope and handed it to the photographer.

'Thank you,' Mundon said. 'Don't worry. I'll send them straight back.'

'No problem. I'll trust you. You've got an honest face.'

'Well, it's the only one I've got, so I'm stuck with it. When were they taken?'

'The wedding picture was obviously seven years ago. The beach picture was two or three years before we married. The awards ceremony was four or five years ago.'

As Mundon placed the frames neatly together for their hostess, he noticed traces of a powdery residue at the edge of the table. He wetted the tip of his forefinger, dabbed it on the powder and licked it. He decided to keep his observations to himself.

'I think I'm done,' he remarked.

Colton shook Deborah's hand. 'Thanks for everything, Mrs Barron, and once again our apologies for disturbing you at a time like this.'

'I understand you have a job to do.'

'May I leave you my phone number in case something occurs to you?' He handed her a business card. 'If anyone else from the press troubles you, just tell them *The Post* were here and we've got the whole story. Hopefully, no one else will bother you then.'

As the double gates opened and the pair crossed the road to reach their cars, Colton expressed delight that they'd secured an exclusive interview with the widow.

He beamed at Mundon. 'I thought that went very well from our point of view.'

Mundon agreed. 'Yes. Shame she wouldn't pose for us. You didn't see what I saw on the table, did you?'

'No, what's that?' asked Colton, as he caught a glimpse of Leyla, still sitting patiently inside her car.

'She's been a naughty lady. There were traces of white powder on her coffee table. It was cocaine.'

* * *

After emailing over his report about the heartbroken widow whose husband appeared to have no enemies, Colton drove home. On the way, he stopped the car in a Tottenham side road to call the news desk.

'Was my copy all right, Clemmie?' he asked.

'Yes. It was fine. The pictures were brilliant. We loved Loretta Kay's letter. It's going to make a big spread in tomorrow's paper. Was the wife a hard nut to crack?'

'It was tough getting into the house. She'd made up her mind she wasn't going to talk, but when I explained I'd been with her husband, it smoothed the way for us.'

'Cool. Well, your copy was great. While I've got you on the line, Nick, there's a report in the *Standard* about the Porsche. Someone discovered it was registered to a man in East London. But when the *Standard* reporter went to the man's address – a flat in Bethnal Green – no one knew who he was talking about. I've sent Kate McMillen over there in case she can wheedle anything more out of the residents.'

Chapter 8

Ten miles away from Pine Tree Avenue, in a dilapidated warehouse in the heart of London's East End, businessman Vince Diamond was leaning back in his black leather office chair, slurping from a mug of instant coffee.

Diamond's office was in an alley that led off Fetterlock Lane, a side street along Bethnal Green Road. The entrance consisted of a black iron security grill together with a metal high-security main door.

At the other end of the former leather warehouse and behind heavy steel roller-shutter doors was the lorry drivers' entrance.

Middle-aged Diamond had no need for plush surroundings. He was content to spend his working day in a dingy room with magnolia-coloured walls and paint peeling from the white ceiling. Experience had taught him that, in his line of business, frequent changes of address were necessary.

Sitting on the opposite side of his antique Victorian desk was one of his bodyguards, Clifford Martin, who was reading a copy of that day's *Evening Standard*. An electric fan was whirring away in a corner of the room, trying to disperse some of the intense lunchtime heat.

'Read that last piece to me again,' Diamond demanded, thumping his mug down next to a pile of documents. 'The bit about Border Force.'

All the grimy windows in his first-floor office were open, but he was still perspiring profusely on this sweltering Friday afternoon.

The burly, six-foot-tall employee read,

> *Border Force officers in Calais carried out a routine check on a consignment of toys heading for Dover. They introduced a sniffer dog which eventually stopped at one of the cardboard boxes. The dog barked repeatedly, which led officials to examine the cargo. They found an estimated one hundred kilos of cocaine with a potential street value of around ten million pounds.*

The corpulent businessman with receding grey hair picked up a silver paperknife that he'd been using earlier to open his mail and angrily plunged it into his desktop.

'Bloody nuisance,' he barked. 'All that planning. All that work.'

Martin swept his jet-black hair away from his eyes. 'I know, boss.'

'Tell me again about that sorry excuse of a Dutchman we got to drive the lorry.'

'It says, "Dutch national Hendrick Van Dike, aged forty-nine and from Groningen in the Netherlands, was later charged with importing cocaine into the UK."'

He shook his head. 'That's what you get when you put your trust in a foreigner,' he moaned. 'Pass me that paper.'

After Martin folded the newspaper and passed it across the desk, his boss flattened it out and used it to fan himself.

'Hendrick's thirty-nine, not forty-nine. Why can't these journalists get their facts right? Anyway, we've got another operation coming up. This time the cargo's coming in at Tilbury and I'm putting Freddie Valmar in charge. He never lets me down.'

Martin stroked his chin as his boss's words sunk in. 'He's a good guy, Freddie is, provided he doesn't lose his temper. There was that time he stabbed his next-door neighbour when he played loud music at two in the morning.'

Diamond nodded. 'These nightmare neighbours can be a real problem, especially if you live in a flat like Freddie does.'

'Do you want me to work with Freddie on this new job, boss?'

'Wait up. I haven't had a chance to talk to him about it yet. Let's see what he says.'

Martin tutted. 'I haven't seen Freddie since I came back from visiting my folks in Jamaica. That was in March.'

'Don't worry. Our luck's going to change. It's bound to. On this next job, we're going to be bringing in some kayaks.'

Martin's face was blank. 'What's a kayak?'

'It's like a canoe, but you kneel in a canoe and sit in a kayak. Anyway, we're hoping the smell of the polyethylene will mask the smell of the gear.'

'What does a kayak smell like?'

'Candlewax.'

'Suppose there's a chance it'll hide the smell.'

Diamond leaned back on his chair. 'The only good news is that we won't be seeing that bastard bookkeeper no more.'

Martin was once again expressionless. 'Who's that – Barron?'

'Yes. Didn't you hear about it? It's in your bloody paper. His brains were blown out at the Royal Albert Hall.'

'I didn't realize it was him.'

'Yes. He won't be troubling us again.' Diamond hauled his heavy frame out of his chair and crossed the grey vinyl floor. Then he looked out of the window at the red and black graffiti to the left of the alley wall and the council flats to the right.

Martin appeared puzzled. 'I thought he was family. Never heard you diss him before. You said he'd got you out of a load of trouble.'

Diamond turned away from the window. 'I know, but people change. He was fiddling. Do you know I reckon at least fifty grand's gone walkabout since he started working with us? I know there's going to be upset people – my daughter for one. That's how it is when someone dies. But when it comes to sharp practice and skulduggery, he was in a different league.'

'Really?'

'Not a word of a lie. But I've learnt me lesson. No more accountants. I'm handling all the bangers and mash myself from now on. I'll just get a humble bookkeeper in to do some pen pushing at the end of every month.'

Martin shook his head. Barron's name hadn't appeared in the early edition of the evening newspaper, which he'd bought from the newsagent's in Bethnal Green Road. But the shooting incident had made an impression on him. He'd wondered if he knew the gunman who'd been described by the journalist.

Diamond was still facing the window. He was watching two boys with bicycles racing round the small garden at one of the flats.

Martin knew he might be risking his boss's ire by posing the question, but he was wondering if Diamond had any knowledge of the murder. He decided to try a diplomatic approach.

'Me and some of the boys were wondering who could have turned his hand to a job like that,' he said.

'At the hall?'

'Yeah. By my reckoning there's only two or three people in the whole of London who've got the brass neck to risk using a shooter in public like that.'

But his quest for information was thwarted. Diamond's mobile phone rang.

'Yeah?' said Diamond, as he answered the call. 'Oh, it's you, Freddie. What's going on?'

Martin could hear only a faint buzzing sound as Freddie Valmar spoke.

'So this guy's giving you a load of trouble, Freddie? He's refusing to pay up? Well, Cliff Martin's with me.' Diamond eyed his crony from across the office. 'What've you got on this afternoon?'

Martin raised his hands in an open gesture to show he was available to work.

'You're in the Downs Tavern in Hackney? I'll send him over to you. And Freddie – nothing too heavy. Don't want the Old Bill breathing down our necks.'

Chapter 9

Three children in shorts and sunhats were basking in the sunshine as Nick Colton arrived at the Royal Albert Hall the following morning.

Oblivious to all the worries of the world, they were sitting on the steps beneath the Prince Consort's statue.

Their mothers, in colourful summer tops and skirts, began handing out ice creams to them. An American couple were chatting excitedly about the historic hall, opened in 1871, which is topped by a glazed, iron dome.

They were gazing at the mosaic frieze which wraps around the oval-shaped building.

It was forecast to be one of the hottest days of the year. Temperatures were set to reach a sweltering thirty-four degrees Celsius in this part of West London.

A news website had reported that Britain's seaside beaches had been packed since 10 a.m. Fire crews and animal welfare staff were busy rescuing dogs from cars. A water shortage had been declared at the Glastonbury festival.

His return to the hall evoked memories of the disturbing events of Thursday evening, but he felt he had little choice. He doubted the competence of DCI Haynes and strangely felt a personal obligation towards David Barron to help track down his killer… although their meeting in the auditorium had been just a brief encounter.

It was just after 11.30 a.m. when he entered the hall through the south entrance. Excited spectators were milling about, waiting for a classical music recital in the Elgar Room.

He crossed the foyer, turned right and found himself in the brightly lit box office. He was greeted by the welcoming smile of a dark-haired sales assistant, whose badge bore the name Liz Martin.

He smiled back at the woman, who appeared to be West Indian. 'I wondered if you could help. I wanted to contact a couple of people who were here on Thursday night.'

'The night of that appalling murder?'

'That's right. All three of us were eyewitnesses to the shooting and I need to speak to them.'

Miss Martin grimaced. 'As I'm sure you're aware, we can't give out customers' personal details. Data Protection Act.'

'It's to help the police.'

'I'm sure it is, but my hands are tied.'

He grinned again.

'Were you here yourself on Thursday night?'

'I was, as it happens.'

'Then you may remember them. The woman was in her early thirties, had blonde hair and was wearing a black dress. She was carrying a black clutch bag with a gold chain. He was a stout guy, ginger-haired and with wire-framed glasses.'

She shook her head. 'We sold nearly five thousand tickets for Loretta Kay. You surely can't expect me to remember someone just because they'd a chain on their bag or ginger hair and glasses?'

He was encouraged to think he was making progress. He sensed her initial ice-cold response was melting.

'If you were here, you'd remember this couple. They were late bookers who were desperate to change one of their tickets so they could sit together. They'd been allocated seats J51 and L97. They'd have been kicking up a fuss.'

'Let's see if they're on the computer. Right, here's L97. You're right. This seat for Thursday night was allocated to a lady who also bought a ticket for J51. They booked by phone at the last minute, and she paid for both tickets.' She made a sudden intake of breath.

'Oh my God! I've just remembered. This was the seat where the guy was shot, isn't it?'

'That's right.'

'I think I should call the manager.'

'No need to bother him. Can you just tell me the name and address of the woman who paid for the two tickets?'

She tapped several of the keys before glancing back at the screen. She waited several seconds before saying, 'Here we are. Yes, this lady paid for the tickets by credit card. Can you explain why you're trying to contact her?'

He sighed. 'I'll be frank with you. I was sitting right next to David Barron, the man who was killed. I promised to help the police find this couple, who might have vital information that can help them.'

Miss Martin looked blank. 'You're not police though?'

He shook his head.

'I really think I should get hold of the manager,' she said. 'Wait one second.' She disappeared behind a screen, which presented him with a golden opportunity.

He barely had more than a few seconds. He hauled his body onto the wooden counter and, after planting his left hand firmly down on her desk, twisted himself round to view her screen. Almost at once the sound of footsteps signalled Miss Martin's return.

He jumped back to the visitors' floor, jarring his right foot as he did so.

Miss Martin spoke with an apologetic tone. 'I'm sorry, sir. Our ticketing manager's busy right now. You'll have to come back.'

'All right. Thanks for trying,' he said while walking away.

Colton was feeling pleased with himself as he left the building and made his way down Exhibition Road to South Kensington Underground Station. He punched the air in triumph, taking a passing woman pedestrian by surprise.

During the brief seconds in which he'd caught a glimpse of the computer screen, he'd learnt that the woman in the black dress lived in Woodmeadow Road, South Norwood and she was called Jasmine Smart. He'd come away without her companion's name, so he had to trust his luck would hold and that the meagre information he'd gleaned would bear fruit.

* * *

Two hours later, after collecting his car from a railway car park, he was driving down South Norwood Hill, a long, busy commuter road in south-east London, searching for Woodmeadow Road. He eventually found the turning on the left and travelled along it until he found the address he sought.

He'd visited this vibrant suburb before with its elegant Victorian and Edwardian houses and flourishing bars and restaurants, a sign of the area's growing gentrification. Jasmine's home was a semi-detached house in a tranquil street, close to playing fields.

He parked a few metres away and strolled over to the house, which was fronted by a low-lying hedge. Pink camellias and blue lavender flourished in flower beds beside a lush green lawn. A monkey puzzle tree, in all its twisted glory, held sway in the centre of the plot.

He opened the white wooden gate and followed a narrow stone path that led to the white, double-glazed front door. He rang the doorbell, wondering all the time how he was going to explain his presence.

To his immense surprise, a man he didn't recognise came to the door. Instead of a stout man with ginger hair and glasses he found himself face to face with a taller man who was slim, casually dressed, clean-shaven and with long, grey, straggly hair.

The householder spent a moment surveying his visitor. 'Yeah?'

Colton stroked his chin. 'I'm looking for Mrs Smart – Jasmine Smart?'

'Who wants her?'

'My name's Colton – Nick Colton.'

'Hang on.' The sullen householder retreated inside and, seconds later, the woman who'd waved to him and Greta at the concert emerged. He recognised her straight away, although her demeanour was rather different from the concertgoer in the elegant black dress. Her blonde hair was now slightly bedraggled, and she was wearing a pink top and jeans. She wore no make-up but nonetheless had an attractive face.

She was alarmed when she recognised Colton. 'What are you doing coming here?' she hissed as she led him back to the gate. 'This is my home where I live with my husband.'

He blushed. 'I'm– I'm sorry,' he stuttered. 'But I've got to talk to you.'

She glared at him. 'I'm still living with my husband. I was meant to be on a girls' night out on Thursday. Anyway, I'll give you Craig's number. Have you got a pen?'

As he jotted the mobile number in his notebook, he remarked, 'I've been trying to work out how the guy who swapped tickets with you came to get shot.'

'So are the cops. It's been a nightmare. They've been on my back for the past two days.' Glancing behind her, she noticed her husband standing in the doorway.

He glared at her. 'Who is he? What's he want?'

'Gotta go,' she said, darting back into the house with her husband and slamming the door.

He returned to his car and phoned the number Jasmine Smart had given him. It went straight to voicemail.

'Damn!' he exclaimed. 'We're getting nowhere fast.'

He was about to start his car engine and head back to Greenwich when his phone rang.

A gravelly man's voice announced, 'Someone just phoned me.'

'Craig?'

'Yeah. Who are you?'

'Craig, I'm Nick Colton. I was at the Loretta Kay concert on Thursday night. I was sitting next to David, the guy who got shot. Do you remember?'

'Yeah, of course.'

'This might sound ridiculous but, since I was with the poor guy in his final moments, I feel responsible, in a way, for finding out what happened. He was sitting in the seat that you were supposed to take.' There was a long pause. 'Craig, are you still there?'

'Yes, I'm still here. You know it's unsettling to have a stranger call me up and ask me a question like that. By the way, how did you get my number?'

'Jasmine gave it to me. I've just been to her house.'

'God, you shouldn't have done that. You know she's–'

'Married? Yes, I've sussed that. Don't worry – I'm a man of the world.'

'So long as she's all right.'

'She should be. We spoke in the garden. She gave me your number – that was it.'

'Listen, I've had the cops onto me. What was your name again?'

'Nick. Nick Colton.'

'Nick, I've just realized who you are. You're the journalist, aren't you? Someone pointed out your article in *The Post* to me.'

'Yes, by an amazing coincidence, I was right there when the action happened. Must be a first!'

'Mr Colton, do you have a few minutes? I'd like to talk to you about the other evening. Are you free now?'

'Yes, I'm fairly free. Whereabouts are you?'

'I'm in Dulwich.'

'And your name's Craig?'

'Yes, Craig Arnold.'

'Give me forty minutes and I'll be over.'

'OK. I'll text you the address. I've got something really important to tell you.'

Chapter 10

Craig Arnold lived in the up-market London suburb of Dulwich Village, which was four miles to the north of Jasmine Smart's home in leafy Woodmeadow Road. His home was a three-storey townhouse located a short distance from North Dulwich railway station and five miles from the centre of London. It lay in a quiet close just a few metres from a main road which it ran parallel to.

Arnold, who was in his late twenties, was cleaning his blue Volkswagen Polo on the drive when Colton drew up a few minutes before three o'clock. He didn't notice the journalist at first as he was concentrating so much on his task.

Perspiration was dripping from his brow as he toiled, causing his glasses to slide down his nose. He had to keep stopping to push them back. Drops of soapy water had splashed over his white shirt and black trousers.

'You can have a go at mine when you've finished,' yelled Colton, as he parked opposite the house and stepped out of his car.

'Sorry!' Arnold replied. 'I've been rushing to clean it before you arrived. I'll knock it on the head now.'

He picked up his plastic bucket and pushed open his solid wood front door. 'Come on in.'

Arnold led him upstairs to an open-plan kitchen and living room with views of the tree-lined street outside. The room's untidy state reminded Colton of a jumble sale.

'Sit anywhere you like,' said his host as he emptied his bucket in the sink.

The only space that seemed to be relatively unencumbered by piles of clothing, newspapers and other clutter was a seat in the middle of a black leather settee. He picked his way across the littered floor until he reached it. He moved aside a Metro Harvest shopping bag, an old copy of *The Post* and a Loretta Kay Soul Classics DVD.

'Big fan of Loretta Kay?' he asked, waving the DVD.

'Jasmine more than me,' he replied. 'She brought it over for me to hear.'

Once Colton had made himself comfortable, his host asked whether he'd like a hot drink.

Colton beamed at him. 'Coffee would be great. White, two sugars, please.'

A few minutes later, Arnold was sitting on a grey couch opposite Colton. Each was slurping coffee from a mug.

The host smiled. 'Interesting job you've got.'

'Some people think so – not everyone.'

'You were really in the right place the other night.'

'Yeah.'

'How did you find out where Jasmine lived?'

'From the box office at the hall.'

'What? They told you straight out?'

'Not exactly. So how long have you lived here then?'

'Three years. I bought it because it's not far from the city.'

'You work there, do you?'

'Stocks and shares with a firm called Springfield Mead. Twenty minutes to London Bridge if I catch the right train.' He paused while he took a sip from his mug. 'First of all, I realize it doesn't look very good – me going out with a married woman.'

'I meet all kinds of people.'

'I know. I just want to explain something. When I met Jasmine, I didn't know she was married. Actually, she was going through a bad patch with her husband. She wants to end it with Alex, but she's waiting for the right opportunity. Then she'll be moving in here with me.'

Colton grinned as he sipped his coffee. 'I've met Alex. Can't say I was too impressed.'

'Why? What was he like with you?'

'I only met them for a few minutes by their front door, but he seemed a little controlling.'

He nodded. 'That's him in a word. Controlling. She's frightened of him.'

Colton was about to ask him about the events of Thursday evening when the room was filled with the sound of a car door being locked. It was the zany ringtone on Arnold's phone.

He responded to his caller by saying, 'Yeah? You can forget it. You've got more chance of finding a pig in a mosque.' Then he abruptly hung up.

'Sorry. Some idiot who thinks I owe him money. Where were we?'

His visitor sipped more of his coffee. 'You were saying Jasmine's frightened of her husband.'

'That's right. He's the kind of guy who acts first and asks questions later.'

'So how come you couldn't get two seats together for Thursday?'

'We phoned the box office three weeks ago and all the seats were gone.'

'They sold out very quickly.'

'So we kept phoning and phoning, asking about cancellations. Eventually we managed to get two seats in different parts of the theatre.'

'You were originally supposed to sit next to me in L97.'

'That's right.'

'So on Thursday evening you arrived early in the hope of getting someone in Block J to swap with you?'

'Yes. We decided Jasmine should take seat J51 as she had gone to all the trouble of continually calling the booking line. It was down to me to try to swap with someone.'

'So how did you come to swap with David Barron?'

'Well, I suppose we were lucky. I asked one guy who was sitting six or seven places away. He turned me down. Then Mr Barron arrived and took the seat directly next to Jasmine. I asked him if he'd swap and he agreed, on the proviso that he'd have a reasonable view of the stage if he moved. He checked the view from Block L and was happy with it, so we switched.'

'Kind of him really.'

Arnold slurped down several mouthfuls of coffee. 'Yes. He was brilliant. Jasmine was over the moon, and we were mortified when we heard the shots and saw him lying in the seat, covered in blood.'

Colton sighed. 'It's a sight I'll never forget.'

'Good on you for trying to give chase.'

'I did what most people would have done. Didn't do any good though.'

'Well, at least we know the guy drove a silver car. That's what you put in the paper, didn't you? A silver Porsche?'

'That's right. But the cops are playing it down. They're not sure if the tradesman in overalls was the gunman. Other witnesses have come up with other suggestions.'

'But you're the press, aren't you? You wouldn't get something as important as that wrong.'

'I'm flattered you think that, but the press don't possess prodigious powers of observation. I'm afraid we're human like everyone else and just as prone to making wrong assumptions when it comes to witnessing an event such as a shooting.

'Listen, I'm going off to see my family in Greenwich shortly. I haven't seen my kids properly for a while, but I need to ask you this. I suppose it's the sixty-four-billion-dollar question. Was the bullet that killed David intended for you?'

There was a pause. Then Arnold put down his mug and stared at the journalist.

'I can't rule it out,' he said. 'There's been nothing else on my mind since Thursday evening. It isn't an easy question to answer.'

Colton raised an eyebrow before drinking some more of his coffee. 'Why? Is there someone with a grudge against you?'

'I've only said this to the police and I don't want it going in your newspaper, but I think Jasmine and I were followed when we drove to Kensington. I glanced in my mirror and there was a car that could have been a silver Porsche behind us. It stayed with us until we reached Exhibition Road – just a few hundred metres from the hall; then it disappeared from sight.'

'You didn't see it turn off?'

'No. One minute it was there. The next minute it wasn't.'

'Who knew you'd booked tickets to see Loretta Kay?'

'Well, as I say, I've been spending a lot of time thinking about this. The staff at the hall knew, obviously. All my friends and family knew. Jasmine mentioned it to her mother and sister, and two of her female friends.'

'So her husband, Alex, didn't know?'

'Well, here's the thing. He regularly goes through her handbag.'

'What a creep!'

'He spotted the tickets and demanded to know who she was going with. She lied and told him she was going with a woman friend, but she's not sure he believed her. She's twice caught him going through her phone. Somehow, he seems to know my name and number.'

'Does he know what you look like?'

'As far as I know, he's never seen me.'

'This Alex must have been furious when he found she was having an affair.'

'Of course. She's consistently denied it, but he doesn't believe her.'

Colton tutted. 'Life must be bloody difficult for her and her husband.'

'She's in a right state, as you can imagine.'

'Children involved?'

'Yeah, two.'

'What was he doing while you two were waiting to see Loretta Kay?'

'Watching television at home. EastEnders and soccer. That's what he told her, anyway.'

Colton stroked his chin, wondering how individuals could live with each other when their lives were tainted by deceit.

'So, Craig, you think the man I saw driving off in the Porsche might have been following you earlier?'

'Exactly.'

'Was it a Porsche Boxster?'

'I'm sorry. I'm not very with good cars. I just drive them.'

'And clean them.'

He laughed. 'Yes, and clean them.'

'So it could have been a similar car – such as a Mazda MX5, for example?'

'Possibly.'

'Could you see the driver's face? Did he have black hair and a beard?'

'I couldn't tell.'

'While he was following you, you didn't by any chance take his registration number?'

Arnold shook his head before finishing his coffee.

'Jasmine could have turned round and taken the number I suppose, but I'm afraid we didn't think of it. After the driver turned off, we decided he probably wasn't following us after all.'

'But now you're not sure?'

'No.'

Colton put his empty mug down on the floor between a pile of books and two stacked chairs.

'And there haven't been any other strange events – no poison pen letters or funny phone calls?'

'No, nothing like that.'

'Have you spoken to the police about the car that you saw following you?'

He nodded. 'Yes, but they only interviewed me for five minutes. They kept asking about two Afro-Caribbean guys that several witnesses had seen near the doorway a few minutes before David was killed. I was completely honest with them. I never saw those two men.'

Colton wondered if Arnold was being entirely truthful. Apart from a brief glimpse of him on Thursday evening, the man was entirely unknown to him. So why should he be totally frank and honest with his visitor? However, there was something about Arnold that he liked. He was amiable, down to earth, and seemed genuinely shocked at Barron's death.

Colton asked, 'As far as you're aware, Alex Smart's the only person who might have known the actual seat numbers that had been allocated to you and Jasmine?'

'No, he's not the only one. After her husband rifled through her handbag, he dumped the tickets on a side table. They've had tradesmen in the house and her relatives have been round. Any one of them could have seen the two tickets and noted down the seat numbers.'

Chapter 11

When Nick Colton arrived back at his home in Greenwich, it was nearly 7 p.m. The street was crammed with vehicles and he had to park fifty metres from his front door.

Often this would send him into a bad mood, but this evening he was unconcerned. He'd made progress with his inquiries and he felt elated. He'd refuse to let anything mar his moment of glory.

Greta rushed forward to greet him as he entered the living room, planting a kiss on his cheek. Their children, Riccardo and Ashleigh, ran to hug their father.

'We've missed you, Daddy,' said six-year-old Ashleigh.

He gathered her in his arms and swung her round the room.

'I missed you too, darling. Sorry. I got held up.'

As the children resumed watching television by the bay window, he made himself comfortable on a couch by the kitchen door.

Once she'd made tea for them both, Greta sat beside him, eager to hear how he'd spent the day. He explained how he'd learnt the names and addresses of the ticket-swapping couple and visited them both.

He also explained how the boyfriend, Craig Arnold, believed the driver of a silver car followed the pair through south London.

Greta smiled as she sipped her tea. 'I knew it. I suspected all along that the gunman hit the wrong target. David was just in the wrong place at the wrong time.'

Nick shook his head. 'I don't know, darling. I get the impression the detectives aren't interested in my statement about the man in the Porsche or Craig Arnold's account of being followed. All that DCI Haynes is interested in apparently is two men seen acting suspiciously in the corridor a few minutes before the shooting.'

He drank a few sips of tea. 'I've got a lot of time for our police, Greta. They've got a difficult job and, on the whole, they do it brilliantly – although only something like three quarters of murders ever get solved.'

'Nick, what happened at the hall is as clear as night follows the day. Someone is bearing a grudge against Mr Craig Arnold and it's probably the angry husband, Alex. He learns they are travelling to Kensington to watch a show. He follows them in a car that's maybe borrowed from a friend and he finds the man sitting in Block L that he believes is a threat to his marriage.'

Colton interrupted to say, 'If it was Alex, he knew that they had been allocated seats J51 and L97. He spots Jasmine in J51, so he assumes the man in L97 is the boyfriend. Is that what you think?'

'That's right. Maybe he doesn't know what Craig looks like, but he sees a man sitting in Block L. That's good enough for him. He shoots and runs. But he makes a silly mistake. He kills the hard-working accountant.'

Colton shook his head. 'If your theory's correct, why did the gunman need to follow them by road? As I've found out myself when chasing showbiz stars, it's incredibly difficult to keep up in London traffic – unless you've got a motorbike or scooter. Why did he do that? If he knew about the tickets, he would have already known they were going to the Royal Albert Hall and the time of the performance.'

'He obviously wanted to strike before the hall filled with people. Maybe he was going to shoot him near the entrance and he wasn't quick enough and had to search for Craig inside. I don't know. I didn't plan his strategy. I'm just thinking that, if Craig was having an affair with Jasmine, her husband's got a clear motive for murder.'

He yawned. 'I've briefly met the husband and he has some resemblance to the guy I followed. Anyway, whoever was behind the murder, the husband must have thought the original seating arrangements very strange. I mean, what couple of lovebirds go to watch one of the world's top soul singers and sit twenty metres apart?'

'Darling, that's why Craig approached people and asked to swap tickets.'

'Yes, I know.'

He yawned again. It had been a long day. Their debate about the seats had been raging intermittently over nearly three days. His wife was convinced the accountant died in error. He, on the other hand, wasn't so sure. He knew from his Totteridge visit that Barron wasn't some lowly backroom accountant but a high-flying financial wizard who ran a successful business and enjoyed a luxurious lifestyle.

Could he have made an enemy of one of his clients? Could he have become entangled with criminal activity in some way – possibly fraud?

'The person I feel most sorry for is Deborah Barron,' he said. 'Her whole life's suddenly in turmoil. She's well-off and clearly well-provided for. But she's thirty-eight and lost the love of her life. She's now got to take responsibility for her late husband's business or dispose of it. She's got to manage the upkeep of a seven-bedroom house, deal with police questions, plan the funeral…'

Greta took both teacups into the kitchen and returned to the couch.

'That Deborah's thirty-eight, I think you said.' He confirmed she was.

'That's only two years older than me. She's young. She's got time to find love again.'

Colton's mobile phone rang. Luke Foster's name appeared on the screen. For a moment, he considered letting the call go through to voicemail. Then he picked up.

'Luke, everything all right?'

'Yeah, fine, mate. I'm at home. I've just been reading the news online. There's a report in one of the Sunday papers saying the cops have found the Porsche you told them about. It was parked in a lane in Crouch End.'

Chapter 12

DCI Harry Haynes swept his dark hair away from his face as he stepped out of his room on the Monday, and cast his eyes up and down the open-plan CID office at Kensington Police Station.

'Have you seen DS Khan this morning?' he asked a detective constable sitting near his door.

'Yes, sir. She's gone to the coffee machine.'

'Ask her to come and see me when she gets back, will you?'

'Yes, sir.'

A few minutes passed. He drew apart some of the vertical blinds and glanced out of his window. For a few moments, he watched the lines of endless traffic crawling along the Earls Court Road. He was glad to be hidden away in his office on the third floor of the six-storey, 1950s building – marginally detached from the constant noise and pollution below.

'At least the heatwave seems to be over,' he told himself as he unwrapped a piece of chewing gum and placed it in his mouth.

He heard a knock. His twenty-six-year-old sergeant, Nadia Khan, appeared in the doorway, greeting him with a cheery, 'Good morning, sir.'

'Good morning,' replied the chief inspector, who'd now rolled up his sleeves and was sitting with his feet up on his desk. He seemed as relaxed as a lotus on a lake.

'Sergeant, I've just received the preliminary report from the pathologist, Dr Richards.'

Clutching a file of documents, she closed the door and sat down on a chair by his desk.

'That's cool, sir.'

Her boss read from a sheet of paper,

> *Results of post-mortem carried out on David Howard Barron at Westminster Public Mortuary. Date of birth, 4 March 1974. Suspected cause of death was gunshot wounds to the head. Manner of death is homicide.*
> *Two bullets entered the left occipital bone and exited the right frontal bone. They were approximately three point three centimetres below the top of the head and three point five centimetres right of the midline. These caused massive damage, including brain swelling and bleeding. This resulted in respiratory arrest and death. There were also complex skull fractures.*
> *A third bullet entered the rear of the neck and passed out through the front, contributing to blood loss. The position of entry and exit wounds indicate he was facing away.*

'Then there's a lot of medical waffle… Ah, here we are.' He read,

> *Initial toxicology tests indicate there were no drugs or alcohol present in the body.*

Nadia Khan stretched and yawned. It had been an exhausting few days since the murder.

'Nothing startling there, sir,' she said.

'No. It's a tough one. We've got no contact between offender and victim. All we've got is ballistics. We know it may be a Beretta from the shell cases that were dropped.'

Haynes paused to glance out of the window before continuing. 'Now I've read the statements from those two boys from Stockwell, Dexter Greaves and Wesley Jacobs.'

Khan removed a report from her folder and briefly studied it.

Haynes continued, 'The gist of it is they were seen acting suspiciously near the door to Block L. Is that right?'

'Yes, sir,' said the sergeant. She smiled confidently. 'So, in both statements they say they were discussing whether they had time to go to the bar for a drink before taking their seats. Jacobs had a knife in an inside pocket when he was searched, but neither was carrying a firearm. In fact, no firearms have been recovered from anywhere in the hall or from any of the concertgoers.'

He removed his feet from the desk and leaned forward. 'I think we can forget about them. Apart from that journalist, Nick Colton, and his wife, how many of our main witnesses have mentioned the guy in the grey overalls?'

'Six have mentioned the man in grey. Two report seeing a man acting strangely in the corridor who ran off after the sound of gunshots. The other four people were outside the building. Broadly, they saw a man in grey overalls who appeared to be in a hurry. Descriptions vary, but most of them recall him wearing grey and carrying a bag.'

He shook his head. 'Not much to go on. How many more witnesses have we got to speak to?'

'Another thirty, sir.'

'OK. Crack on with that. Where are we with the CCTV?'

'Since we last spoke, one of the lads has found some hazy footage of a man in overalls walking very quickly along Kensington Gore towards Queen's Gate. All we can tell is that he's fairly tall. We're trying to get the footage enhanced.'

'No sign of a silver Porsche on the cameras?'

'No, sir. The car we found in Oakwood Lane, Crouch End matches the registration number Colton gave us, but there doesn't appear to be any useful DNA or dabs. The owner lives in Bethnal Green and had reported it as stolen.'

He nodded. 'Whoever drove it has done a clever job with it. What beats me is why a plumber should turn up in a Porsche.'

She folded her arms. 'What better vehicle to park in a Kensington mews, sir? If he'd turned up in an old saloon car, it might have looked out of place.'

'That's a good point. It shows we might be dealing with a rather cunning individual, Sergeant – not the usual toerags. By the way, what did you make of Lauren?'

'The stage door keeper? I thought her statement was very helpful.'

He rummaged among some documents before holding up a scrap of crumpled paper. 'Here we are,' he said.

> *The man was around five feet ten inches tall. He had dark hair, was well-built and had facial stubble. He was wearing grey overalls. He came to the stage door shortly before 7 p.m., claiming to be a plumber.*

'This next bit's interesting,' he said, and read on.

> *I thought I detected an American accent.*

'I probed her for more on that point, but she couldn't add anything. Then she goes on.'

> *He claimed he'd been called to a plumbing leak in the toilets. I told him to wait while I tried to contact the*

manager because he wasn't from our usual firm. But he slipped past me when the florists arrived with bouquets for Loretta Kay and I was distracted. I notified security. At approximately twenty minutes past seven, I saw a man who looked quite like the plumber leave the building through the stage door exit. He rushed past me, got into a white van and drove off in the direction of Knightsbridge.

The chief inspector stroked his chin thoughtfully. 'Unfortunately, she didn't get the registration.'

'No, sir, but she believes it had "Stockwood & Son" or "Stockhill & Son" on the rear doors.'

'Can you check out any firms in London with those names? See if one of their staff was at the hall on Thursday evening. We must check CCTV for the white van as well.'

Khan raised a finger, signalling her agreement.

'So what do you think of our main witnesses' accounts?' Haynes asked.

She took a deep breath. 'Sir, I'm starting to have a few doubts about Nick Colton's version of events. Not in relation to the actual shooting because it seems beyond doubt that the man in grey overalls who tricked his way through the stage door probably fired the gun. I just think Mr Colton followed the wrong man.'

'So the man in the Porsche had nothing to do with it?'

'I don't think we should discount the Porsche altogether, but I'm inclined to believe the statement from the stage door attendant. She is staff, after all, and Colton's a journalist. You know what they're like. He might have embellished his account to make a better story.'

'I noticed he wrote about the events of that night in his article with a certain glee,' said Haynes.

'Yes, sir. I think we should contact the media team at Press Bureau. Perhaps they could issue a new press release, based on the woman's account. We don't have to dismiss the possibility that the suspect fled in the Porsche. We can just say we're now searching for a man in a white van as well.'

'I agree. What did you make of Deborah Barron the other day? She can't think of anyone with a grievance against her husband.'

'I felt sorry for her, sir. She's taken it badly. Perhaps in a few days, when she's had a chance to recover, we could have another chat with her.'

He frowned. 'You never come to terms totally with a loss like that. But I agree with you. We'll need to have another chat with her at some point. We also need to talk to Barron's son, Raymond.'

She nodded. 'I've spoken to the family several times. I've explained how important it is that we chat to him. But no one seems to know where he is. He seems to have disappeared.'

Chapter 13

That same Monday morning, Nick Colton arrived at work early and read through the rival daily newspapers. Many of them – including his own – had mentioned the discovery of the silver Porsche. It had been found parked outside a detached house in a secluded avenue.

After it had remained there for three days, the exasperated owner of the house complained to the police, who recognised it as being linked to the Royal Albert Hall case.

Colton had considered travelling to Crouch End to interview the householder, but in the end decided against it. It was highly unlikely the bogus plumber lived in the area. He almost certainly switched to another car or was picked up by someone. It was also unlikely he would have been seen alighting from the car.

He spent half an hour phoning round a few minicab firms in Crouch End and gave them the plumber's description, but none could recall picking the man up between 7.30 and 8.30 p.m. on the previous Thursday evening.

'You're early. Couldn't you sleep?' asked the silky voice of Katie McMillen from behind her computer.

He stood up and peered across at her. 'Hi, Kate! I got the early train by mistake. Must try to avoid that in future!'

'I loved your piece this morning about the letter Loretta Kay sent the widow, and the pictures with it were fab. We've really thrown our rivals into the shade. I've got the story here. What does Loretta say? "*It's devastating to lose a husband who was such an honest, sincere and kind-hearted person.*" She comes across as a really caring woman.'

He nodded. 'The singer hasn't done herself any harm at all, sending that letter.'

'Nick, she's loved enough in this country already. You only had to flick through the Sunday papers yesterday. They were full of letters saying what a shame it was that a terrible crime had forced them to abandon the concert. Some of the letters went onto say that crime in the UK's becoming as bad as in the US.'

'That doesn't surprise me.'

* * *

An hour later, when all the staff had arrived at their desks, Colton was writing a story about an assault outside a Hackney pub.

His desk phone rang.

'Nick, Chris Lane here. Are you free at the moment? I wanted to have a quick chat with you.'

'Yeah. Are you in your office?'

'Yes. Do you want to drop round?'

Five minutes later, Colton strolled out of the newsroom, elbowed his way through the double doors and made his way along the corridor that led to Lane's small office at the end.

Lane had had a successful career as a reporter on three different national newspapers before being promoted to the position of *The Post*'s news editor ten years ago. For the past two years, he'd spearheaded the investigations team, a small unit of journalists employed to make in-depth studies of issues in the news. The team had received awards for their trail-blazing report into puppy farms and the exploitation of immigrants by people traffickers.

'Good to see you,' said plummy-voiced Lane, rising from his desk to shake Colton's hand. He had a somewhat spartan but comfortable office with views across the wharf.

One wall was filled from floor to ceiling with encyclopaedias, maps and books about law, surveillance, phone tapping, and criminal gangs. Framed sets of past front pages of *The Post* were neatly arranged over a second wall.

Colton made himself comfortable on a chair. Lane sat at his desk and perused a set of photographs before casting his eyes towards him.

'I gather you're going to visit Ealing for us this week regarding the MP's affair?'

'Tomorrow actually, Chris.'

'Good. Now, you're certain of the area where the secret liaisons took place, are you?'

'All I've been told is that it's the Uxbridge Road area of West Ealing.'

'Yes. I'm sorry I can't be more specific, but it was a long time ago. This woman, Sadie, remembers it because there were bric-a-brac and souvenirs in the window.'

'Is it someone's home?'

'She was very vague. She thinks so.'

'All right. I'm up for a challenge.'

'That's great. Here are some individual photographs for you of Sadie and old Polebrook. I just want you to give the premises the once-over. See if any of the neighbours remember seeing them. Maybe, if there's a pub nearby, ask in there. But our watchword's discretion.'

Colton frowned. 'If I find the house with strange objects in the window, do you want me to go in and ask a few questions?'

Lane, who was short, tubby and with receding grey hair, shook his head. 'No, I don't want us to risk giving the game away at this stage. This is just a gentle pry. We don't want to show our hand yet. We certainly don't want to tip off the MP or any of his cronies about what we're up to. Is that understood?'

'Yes, Chris.' Colton was annoyed by the sharpness of his tone. He was a respected reporter and felt Lane – for all his past achievements and national newspaper awards – should treat him with more respect. However, he decided he didn't want to make it an issue at that moment.

Instead he asked, 'Is there anything else I need to know?'

'Well, just for background, this woman approached us. Says she's Sadie Robinson, a beautician and a member of Ealing North-West and Ruislip Conservatives. She's twenty-eight and lives in Ruislip.'

'And all this has been checked out?'

'Yes, of course. Have you met our reporter, Denise Barton-Jones?'

'Yes, I've met her a few times.'

There was a knock on the door.

'Come in!' Lane bellowed.

The face of *The Post*'s lawyer appeared in the doorway. 'Oh you've got someone with you. I'll come back,' he said.

As he closed the door, Lane hollered, 'Shouldn't be long, Mike.' He turned towards Colton. 'That was the lawyer, as you've probably guessed. He's not very happy with a piece we're meant to have in the paper tomorrow. Never mind! Where was I?'

Colton tried to be helpful. 'Denise. You were talking about the reporter Denise.'

'Oh yes. She's met Sadie several times and has got her on tape. Basically – and, obviously, this isn't to go anywhere outside these walls – this Sadie claims she was Oliver Polebrook's sexual plaything for more than a year. We've got dates, times and a lot of personal information about Polebrook. It all seems to stand up.'

'I'm flattered you want to include me in the investigation.'

'Well, Nick, you've got a good reputation and long experience. Denise is a bloody good operator but she doesn't have your experience. A year ago she was on a daily rag in Liverpool. I just want you to see if you can find this building. It's meant to be the place where they held their shenanigans in the spring of 2017. If it all works out, we'll approach the people who own the building and take a photograph. Then we'll be able to say, "This is where the Cabinet minister and the beautician had their sex sessions."'

Colton smiled. 'The minister and the make-up girl,' he said to himself.

Lane handed him a manila envelope. 'The pictures are all in there. There's two of the girl and one of Polebrook.'

Colton took them out and studied them. One, which was dated on the back 'April 2017,' showed Sadie standing with a broad smile alongside another woman. She was dressed in a bright red, ski-style jacket and grey slacks. She was short, red-haired and sharp-featured.

The second photo was a head-and-shoulders photograph which appeared to have been taken a few years earlier. Her face was slimmer and showed fewer signs of the ravages of time. The third image was of the MP in a dark suit shaking hands with the Prime Minister.

‘Of course, she wasn’t in her ski jacket when she was shagging the future Chancellor of the Duchy of Lancaster. He forced her to dress as either a French maid or a saucy nurse.’

‘Did he? The randy old goat,’ Colton remarked.

‘Yes, and apparently he’d dress up as a fireman or policeman.’

Chapter 14

The following day, Nick Colton was relieved when he woke up and heard on the radio that the first hours of the morning would be cooler. He never relished driving on London’s congested streets in stifling heat.

The journey from Greenwich to Ealing was just eighteen miles, but it involved travelling through the heart of London and along some of Britain’s most gridlocked roads. It was nearly half past eleven by the time his Volvo reached the Uxbridge Road.

He parked in a side road and studied a map. It was only then that he realized the immensity of his task. Uxbridge Road is a twelve-mile route that intersects Ealing, beginning at Shepherds Bush Green and ending in Hillingdon. Knowing the premises he sought were in West Ealing reduced the search area to some extent.

But he needed to cover an urban district that stretched for several miles. And he had to include in his quest a myriad of side streets branching off from both sides of the main route. No wonder he’d been called in – no one from the investigations team would have relished the prospect of spending a whole day, or maybe several days, touring West Ealing.

The borough of Ealing, once dubbed 'the Queen of the Suburbs,' first became a town during Queen Victoria's reign. Now it had been swallowed up by metropolitan London with endless blocks of flats and shops.

As the temperature rose to twenty-one Celsius, he set off in a logical manner, first scrutinising the streets to the south of the Uxbridge Road.

Then he returned to his starting point, surveying the main thoroughfare as he went, and began tackling the streets to the north of the highway.

Four hours and several litres of unleaded fuel later, he had nearly completed his gargantuan undertaking. But he was becoming disillusioned.

He'd just stopped for the third time in a street called Azalea Gardens when, from the corner of his eye, he noticed a building exhibiting a motley collection of objects in its bay window. It was a house occupying a corner position at the junction of Azalea Gardens and Hawthorn Drive. He left the car and stepped across the street for a closer inspection.

It was an antique shop that had fallen into a state of decline. Some of the dark-green paint on the woodwork around the front and side-street windows was peeling. The sign above the door was faded. It took him a moment to decipher the words 'The Old Emporium'.

The shop's windows were filled with treasures from times past – an assortment of objets d'art to lure in passers-by. In the main front window were Victorian lamps; furniture from the 1930s; and radios from the 1950s. Propped up behind them were several landscape paintings.

The side window was a showcase for clocks, glassware, jewellery and nautical instruments. An ancient hunting horn took pride of place in the centre of the display. Strangely, both shop windows were bordered by faded, burgundy curtains.

He knew at once this was the building he had been seeking and he could understand now why, despite the passage of time, it had been retained in Sadie Robinson's memory. It was the kind of building that was hard to forget.

Suddenly he realized he wasn't alone. Two elderly women were walking down the street towards him, away from the Uxbridge Road. They slowed their pace as they approached and, for a moment, he wondered if they were going to enter the shop.

But instead, they pushed open a side door on the left of the building and went inside. He stepped over to the doorway and watched with curiosity as they climbed a set of stairs and disappeared at the top. It was only then he noticed the word 'Tearooms' displayed above this second entrance to the building.

He could hear voices and the clinking of cutlery coming from the first floor. Then a waitress appeared on the top stair.

'Can I help?' she asked, peering down.

'Are you open?' he asked.

'Yes. Tea, coffee, rolls, sandwiches, pasties,' she recited.

Forgetting Chris Lane's advice, he clambered up the stairs and found himself in a dingy café with barely enough room for a dozen customers. There was a small kitchen and counter at the far end. The two women were seated by a window overlooking Azalea Gardens. They were the only clientele.

After taking a table by the stairs, he ordered a tea and a ham sandwich, and waited for his order. When the waitress brought them, he drew the photographs from his pocket.

'Do you by any chance know this lady?' he asked the girl, who was in her late teens. She was short, had blonde hair tied back behind her head and laughed like a toddler on a picnic.

'Can't say I do,' she said. 'Unless she taught at my school.'

'No, she's a beautician.'

'Don't sound like any of our teachers. They're mostly nuns!' she said, her laughter ricocheting round the tearoom. 'Who's the guy?'

He lowered his voice. 'That's Oliver Polebrook, the MP.'

'Never seen him,' she replied loudly. The two old ladies peered across. Colton caught their glance, and they quickly resumed their conversation. Chris Lane's haughty tones seemed to echo through his mind, 'Our watchword's discretion.'

'Has this always been tearooms?' he asked her.

'For the past two years. It was hired out as a meeting room before that. You'd better talk to Mr Sharma downstairs.'

'Does he run the antique shop?'

'That's right. He's the freeholder. He'll put you straight.'

'Was there ever a drinks cabinet and bed up here?'

'You're winding me up. What's this place meant to have been? A bloody knocking shop? My mum used to serve teas and coffees to the people holding meetings up here and she'd have definitely told me if there'd ever been a bed and a cocktail cabinet.'

After enjoying his snack and paying his bill, Colton descended the stairs. He stopped for a moment outside the shop and recalled Lane's advice. He decided the award-winning editor was being overcautious. Discretion does nothing to encourage those with knowledge to impart it, he decided. If you don't ask questions, you'll never get people to open up and vital information may lie secret for ever.

Sensing his conversation with the freeholder might reveal some crucial facts, he activated the voice record function on his phone and placed the handset in his inside pocket. Then he pushed the door and entered the shop as a bell tinkled above his head. An elderly Indian man with grey hair and a sombre expression was sitting behind an antique desk at the rear.

'You lost?' asked the shopkeeper, who was wearing a slightly soiled grey shirt.

'Why do you say that?'

'I noticed you hovering around just now.'

'I wanted to ask you something. I was upstairs in the tearooms and the young lady said you might be able to help.'

'I'm guessing you're from the press.'

Colton's face fell. 'Now why would you think that?'

'I can always tell.' He pointed to Colton's neck, where his top shirt button was unfastened and his tie hanging loosely. The journalist nodded and smiled.

The shopkeeper stood up. 'How can I help?'

Colton removed the envelope from his pocket and showed him the photographs. The shopkeeper studied them carefully.

'That's Mr Polebrook the MP. Never trusted that bastard. What's he been up to?'

'I was hoping you might be able to tell me.'

He continued studying the photograph. 'I went to see him at his surgery a few years ago about my planning application for an extension and he didn't raise a finger to help me.'

Then Mr Sharma became silent. His sharp, brown eyes were poring over the pictures of the beautician.

'That's Mercedes,' he declared before gazing at Colton. 'Is she in some sort of trouble?'

'I don't know. Possibly.'

'You're being rather cagey.'

Colton knew he had to choose his words carefully. 'This lady's meant to have visited this building a few years ago and she may have been in the company of the MP.'

'She's been here all right, but not with the MP.'

The journalist felt he should be more open with his host, in the hope of gaining some information in return.

'OK. I'm Nick Colton and you're right. I'm a journalist,' he explained.

'Raj Sharma. Pleased to meet you,' the shopkeeper replied.

'Was she a customer?'

'No. It's like this – I own the building and rent out the first floor. For the past two years, it's been tearooms. But over the years I've rented it out to various organisations. Mercedes came as a member of a self-help group. I think they were people who had problems with alcoholism.'

'We know her under a different name – Sadie.'

'I only knew her as Mercedes.'

'Do you know her surname?'

'No.'

'But you're completely sure that's Mercedes?'

'On my children's lives.'

'Was Mercedes friends with the MP?'

'Not as far as I know. Look, I'll let you into a little secret. I got to know her a little bit over a short period of time. Sometimes she'd arrive early and come to me for the upstairs key. That girl lived in a bit of a dreamworld and would say all sorts of strange things.'

Colton raised an eyebrow. 'What sort of strange things?'

'Well, she believed there were snakes in her garden, and she talked a lot about them. It was pure nonsense!'

'But you can't rule out that she might have known the MP?'

'Ealing's a small place. Everyone knows everyone. She told me she went to some of the Conservatives' meetings, so she probably met him.'

'Did the MP ever visit this building, as far as you know?'

'Never. I'd have heard about it if he'd been invited. And if he ever entered the building, I'd have probably had him thrown out.'

Chapter 15

The half-naked man sat shivering on a small chair in the former leather goods warehouse. He'd been blind-folded, his hands were bound behind his back and, for good measure, he'd been tied to the chair.

He'd been driven in a grubby lorry to this inhospitable place – the former overseer's office – against his will.

Now, slowly, he was beginning to guess the identity of his abductors from the sound of their voices. Standing over him, shouting and firing questions, stood Freddie Valmar, a burly forty-two-year-old Londoner who worked for the Diamond family as their 'enforcer'. He was smoking a cigarette and frequently blowing smoke into the man's face.

Beside him, and slightly taller, he recognised the deeper voice of Valmar's associate, Clifford Martin, who had rings on most of his fingers and a gold medallion round his neck. Based on what he'd heard during an earlier discussion, he knew Martin was holding a knife or a cricket bat.

Valmar bent down until his unshaven face and wire-framed glasses were just inches from the man's pale, worried expression.

'Now I'm going to ask you just once more why you'd got a cop's private number on your mobile.'

'I told you before, Freddie. He nicked my daughter when she got done for shoplifting down the Roman. I gave him a buzz a few times over a court date and forgot to wipe him off the phone after.'

'You're lying, mate! Now we really don't want to hurt you…'

'No?' replied the man, who was sitting in an empty ground-floor room with bare floorboards and no furniture. 'From where I'm sitting, I find that hard to believe.'

Valmar slapped his face. 'Don't be cocky with me, pal. All right, I think it's time we show you we mean business. Cliff, have you got your persuader?'

Martin held up a cricket bat which he'd placed on the floor before tying the man's hands.

'I'm sorry, Freddie. I've pulled a muscle in me shoulder.'

Valmar scoffed. 'Come on. Give it here,' he demanded. 'Knowing you, you couldn't hit an elephant's arse with a banjo.'

He snatched the weapon from Martin and struck the man on the head with it. The man cried out in pain. He then struck a second, more vicious blow which sent him sprawling onto the grimy floor, accompanied by the chair.

Valmar stepped forward. He trod on his victim's right hand until there was a crunching sound and he howled in pain.

'Do you want to reconsider what you just said about the copper or shall we fetch the pliers?'

'As God is my witness, I'd got that copper's number to find out about my daughter's court case. Honest!'

Valmar gestured for his colleague to put the victim's chair upright and place him back on it, which took several minutes. Then the pair stood staring at the man.

'Do you think he needs a bit more persuading, Cliff?' asked Valmar.

The muscleman shrugged. 'It's your call,' he said.

Valmar raised the bat in the air.

Heavy footsteps could be heard outside the room. Then a voice demanded, 'Hold on!' and Vince Diamond marched in.

'Let him go!' he insisted.

Valmar turned his back and took a few steps away. 'For God's sake!' he whined.

'I said, let him go!'

Martin shrugged his wide shoulders. He removed the navy-blue blindfold and proceeded to untie the man's hands.

Diamond stepped further into the room. 'You got the wrong man. This ain't the guy.'

Valmar spun round. 'How do you mean?' he demanded angrily.

'It's all right, Freddie. You weren't to know. I'll tell you all about it later.'

Valmar took a few paces with his head in his hands. 'I don't believe this. We've gone to a lot of trouble. We picked up this guy in Hackney. We bring him here and grill him for an hour. Now you tell us it's the wrong geezer.'

Diamond shrugged his shoulders. 'Shit happens. Get over it.'

Valmar rolled his eyes. 'Is that all you've got to bloody say?'

'Freddie, drop it. It ain't him. It's the wrong man. Send him on his way.'

Diamond walked back to his nearby office. Valmar glanced at Martin and shook his head. The man remained sitting on the chair, rubbing his wrists and appearing dazed. A fusion of blood and perspiration was dripping down the side of his head.

'It's all right, mate,' said Martin, as he placed the bat on the floor. 'You can go.'

'Where are my clothes?' the quivering man asked. Without a word, Martin collected them from a corner of the room. The pair watched without saying a word as the man dressed hurriedly.

'I'd go home and take an aspirin,' Valmar remarked before the man, trembling and shaking his head, stumbled out through the door. Once in the corridor, he became disorientated.

'Show him the right door,' Valmar said.

Martin darted out and showed the grateful man the exit. Then he returned.

'I'm pissed off,' Valmar fumed quietly. 'I'm sure that was the guy who's been tipping off the cops about our jobs.'

Martin gave a blank expression. 'The boss says different.'

'Maybe he does say different. Maybe he's right… but what if he's wrong?'

Martin grimaced. 'Don't say that. He's all right is Vinny.'

Valmar sneered but held his tongue.

Martin looked him in the eye. 'Hey, you don't think that guy will squeal?'

'Not much chance, I'd say. We know where he lives. But in the unlikely event he does, I'll break every bone in his pathetic body. Let's go into Vinny's office and have a word with him.'

A few minutes later, all three men were sitting round Diamond's desk.

'Sorry, lads,' Diamond began, puffing on a cigar. 'I just got a phone message confirming who's been tipping off the cops about our import operations.'

Martin's eyes lit up. 'Who is it then?'

'Don't want to say more at the moment. I've just got to check one more thing. By the way, Freddie, you did a good job in Hackney.'

Valmar smiled weakly. 'Thanks, Vinny.'

Diamond grimaced. 'What's the matter, Freddie? You're like a man who's wolfed down a doughnut and didn't find the jam.'

Valmar shrugged. 'It's nothing, Vinny.'

Diamond continued, 'You went a little too far at the pub, in my opinion. We didn't really want the guy to end up in hospital. Something like that brings too much attention. Puts us in the media spotlight, so to speak. But it's had the desired effect.'

'Yeah?'

'He's called us from the Homerton. He's promised to give us what he owes and pay on time in future.'

Valmar nodded. 'Very good, Vinny.'

Diamond continued, 'I'm a fair man. If I do a guy a favour, helping to care for his business and keep trouble away, all I ask for in return's a little recompense. Isn't that right, Cliff?'

Martin grinned. 'A fair day's wage for a fair day's work, my old grandad used to say.'

Diamond agreed. 'Your old grandad was right, Cliff. By the way, now I've got you both here, the shipment from Belgium's coming in next Wednesday, 10 July. I want you both here to open up the doors and unload the kayaks and toys.'

Valmar became pensive. 'What time, Vinny?'

'All depends.'

'On what?'

'On what time the boat gets in. How long it takes the lorry to pass through the port. How long it takes to drive here from Tilbury. I'd show up at about 7 a.m. and be ready for a long wait.'

Valmar stroked his chin. 'You won't be here, Vinny?'

'Don't know yet. I've got one or two problems to sort out. My boy might be here. We'll see.'

'How *is* Mickey?' Martin asked. 'Haven't seen him for a while.'

'He's been working for us out in Essex.'

Martin made no reply. His curiosity seemed satisfied.

Valmar and Martin stepped out onto Bethnal Green Road and turned left. They were heading for their usual lunchtime haunt, the Joiner's Arms, close to the church where the Kray twins' funerals were held two decades before.

As they walked, Valmar said nothing. He was engrossed in his private thoughts. He was thinking that diamonds might be forever, but sometimes they needed to be cut down to size.

Chapter 16

The sun streamed through the gaps in the curtains as Nick Colton lay sleeping beside Greta early on Wednesday morning. It flickered across his face, rousing him from his slumbers.

His thoughts immediately returned to the corner house in Ealing. The tearooms. The antique shop and the owner's recollections.

His problem today would be how to break the news to Chris Lane that the Sadie Robinson story was flawed. His conclusions wouldn't be popular. Weeks of hard work had gone into the investigation. Now the prospects of Cabinet minister Oliver Polebrook being exposed as a lecherous love-cheat were looking less and less likely.

Soon after he arrived in the newsroom, he phoned Lane's extension. But the phone went to voicemail, and he discovered Lane had left a lengthy message, explaining he'd be out of the office for most of the day. Colton simply left a request for him to call him and hung up.

* * *

Two hours later, Clemmie Jones marched across the room with a slip of paper in her hand and sat down with a broad smile on the edge of Colton's desk.

'Nick, darling, how did you get on with your job for Chris?'

He shook his head. 'On the plus side, I found the place.'

'Oh great.'

'The trouble is the owner swears blind Polebrook's never been there, and it seems as though the girl might have had – how shall we put it? – issues.'

'Oh well, you need to talk to Chris about that, obviously. He'll be in later. Meanwhile, I've got a message for you. Someone called the night-desk last night giving the name Raymond Barron. Is that some relative?'

His face lit up. 'That's David Barron's son. I've been trying to get an address for him.'

'Well, here you are. Flat One, 245 Elmdene Avenue, Highgate. They've also written down his phone number for you. He knows your name and he's eager to talk. I suggest you see if Tommy's free.'

'That's cool, Clemmie. Thanks.'

Before returning to her desk, she added, 'By the way, you've done well with the Barron stories. Keep it up!'

Colton wandered over to the picture desk, where Tommy Mundon was helping to answer the phones.

He greeted Colton with a chirpy 'Hello, mate' as he ended a call.

'Are we going off somewhere nice? Somewhere exotic?'

'London borough of Haringey.'

'Oh dear. We get all the best jobs, don't we!'

'It's the posher part. Highgate.'

'Ok, mate. Have you got your jam jar?'

'No, I came on the train.'

'All right, chum. We'll go in mine. I'll just get me gear and we'll be off.'

* * *

Ten minutes later, the pair were travelling in Mundon's BMW through Bethnal Green, Islington and Holloway until they reached Highgate – a district close to Hampstead Heath containing historic woods, a park and one of Britain's most famous cemeteries.

By eleven thirty, they reached their destination – a leafy avenue off the busy Archway Road. Colton had taken the precaution of phoning Raymond in advance. When they reached the red-brick Victorian house, he was already standing by the open front door, ready to greet them.

'Good of you to come,' Raymond called out as Mundon parked and the pair walked up the tiled path. Their host led them through a spacious hallway with high ceilings, and into a light, opulent living room.

It was furnished with two white leather settees, a wall-mounted television, white shelves laden with books and a solid-oak coffee table. Framed pictures of sports cars graced the white walls. Two Stratocaster guitars and two suitcases were in the front bay.

At the other end of the large room, patio doors gave access to a long, narrow garden, mainly laid to lawn.

'So sorry about your father,' Colton said, gazing awkwardly at Raymond. 'Oh, this is one of *The Post*'s photographers, Tommy Mundon.'

'Pleased to meet you both,' he replied, shaking their hands.

'Yes, you've got our sympathy,' said Mundon, who had one camera round his neck and was holding a black leather bag containing a second one.

Raymond appeared despondent. 'Yes, well. We're hoping to hold the funeral in Golders Green in a couple of days. Maybe I'll feel a bit better after that.' He gave a weak smile. 'Anyway, tea? Coffee?'

Colton gazed at his colleague. 'I think we'd both prefer coffee, wouldn't we?'

'Coffee would be grand,' said the photographer. 'White, two sugars.'

'The same,' said Colton. 'Thanks.'

As Raymond strode off to the kitchen, the pair made themselves comfortable on the settee. Mundon placed his two cameras on the floor before going to examine a photograph of a red car above the stone fireplace.

When their host returned with three mugs of coffee and a sugar bowl on a silver tray, Mundon asked, 'Is that Ferrari the 458?'

'That's right. Beautiful car,' Raymond agreed as he handed out the coffees. 'I'm saving up for one.'

'First unveiled in 2009 at the Frankfurt Motor Show, I believe.'

'Think so.'

Mundon sat down. 'Your dad had a Ferrari.'

'Yes, he had a California. You've obviously been up to Totteridge and seen it?'

'Yeah.'

As they spoke, Colton took a moment to study Raymond. A shy, earnest-looking man in his mid-twenties, he reminded him of the father, David. He wore black-framed glasses, was slightly overweight and had receding dark hair.

'I've only just got back from Dubai, Mr Colton, and–' He was interrupted by the rap music ringtone on the phone in his pocket.

Their host muttered, 'Forgive me' before walking over to the patio doors and answering the call.

'Yeah? Got back at eight o'clock last night. Got the Gatwick Express to Victoria and the Tube to Highgate … Yes, absolutely knackered. So the coroner's said it's OK for Thursday? That's cool … Yes. I'm definitely buying the flats. Got an appointment with the lawyer tomorrow … Yes, bloody good investment. It was Dad that put me onto it.'

There was a pause before he said, 'Hell of a shock at first, of course, but I've started to get over it a little now. How are you?' Another pause. 'So Fiona's been a great support, has she? And what about Grandma Alma? She's been a tower of strength, has she? That's wonderful. Thank you so much for keeping me up to date with what's been going on. I'd better go. There's someone with me. I'll give you a call later. Bye!'

As he walked back, he explained it had been his stepmother, Deborah, on the phone. 'Haven't spoken to her for a couple of days. She just wanted to check I was OK and let me know about the funeral arrangements. Fiona's been very supportive and so has my grandmother.'

Colton raised an eyebrow. 'Fiona?'

'Yes, Fiona Blake. Deborah's housekeeper.'

Raymond sat on a chair in the front bay with one of the coffee mugs. 'I'm glad you've come, Mr Colton. I wanted to thank you for being with Dad as he died. I appreciate that you tried to help him.'

The journalist shrugged. 'I merely moved him back into his seat after he slumped forward.'

'Yes, I read your article. I know you'd have done more if you could…' His voice trailed off. The memory of the fateful night was still a painful one. 'I wanted to thank you for being there.'

Colton looked downcast while sipping his coffee. 'Unfortunately, there was nothing anyone could do. If you want to know how your father seemed before the incident, I can tell you he was very happy with life. He was mainly talking about Loretta Kay, how she was a living legend. He was praising her as still note perfect and saying she was a great example of how the human spirit thrives.' He added, 'His death was instant. No lingering pain, if that helps.'

'Thank you. That means a lot. Mr Colton, before we go any further, I should mention that the police are coming over here. I received a call from a sergeant called Khan – Nadia Khan. She's been leaving messages for me on my landline several times a day since it happened. I'd been in two minds whether to cut short my trip, but I was over there buying into a development project suggested by my father. I felt he'd have wanted me to complete the deal before coming home.'

Colton shrugged. 'DCI Haynes is the detective I dealt with. Miss Khan must be working with him.'

'That's more than likely. Anyway, I didn't just invite you round to thank you. Mr Colton, I also wanted to tell you that I want as much publicity as possible about the shooting so we can catch the man. I won't call him a man. He's vermin. He shot my father from behind when he'd got absolutely no chance. I want him caught and punished.'

Mundon nodded. 'That's quite understandable. He has not only destroyed your father's life.'

Raymond drank some of his coffee. 'That's right. The entire family's devastated. My parents divorced when I was ten and I'm twenty-four now, but both my own mum and stepmum are devastated.'

Colton bent forward. 'Are you close to your stepmother?'

'Yes, I am, actually. She's always been very welcoming towards me, although my mother won't talk to her.'

Colton cautiously removed his notebook from his pocket and began writing. 'Do you have any idea about why your father was killed?'

He shook his head. 'I'm completely mystified. The way he was shot makes it look like a professional operation – the kind of thing you see at the movies. Dad had no enemies, as far as I'm aware. I'm really having problems getting my head round it. Mr Colton, he was the most kind, loving, devoted father a man could want. I'll never get over what happened.

'I don't understand how my father came to be targeted. The information about my father's attendance at the concert was well-known to the family and his close circle of friends. But, as far as I know, no one outside this group of people knew he would be going.'

Mundon slurped down a mouthful of coffee. 'You don't think any of his employees knew he was going? Perhaps one of them had a grievance.'

'No,' said Raymond. 'I can't think that any relative, friend or employee of my father's could be behind what happened. This was Loretta's second concert, wasn't it? She performed at the Albert Hall the night before. He'd tried to get a ticket for that one but failed and had to settle for seeing her Thursday performance.'

He was close to tears as he turned towards Colton.

'He'd been so excited about seeing her. He also had a ticket for the Cardiff concert, which is taking place tomorrow.'

Colton shook his head. 'It looks as though someone passed information about his concert trip to an assassin. If it wasn't someone in your family or in his close circle, who else could have been privy to that information, Raymond?'

'Maybe someone at the ticket office blurted out the information to someone,' Mundon suggested.

Colton put his notebook and pen down on the coffee table. 'Raymond, can you think of anyone at all who could be behind the death of your father?'

Mundon muttered a few words about needing pictures. Without asking Raymond, he took a Canon camera from his bag. Then he squatted in front of Raymond and focused. As his subject made no complaint, he took several shots from various angles.

'No, of course not, Mr Colton,' he was saying. 'My family are all decent people. They're not all angels, of course. I mean, there's Grampa Vince.'

Colton raised an eyebrow. 'Who's Grampa Vince?'

'Deborah's father. He's a bit of a wheeler-dealer.'

Mundon, whose family had strong ties with the capital's East End, stroked his chin. 'That's not Vinny Diamond, is it?'

'Yes,' their host conceded. 'I know he's got a bit of a reputation…'

The photographer gave an exasperated sigh. 'Not much,' he grumbled.

'…but there's no way he'd let anyone harm a hair on Dad's head.'

Colton was surprised by this disclosure. After years spent writing about the notorious families involved in London's criminal underworld, there was one name that stood out. It was a name that struck fear in people's hearts – even the callous hearts of fellow criminals. Vince Diamond.

Chapter 17

Although astonished to hear that David Barron's widow was the daughter of a London gangster, Nick Colton knew he had to press on with the interview. He didn't know how much time he'd got left with the dead man's son. The police might arrive at any minute.

'Can you explain what work your father did for Vince Diamond?' he asked impassively, picking up his notebook and pen and preparing to write again.

Raymond nodded. 'They worked together. Dad was his accountant. I know Grampa and Deborah's twin brother, Mickey, have been criticised a little in the press, but they're just highly successful entrepreneurs in the toy import business. Dad constantly gave them both valuable financial advice and he and Grampa were like brothers.'

Colton broke off from taking notes.

'You seem pretty certain that no one in the family could be connected with the attack on your father,' Colton said. 'But was there anyone else who might have had some kind of grudge? You know, maybe a client of his? Someone from your father's past?'

'Not that I know of. I'd always assumed that everyone loved and respected my father.'

'No one angry at being denied a pay rise or feeling they were being unfairly treated?'

He shook his head.

Colton continued, 'So only close and intimate friends knew he was going to the second of the two Loretta Kay concerts in London?'

He waggled his finger. 'That's not quite right, Mr Colton. I've just remembered something. The Loretta Kay Fan Club did a write-up about Dad in the spring issue. In it, Dad was quoted as saying he hoped to see Loretta at the Albert Hall in June.'

Mundon broke off from pressing his shutter button. 'Only die-hard fans will have seen that, Nick.'

Colton agreed. 'Yes, that's a fair point. The magazine's almost certainly got a restricted circulation. Raymond, I know what I was going to ask. Have there been any unusual incidents in recent weeks or months? Any suspicious behaviour?'

Raymond thought for a moment. 'The only strange incident was the man from the water company, but I expect my stepmum's told you about that.'

Colton's face was blank. 'No. Would you like to tell us what happened?'

'Yes, of course. It was about a month ago. My stepmum told me she heard the intercom buzzing. It was late in the day – about 5 p.m., just before Dad was due home. A guy claimed to be from Thames Water and that he needed to come in. He claimed some of the neighbours' drains were blocked and believed they were connected to ours.

'Deborah was rightly suspicious and refused to let him in. Later, she spoke to the neighbours and none of them had any drainage issue. She also called Thames Water and they said none of their staff had been in the area.'

The two visitors stared at each other in silence on hearing this second startling revelation. Mundon was about to comment, but his colleague raised a finger to stop him.

'We need to know the precise details. Do you recall the exact date of the incident?'

'I could ask Deborah, but I think it was either 28 or 29 May.'

'Can you check?'

'I'll phone her right now.' Seconds later, his phone connected with Deborah and he switched to loudspeaker. She confirmed the man called at ten minutes past five on 28 May.

Colton raised his voice.

'Mrs Barron, it's Nick Colton. Do you remember the exact words the man used when he spoke to you?'

'Well, let's see if I can remember. He said he was from the water company and then said, "I need to come in to check your drains. Some of your neighbours' drains are blocked and I suspect it's your drain that may be to blame." Then I just said there was no problem with our drains. I told him to go away and come back when he'd made a proper appointment.'

Colton asked, 'And how did he react to that?'

'Well, he was annoyed, but he could tell I was adamant.'

'Did the man have any particular accent?'

'Now you come to mention it, I think I detected a slight Irish tone to his voice.'

'And have you ever had any suspicious callers before or since?'

'No. I've had a fair number of tradesmen call round offering to cut our trees or clean our block paving, but nothing else. If I'd thought about it, I could have mentioned this man to you when you called round the other day.'

'Did you or anyone else see what this fellow looked like?'

'There's a hazy image of a man in a black hoodie on one of our CCTV cameras.'

'Any idea of the height or size of the man?'

'No. The image is too indistinct.'

Mundon interrupted to say, 'He didn't drive off in another Porsche, did he?'

'I heard that remark about a Porsche,' said Deborah. 'We've got no CCTV of any vehicle. When I spoke to the neighbours about the drains, I asked if they'd seen a man or a car. Neither had.'

'One last question. How did this make you feel?'

'Once I knew there was no drainage problem, of course I was worried. But then I just put it down to the sort of criminal behaviour you get these days. There are a lot of bogus callers trying to con their way into people's homes. If they get in, they steal your jewellery or TV. I'm still not sure if he was a burglar or if it was something more sinister.'

Colton thanked her for speaking to him. Raymond told her he'd call later before hanging up.

Mundon, who by now had a collection of thirty or forty images, sat down and packed his camera away in its case. 'Just as well she didn't let him in, Raymond,' he remarked.

'Yes,' the young man admitted. 'The same thought crossed my mind.'

Colton had a stern expression. 'The obvious implication is that this was an initial attempt to harm your father. After this rebuttal, that man may have carried out some research and discovered your father was going to the concert.'

'Yes, maybe it was a case of second time lucky for him.'

'There's just one issue I haven't covered. This is important. Did your father go out walking much?'

Raymond paused for a moment to think. 'Not much at all. He drove to his office in Muswell Hill and home again.'

'He just walked to the car and back then?'

'Yes. He drove straight into his car park at work.'

'Is there good security at the car park?'

'Yes. The gates open automatically and there's a high wall round it.'

'And did he go shopping on his own? For instance, would he ever traipse down to the corner shop on his own for a pint of milk?'

'Never. My father hated shopping.'

Colton was about to ask their host a few further questions when the doorbell rang. Raymond went to the window and peeked through the white vertical blinds.

'A tall guy in a suit and a woman. Must be the cops,' he concluded.

The two visitors stood up. 'I guess it's time to go,' said Colton as his colleague seized his camera and took one last picture.

'Thank you – both of you,' said Raymond, shaking his hand warmly. 'I do appreciate what you've done. You've got my phone number. Please call me if you need any further information.'

Colton had decided by then that Raymond was a kind-hearted, amiable soul. He reminded him so much of the polite stranger in seat L97 that he'd known for such a short time.

As Raymond went into the hall, Mundon groaned. 'Bloody nuisance that, the cops turning up. Hope I've got enough pictures. I was going to take him into the garden where the light's better.'

After a mumbled conversation in the doorway, Raymond returned.

'The detectives want to talk to you outside,' he revealed. 'Don't know what it's about, so I'll say goodbye.'

As soon as the pair stepped out of the front door and set foot on the path, they were confronted by an aggrieved chief inspector.

'Mr Colton, we meet again,' said DCI Haynes. 'I'm afraid I'm not very happy with you. This is my colleague, DS Khan.'

The journalist and the sergeant exchanged glances as they stood together on the path. Mundon stepped onto a corner of the unkempt front lawn.

Colton looked blankly at DCI Haynes. 'I'm sorry, Chief Inspector, but I'm not sure how I've offended you.'

'Coming round here talking to one of our potential witnesses. That's how. We've been trying to reach him for nearly a week. You've also been to see the Smarts in South Norwood and stirred up a right old hornets' nest. This is a murder inquiry and we're being hampered by the bloody press.'

'Just following up leads on the Barron story, Chief Inspector. Making responsible inquiries on matters that are in the public domain. No one's been charged so far, have they? So there's nothing off limits as far as I can see.'

'You're making our job ten times harder. That's all,' he said, pushing the front door open and marching inside.

DS Khan smiled. 'He's under a lot of pressure,' she whispered. 'I've been trying very hard to speak to this Mr Barron and, until now, he's proved rather elusive.'

Mundon took a step towards her. 'The young lad's been in Dubai.'

She nodded. 'So I gather. I've been reading your pieces with interest, Mr Colton. There's a chance I might need to give you a call at some point. Is there a number where I can reach you?'

Mundon laughed. 'He's always either in the office or the pub.'

Colton passed her a business card. 'Here's my number. Please call me any time.'

Chapter 18

It was nearly half past one by the time Nick Colton and Tommy Mundon drove away from Raymond Barron's home in Elmdene Avenue.

The photographer glanced across at his colleague. 'We don't have to rush back, do we, old chum? I'm a bit peckish.'

'So am I. A lot of the pubs round here are closed. Let's find a café on the way back. That'll give me a chance to sit and write down a few words.'

Amid the blistering heat and the throb of traffic, Mundon parked directly outside a café which was halfway along Junction Road in Upper Holloway. He turned off the engine.

Colton stepped out, clutching his notebook and pen. 'You know there are white zigzag lines here, don't you?'

'It's all right, Nick. I'll be keeping a close an eye on the motor because of my gear.'

After they'd chosen a table in the window, they ordered two coffees and two mixed grills. Colton took out a pen and began furiously writing in his notebook.

'Well, that's a revelation,' said the photographer. 'Fancy your concert friend's wife being the daughter of old Vinny Diamond. I used to go to school with him.'

Colton folded his arms. 'Yes, bit of a shock. The Diamonds are meant to be one of London's best-known crime families.'

'Not half. What's your story then – the Diamond family or the bogus workman?'

Colton put his pen down. 'Both. I'll nose the story off with, "Tragic accountant David Barron worked for one of Britain's most notorious crime families". Then the third or fourth sentence will tease the reader about the mysterious Irishman who tried to trick his way into the murder victim's home.' He paused to drink some coffee. 'You can see that Barron was a difficult target. Automatic entry at his home and work. Toughened glass in his Mercedes. Never goes out on his own.'

Mundon glanced at his car as a bus driver was trying to get past it. 'I don't blame him – what, with all the crime in London.'

'What did you make of Raymond?'

'I thought he was a very decent, likeable young man. I felt sorry for him – losing his dad when he's only in his twenties. And he's obviously got good taste in motors.'

When they returned to the office, there was a note on Colton's desk, asking him to call Chris Lane urgently. He managed to reach the investigations editor on his mobile. From the sound of loud voices, laughter and the clink of glasses, he gathered Lane was in the office pub, The Bosun's Wife.

'Can you see me in my office in half an hour, Nick?'

'No problem.'

After finishing his story about Barron's links to the crime family, he left the newsroom clasping his notebook and the photos of Polebook and Sadie Robinson. He reached the corridor that led to Lane's office and immediately became aware of the stench of alcohol, indicating Lane had recently passed this way a few minutes before. He knocked on the door and peered into the office.

'Ah, young Colton!' yelled Lane. 'I hear you found the mystery house but there was some kind of problem. Come in and tell me all about it.'

Colton sat down and inspected his notes. 'It took me hours to find the house.'

Lane slumped back in his chair. 'What did you do? Drive around?'

'Yes. But eventually I found what I thought was the right place. It was in a quiet street in West Ealing called Azalea Gardens. There's a side road called Hawthorn Drive and the premises are on the corner of the two streets.'

'Sounds right. Sadie said it was on a street corner.'

'Right. Well, it's actually an antiques shop, The Old Emporium.'

Lane was shaking his head. 'That doesn't sound exactly right. It's meant to be an ordinary suburban home.'

Colton ignored the remark and continued, 'The building's owner rents the first floor out. It's currently tearooms, but two years ago it was a meeting room.'

'Sadie told us she and Polebrook used to go upstairs. He'd ply her with booze from a drinks cabinet and then he'd have his wicked way with her on a double bed.'

Colton frowned. 'I'm sorry, Chris. Sounds like fantasy to me. I went inside the shop and spoke to the owner.'

'You what?'

'I began by making a note of everything in the shop window. While standing there, two old women entered a side door and went upstairs to the café. The waitress noticed me and invited me up.'

Lane was becoming agitated. Colton felt like a child who's built a sandcastle on the edge of an advancing tide.

'I gave you strict instructions not to go in. I didn't want to risk giving our hand away at his stage. Because you know what could bloody happen. The MP will get to hear what we're up to, talk to his legal cronies and get an injunction to halt the story.'

'Of course, I was aware of that.'

'Doesn't bloody sound like you were. So what exactly did you do?'

'I had a tea in the café and learned from the waitress that the shopkeeper downstairs owns the freehold. She didn't recognise Sadie or Polebrook from the pictures. Then I called at the shop and spoke to Raj Sharma, the Indian guy who owns it.'

Lane was leaning forward on his desk with his head in his hands.

'All right. You've gone against everything I said. What did this Mr Sharma tell you?'

'Well, he recognised both Sadie and the MP from the pictures.'

'Now we're getting somewhere.'

'But he said the MP's never been there. And here's the key thing, Sadie was attending a self-help group for recovering alcoholics.'

Lane sneered, making the sound of a punctured balloon.

'How did the antiques man know whether or not Polebrook had ever been there? He wouldn't have been at the meetings.'

'Chris, he says he dislikes Polebrook intensely and would never allow him in the building. He told me he'd have heard if Polebrook had attended. In any case, all the spiel about booze and a bed seems to be nonsense. I'm afraid this girl sounds like a fantasist. Mr Sharma said she had claimed to him there were snakes in her garden.'

'A fantasist? I've had Denise Barton-Jones taking her out for meals and drinks. We've got the girl's life history. We've been watching the MP's home. We're on first name terms with the girl's parents and friends and we were all set to go with the story. Now you're suggesting the affair's been entirely made up?'

'I'm afraid so,' said Colton. 'To be honest, Chris, I doubted the whole story from the outset. I mean, it's not impossible, but highly unlikely that a senior Tory, who's in the Cabinet, would have the time or the inclination to become involved with a woman in her twenties from a completely different background. But you add to that the fact she's got a snake obsession, I'm afraid I can only conclude it must be fiction.'

He paused before adding, 'By the way, Mr Sharma doesn't know her by the name Sadie. He knows her as Mercedes.'

'Mercedes?' Lane began ranting like a deranged fishwife. 'We've been working on this story for three months and you come along and put the whole investigation in jeopardy. You barge into this Ealing building, babbling to anyone who will listen. You were meant to make discreet inquiries – not dash in like a fox in a henhouse.'

Colton was annoyed at the direction in which the discussion was moving but strove to remain calm.

'Chris, that's an exaggeration. I was put in a difficult situation by the waitress. If I hadn't gone in and chatted to her, she'd have been suspicious. Then, after telling me about Mr Sharma, it would have been doubly suspicious if I hadn't spoken to him. In any case, if you don't ask any questions, you rather limit your ability to find any answers.'

These remarks seemed to placate the investigations editor a little.

'All right, Nick. I can see the point you're making. So what you're saying is that Sadie Robinson's got knowledge of this building because she went to a self-help group there for a while. That's how she remembers little facts like the burgundy curtains, the Victorian lamps and the 1950s radios. And she's woven it into her tale about Polebook?'

'Exactly.'

Lane continued, 'Polebrook's never been there, there was never a bedroom and Sadie shows signs of possible instability.'

'That's right, Chris. I've recorded my chat with Mr Sharma because I thought it would be important.'

'Good. I'll listen to that in a minute. Denise would want to hear it too. Mercedes, you say? I suppose Sadie could be a diminutive form of Mercedes. I'll get Denise to check with Sadie about her name.'

Colton was astounded to hear that Lane didn't seem to have taken one of the most fundamental steps of obtaining the woman's birth certificate, but he said nothing.

'All right. Let's leave it there. I'm sorry I raised my voice, Nick, but we've worked hard on this one and there's a good chance we may have to scrap the whole project now. Can you send me a memo, outlining what you've just told me?'

Colton nodded. 'I'll do it this afternoon.'

'Good man.'

Chapter 19

DCI Harry Haynes's white Audi glided into Fetterlock Lane at half past nine in the morning on Thursday 4 July and came to a halt at the side of the street.

'This bloody heat's unremitting,' he complained to his sergeant, who was sitting demurely beside him. He mopped his brow with a white handkerchief.

Khan agreed. 'The TV weathergirl said today could be one of the hottest days of the year, sir.'

'I don't doubt it. The place we're looking for, Diamond Enterprises, is just round the corner, if my memory serves me. I think we'll leave the car here. Do you know much about Vince Diamond, Sergeant?'

'Only what I've heard in the police canteen and in the pub, sir.'

'He might remember me. We've crossed paths before. He's got a list of previous as long as my arm and he's quite capable of disposing of anyone who gets in his way.'

The pair walked a short distance until they reached a series of posts, preventing vehicle access. The lane then split into two footpaths. One on the right led to a parade of council flats. The left-hand path led past a series of half-dilapidated warehouse buildings. They followed the second path which took them to the grey high-security door of the Diamond family's premises.

'Right. Let's see if we can attract someone's attention,' he said as he pressed a doorbell.

After a minute, a voice demanded to know who the caller was.

'Police. Open the door, please,' Haynes insisted while putting some chewing gum in his mouth.

Clifford Martin drew back the bolts, turned the key and pulled open the door. Haynes waved his warrant card and the tall, muscular West Indian stepped back as the chief inspector walked in, followed by his sergeant.

Martin's face was blank. 'I'm not sure if the boss is free.'

'Can you tell him we're here?'

'Who are you exactly?'

'DCI Haynes and DS Khan from the Met.'

While Martin climbed the rickety stairs to the first-floor office, the pair stared round the vast goods depot that lay open before them. Toys and clothing were stacked on rows of shelves into the far distance. Beyond the shelves, they could see three lorries and, beyond them, the steel roller-shutter doors of the goods entrance.

A few seconds later Martin appeared on the landing. 'Do you want to come up?'

At the top of the stairs a corridor led to a small suite of rooms. The doorman directed them to the first door on the right where Vinny Diamond was lounging behind his antique desk, engrossed in a phone call. Most of the room's grubby windows were open, allowing a gentle breeze to waft in.

'Good morning,' the chief inspector announced with a slightly gruff voice.

Martin stepped outside as Diamond glanced up at the pair and quickly ended the call. The businessman smiled and leaned forward in his chair.

'What can I do for you?'

'I take it you're Vince Diamond?'

'As long as I keep taking the pills.'

Haynes took a few steps across the bare floorboards until he was a few feet from the desk. 'DCI Haynes and DS Khan,' he stated, showing his warrant card.

Diamond was expressionless. 'I can't help you. I told your colleagues I'd got no information.'

'What colleagues would you be referring to?'

'The two guys from Hackney nick who called round three days ago. They were asking about an incident at a pub.'

'We're not here about that. We're from Kensington and Chelsea CID. We're here about a murder.'

Diamond looked at them blankly. 'I don't think I can help you there either.'

'Your late colleague, David Barron,' Haynes said with emphasis.

Khan, who'd been standing in the doorway, stepped forward to join the chief inspector.

'He wasn't a colleague. He was my accountant…'

'…and your daughter's husband.'

'Granted. But I know nothing about what happened to him in Kensington. Very sad, obviously. The whole family are upset, but I can't help you. I hadn't seen him in weeks.'

'Well, I've heard different,' said Haynes. 'I've heard you had a disagreement.'

'Over what?'

'Over money. I've heard you had a stand-up row with him and accused him of fiddling the accounts.'

'It sounds like you've been talking to the man's staff.'

'You don't deny having a row with him?'

Diamond leaned back in his chair. 'You're right. Words were exchanged. Not uncommon in business. I was concerned about the way he was conducting the accounts, but there's no way I'd arrange to have the man killed, if that's what you're thinking. My daughter's in pieces. Do you think I'd have him bumped off because of a row over a few quid?'

Khan took a pace forward. 'So, Mr Diamond…' she began.

'Oh she talks as well.'

'…Mr Diamond, we understand it was a row over more than just a few quid. You accused him of siphoning off thousands of pounds.'

'That's nonsense. Me and David was like brothers.'

'Then you won't mind if we have a good look round. We'd like to see your accounts, your files and–'

'Yes, I do mind. I've got a business to run. I don't want people coming in here and snooping round.'

'Surely you don't have anything to hide?' said Khan.

'No. I don't have nothing to hide, but that's not the point.'

Haynes frowned. 'Go and take a butcher's, Sergeant.' She left the room to find Martin leaning on a wall in the corridor, smoking a cigarette.

'Um, er…' he stammered. She ignored him and wandered into the office next door while her boss continued talking to Diamond.

'You've got a bloody nerve, Chief Inspector,' he fumed. 'You need a warrant to carry out a search, as you well know.'

Haynes pulled a paper document from his pocket and handed it across the desk.

'Issued by magistrates this morning. So you've had Old Bill round already this week? Things aren't going well for you, are they, Vinny?'

'I'm not fazed by you people. It's just that you're bad for business – very bad. I'm here trying to make a living running an operation that's totally kosher and I keep getting interrupted.'

'I'd have thought you owed it to Mrs Barron to help the police.'

'I'd help if I could, believe me. But you're speaking to the wrong person. You should be searching for someone with a genuine grudge against David – not talking to someone who had a minor tiff with him.'

Without being invited, Haynes drew up a chair. 'Look, I'm going to need some information before I finish with you. To start with, what's your home address?'

'Why should I give that to you?'

'Because, if you don't, I'll be round here every day, I promise you, until I get it.'

Diamond reluctantly took a piece of paper from a drawer and wrote his address down. Then he handed it to the chief inspector.

'Anything else?'

'I want a list of the names and addresses of everyone in your family who's involved in the business. How many staff you got?'

'Eight. Maybe ten.'

'I'll want their details as well.'

'Don't ask for much, do you?'

'Routine police procedure after a murder.'

'My son Mickey's the only actual family member currently on the payroll here.'

'Right, you'd better get busy then. I want his details and those of every member of your staff. And where are your business records?'

'They're all with Barron & Partners in Muswell Hill.'

'What? Even the recent ones?'

'Well, the recent accounts are here on me computer.'

'I also need to ask you where you were a week ago today – Thursday 27 June between 7 p.m. and 8 p.m.'

'Well, I don't know. Let me think. That was the night I was at my favourite Indian restaurant, the Curry Palace in Southgate.'

'Can anyone vouch for that?'

'I was with my boy. I hadn't seen him for a while, so we met up for a curry. Ask Ashok, the owner. He'll tell you.'

At that moment, DS Khan returned, carrying a cricket bat. 'See what I found tucked away in a cupboard, Chief Inspector. There's blood on the edge, near the bottom.'

Haynes looked Diamond in the eye. 'How do you account for that?'

He shrugged. 'My boy got struck on the hand with a ball while playing for his village cricket team. Some of the blood must have dripped onto his bat.'

Haynes frowned. 'So why does he keep it here?'

'I don't know. Maybe he wanted a game in his lunch hour.'

'If you can't come up with a better story than that, we're impounding it.'

Khan, still carrying the bat, joined the chief inspector as he made his way to the door.

'You're not leaving, are you?' called Diamond in a mocking voice. 'We were having such a pleasant conversation.'

'Yes, we're leaving,' said Haynes. 'But don't worry. I expect we'll be back to see you again sometime soon.'

Once they'd returned to his car, the chief inspector called one of the detective constables and asked him to attend David Barron's funeral, which was being held the next day in Golders Green.

'Just keep an eye on the attendance,' he told the constable. 'I want a list of everyone there.'

In the meantime, a team of forensic staff drew up in a white van, accompanied by three uniformed police.

'Please brief them, Sergeant,' he said. 'Some of their team will have to take the second warrant round to the Diamonds' home in North London. Both premises must be thoroughly searched, and we'll need to seize computers and phones.'

Khan asked, 'You believe Vince Diamond's involved in the shooting of his son-in-law, sir?'

'From where I'm sitting, he's as guilty as a cat in a fishbowl.'

Chapter 20

The young office worker peered uneasily over his shoulder as he walked along Effra Road towards Lambeth Town Hall, the Edwardian Baroque-style building in the heart of Brixton.

He suspected he was being followed.

It was nearly midday. The streets would soon echo to the sounds of office and shop staff queuing for lunch at cafés, pubs and sandwich bars. For now, the pavements were almost deserted as he passed the Grade II-listed municipal landmark across the street from him.

He was making a call on his mobile phone as he passed on his right the Ritzy Cinema at the top of Coldharbour Lane and the KFC.

He cast his eyes back again. The same man with the blue hood was twenty metres behind him. He appeared to be listening to music on some headphones. It was hard to estimate an age. Probably, like himself, he was in his late twenties. He seemed about six feet tall as he strolled along in his dark-blue jacket with its sewn-in hood and grey slacks.

Frequently, whenever he turned round, the hooded man would stop briefly to gaze into a private garden or a shop. But, whoever he was, he remained steadfastly on his tail.

The city professional had taken the morning off to do some shopping. It was such a fine day he'd decided to walk from the shops in Herne Hill to Brixton Underground Station, two miles away. He then planned to travel to his office in the Square Mile.

He first noticed the stranger a few minutes after entering Effra Road, a tree-lined avenue with wide lawns, residential flats and commercial buildings. He was uncertain, but suspected the man may have been following the same route as him from the time he left the shops, where he'd bought a new pair of trainers and a children's book for his niece.

Is it just a coincidence? he wondered. Will he disappear down a side road at any moment? Or is he, by sheer coincidence, heading for Brixton Tube Station like me?

The young professional, who was clutching his purchases in a carrier bag, ended his phone call. Then he passed a Barclays Bank, a fashion store, the famous Reliance shopping arcade, a chemist's and an Iceland supermarket. He removed his jacket and began to carry it. He was perspiring so heavily he kept mopping his brow.

At last, he reached the station entrance, where he rushed down the stairs into the concourse. By the barriers, he swiped his travel pass and manoeuvred his way through. To his consternation, the hooded man also entered the station and approached the same barriers.

Now he had a white cotton scarf covering the lower part of his face.

The office worker felt uneasy. There was something menacing about the hooded man. He felt afraid and set himself a swifter pace.

When he reached the escalators, he made his way down as quickly as he could. Perhaps he was worrying unnecessarily, he told himself. On any morning, a good proportion of pedestrians venturing along Brixton Road were likely to be heading for the station. It's a key transport hub, he told himself. Why should anyone be pursuing him?

At the foot of the escalator, he followed a sign for trains to Victoria and emerged through a passageway onto the platform. He strode along until he found a bench and sat down, placing his bag beside him. The hooded man was at first nowhere to be seen. Then he appeared through the passageway. He strolled towards him. He was getting closer.

The office worker's heart was beating faster as the stranger stopped a few metres away. He seemed to be staring at the blank spaces for posters on the far wall.

He struggled to overcome his nerves. He gazed directly at him, but the man made no effort to return his gaze. He kept his head turned away as though unwilling to show his face. The office worker stared at the ground and so they remained for a while.

Then, as a few fellow travellers appeared on the platform, an overhead sign flickered into life, informing them a train to Victoria would be arriving shortly.

Minutes passed and the sign changed. It now read, 'Stand clear. Train approaching.' The city worker stood up and ventured to the platform's edge, gazing at the other passengers as they too began moving forward. The train was coming clattering through the tunnel. The driver's cab would emerge at any second.

Then suddenly he felt himself being thrust towards the track. Terror pulsated through him. He felt as though a blacksmith's hammer was pounding inside his heart.

He struggled against the momentum, but he'd been taken by surprise. He screamed as he lost his footing and tumbled onto the track. The oncoming train hurtled by with the horrified driver unable to stop.

The air filled with screams as the other passengers realized the man had plunged beneath the electric locomotive. Several rushed to the spot where he'd fallen as the train slowed and came to a halt beside the platform.

Two men took it upon themselves to pursue the hooded man, but he'd sprinted up the escalator and out of the station before anyone could catch him or even snatch a proper glimpse at his face.

* * *

Nick Colton had spent that same Thursday morning busily phoning his personal contacts, collecting as much information as he could about the Diamond family. But it had been a frustrating task. The family were highly secretive. He'd resorted to viewing published news reports on his office computer. By the time his watch showed it was nearly one o'clock, he was ready for his lunch break.

'All right, mate?' asked Foster, who'd spent the morning in court, covering a case involving a couple arguing over the ownership of a home worth two and a half million pounds.

'Yeah, no sense complaining. No one ever listens.'

'I'll listen, mate,' said Foster. Luke Foster had begun his career on a local newspaper in Lancashire, unlike Colton who'd started on a Kent newspaper.

'I know. How did your case go?'

'It's been slow today. The office called me back because agencies are there. Don't think the woman's got much hope. Think she'll end up having to sell up and give the guy half the proceeds. Do you fancy a drink?'

'Best thing anyone's said all morning.' He waved at Katie McMillen, who was reading a copy of the *Evening Standard*. Then he wriggled his hand at her in a drinking gesture.

'Where you going? The Bosun?' she asked. Colton glanced at Foster, who raised his thumb in agreement.

* * *

Ten minutes later, Colton was queuing at the noisy nearby bar while his two friends commandeered a table overlooking the quayside. As he returned with a white wine for McMillen and two lagers for himself and Foster, he removed his grey jacket and placed it on the back of his chair.

McMillen, who was dressed less flamboyantly than usual in a grey trouser suit, asked how his work on the Barron story was progressing.

Colton shrugged his shoulders. 'Well, you saw my piece this morning, didn't you?'

'Yes. What was the headline? Crime family linked to Albert Hall victim?'

'That's right. It looks as if Barron's family life could be a factor in the murder.'

McMillen nodded. 'Sounds likely, doesn't it.'

'But did you see the story in the *Graphic*?' asked Colton. 'They had a reasonable Barron story as well.'

'Yes, the Porsche owner,' said Foster, after taking a sip of his pint. 'Didn't really move the story on a great deal.'

McMillen pouted. 'Missed that. What was that about?'

Colton frowned. 'The car owner's shock on learning his beloved Porsche was the killer's getaway vehicle.'

His phone rang. It was Greta wishing to discuss a problem with one of the children and he moved outside for a better signal.

When he returned to the table, Foster and McMillen were discussing a rumour that their news editor, Clemmie Jones, might be moving to another Fleet Street newspaper. But they spoke in low voices because other staff from *The Post* were standing nearby.

Ten minutes later, Foster's phone rang. He mouthed the words 'news desk' as he listened to Jones outlining some detailed instructions. Like Colton, he decided to take the call outside as the hubbub of conversation was growing louder.

In a short time, he was back, gulping down the remains of his drink and snatching his jacket from his chair.

He appeared flustered. 'Got to go, gang.'

Colton smiled. 'Typical of you. Just when it's your round.'

'Sorry. The desk want me to get down to Brixton. Some poor bloke's been shoved under a train.'

Chapter 21

When Nick Colton reached his office on Friday 5 July, a flotilla of boats were bobbing about in their berths along the nearby quayside. A rusty old barge was gliding silently away across the shimmering water of the dock.

Temperatures that day were predicted to reach twenty-six Celsius.

No sooner had he removed his jacket and hung it on his chair than Clemmie Jones was tapping him on the shoulder and thrusting a piece of paper in his hand.

'An ex-army guy called Ryan asked to speak to you. He says it's about David Barron. Here's his number.'

He beamed at her. 'Thanks, Clemmie. Did he say if it was urgent?'

'No. He just wanted to talk to you. He said he'd got some important information.'

Colton tried to phone the mobile number, but the call continually went to voicemail.

Since he had nothing to do for the moment, he began flicking through the first few pages of that morning's edition of *The Post*. A report about the man killed in Brixton caught his attention. There was a photograph of the body covered in a blanket with a uniformed policeman stooping over it in the dim light. Underground staff had raised the bloodied corpse from the track under police supervision. Then he noticed an object in the picture that seemed strangely familiar.

As he stared at the image, he realized someone was standing by his desk. He looked up. It was thirty-year-old Denise Barton-Jones, the slim, dark-haired investigations reporter. She scowled at him.

'You know they're scrapping the Polebrook story because of you,' she sneered. 'Three months' work down the bloody pan.'

He shrugged as he looked up at her. 'I'm sorry, Denise, but there was no way that woman Sadie could have met up with the MP at that building in Azalea Gardens. It's clearly a figment of her imagination.'

Denise rolled her eyes. 'I've been speaking to her constantly. I've met her mother and two of her friends. There's no way she's a fantasist. Polebrook's even been to the mother's house in Acton.'

'Was the mother there at the time?'

'Well, no. The couple were obviously spending time alone together there.'

'So how does the mother know they were there? Only because Sadie told her so, I imagine. I'm sorry, Denise, but you know very well all sorts of people come onto us claiming to have a great story, and we have to sort the wheat from the chaff.'

She raised her voice. Other reporters peered out from behind their screens to watch the commotion.

'You've just ruined what would have been an absolutely terrific story, Nick. And you've just done it on a whim.'

Denise raised her head into the air and began to march away.

Colton shouted after her, 'If we'd run that dodgy story, the MP would have taken us to the cleaners.'

He resumed reading the Brixton story and realized why his attention had been drawn to the picture.

Foster rose from his seat and strolled over. 'What was all that about, mate?'

'Oh, Denise from Investigations. She was moaning that they've spiked her story about the Cabinet minister Oliver Polebrook. He was meant to have been romping with a beautician at a house in West London, but I checked it out and Polebrook's never been seen there.'

'Denise was really laying into you, mate.'

'I know. Listen, how did you get on in Brixton?'

Foster shrugged. 'Most of the eyewitnesses had gone by the time I got there. You've seen my piece, haven't you? Our snapper did brilliantly. Somehow he managed to get a picture of the body lying on the platform just before it was removed.'

'I saw that. Luke, there's a Metro Harvest bag next to the body. Did it belong to the man who was killed?'

'Why do you ask?'

'Because I saw a bag exactly like it on Saturday – when I was visiting Craig Arnold.'

'The man who swapped seats with Barron?'

'Yes. The words on the bag in green letters said "Metro Harvest". It was a phrase that stuck in my mind.'

'Mate, there must be thousands of those bags in London. There's probably nearly as many of those as there are Tesco and Asda bags.'

'I suppose you're right,' Colton conceded as his colleague walked away.

As the morning wore on, he made inquiries about a seventeen-year-old boy who'd been stabbed in North London, but he was unable to concentrate. All he could think about was that the man murdered in Brixton might be Craig Arnold.

He called British Transport Police to find out when they'd be releasing the dead man's name. But officers were still in the process of identifying the victim and informing next of kin. They didn't expect to release any more details until later in the week.

He dialled Arnold's phone number but his call went straight to voicemail. Then he remembered that Arnold had mentioned working for city stockbrokers Springfield Mead. Surely, he thought, if he called Arnold's office and discovered him there, that would set his mind at rest.

He dialled the firm's number. A polite male voice announced, 'Springfield Mead. Matthew speaking.'

He took a deep breath. 'I'd like to speak to Craig Arnold.'

'I'll just see if he's available. Won't keep you long,' said the voice.

After holding him on the line for nearly a minute, Matthew returned to inform him that Arnold wasn't in the office.

'Can you tell me when he's next due in?'

'Hold on.' After a pause, Matthew said, 'I'll just put you through to someone who can help.'

Seconds later a surly female voice came on.

'I'm sorry,' she said. 'I'm Mr Arnold's manager and we've got no information at this time.' She then hung up.

Without realising it, the woman had partly confirmed Colton's worst fears – that Arnold might be the Brixton train victim. A picture was forming in his head. A carrier bag identical to Arnold's was found with the body. Arnold was absent from work.

Moreover, staff had been told to keep shtum. Normally, the response from a manager would be a cheery 'Try again tomorrow' or 'Oh, he won't be in till Friday, lucky fellow.' No, there was a sinister aura regarding his absence. It was, of course, possible that, all the time, the man was in bed with a cold or upset stomach, but his journalistic instinct told him otherwise.

He kept glancing towards the news desk where Clemmie Jones was engrossed in a phone call. After a few minutes, he seized his opportunity and hurried to her desk.

'Clemmie, I need to talk to you.'

'Not now, Nick. I'm going into conference.'

'Clemmie, it's urgent. I think the man murdered in Brixton was the guy who swapped seats with David Barron.'

She frowned. 'What makes you think that?'

'Oh, a number of reasons.'

'What are you planning to do?'

'I want to call round at his home in Dulwich to confirm my suspicions.'

She nodded as she picked up a sheaf of documents. 'All right, Nick. I haven't got time right now. Go down there, if you must. You'd better speak to Pictures.'

Chapter 22

Craig Arnold's townhouse was as quiet as a monastery at prayer and the street was deserted when Nick Colton drew up outside, early that afternoon. He was alone on this occasion as no photographer had been available.

After trying the bell several times, he returned to his car and watched through his windscreen as traffic passed up and down the street. Colton recognized that, if the man had lost his life at the station, there obviously would be no one at home.

On the other hand, if he had simply taken the day off work, it was again likely there would be no one at home. He would almost certainly be out somewhere, enjoying the fine weather.

But Colton had the uneasy feeling that he would not be seeing Arnold again. And the longer he remained there, the more he convinced himself his instinct was right.

He was trying to decide whether to drive off when a slightly battered red Fiesta trundled into view. A blonde-haired woman was visible at the wheel as it drove into the close and stopped behind his car. He recognised her as Jasmine Smart.

She seemed more presentable than on the previous Saturday. Her hair was tied behind her head, and she was wearing make-up, although still dressed in a pink top and jeans.

'Oh, it's you, Nick,' she said as she locked her car and came towards him. 'You've obviously heard what happened.'

'Well, I've guessed.' He could tell she had been crying. As she approached him, she held her arms out and he gave her a quick hug.

'It's so awful,' she sobbed. 'To be pushed under a train. How on earth did you find out, Nick? The cops have only just told Craig's family.'

'Guesswork. I recognised his shopping bag lying beside him at the station and called his work, who half-confirmed it.'

Jasmine explained she'd called round the previous evening to see Craig. She'd let herself in with a key he'd lent her and watched television while waiting for him to come home.

'I tried his phone several times, but it went to voicemail which is quite unlike him. At 10 p.m., I called the police, who came round and told me he'd died. I couldn't believe it.

'They said they suspected he was pushed onto the track by a psychiatric patient. There've been a few cases of that happening at stations in recent times. Oh my God, Nick. What am I going to do?'

He adopted a serious tone. 'Shall we go inside? It'll be more private.'

Jasmine fumbled in her pocket and produced a Yale key. She opened the door and stooped to collect some post from the doormat. Then she held the door open for him.

She led him upstairs to the cluttered living room that he remembered from before. It appeared someone had attempted to tidy up and he found he was more easily able to sit on the leather settee.

Jasmine, who spoke in an erudite voice with a slight London accent, made an effort to smile. 'Tea or coffee? I'm afraid there isn't any milk.'

'Have you got any cold drinks?' the journalist wondered.

She checked the fridge. 'How about a cold beer?'

'Sounds good,' he replied.

After handing him a can of lager and a glass, she sat down on the couch. 'Sorry about the mess. I haven't had a chance to do the housework.'

He shook his head. 'Don't apologise. Can you tell me why Craig went to Brixton yesterday?'

'Oh, you're not going to quote me, are you? There's no way I can be in the paper.'

He smiled sympathetically as he sipped his drink. 'Don't worry. This is just for background.'

'Craig told me he was taking the morning off and he was meant to be shopping for his niece's birthday in Herne Hill, which is half a mile down the road. He called me on his mobile at about ten minutes past twelve and said it was such a nice day, he'd decided to walk from there to the Tube station. That was the last time I ever spoke to him. Oh, Nick… he was the kindest, gentlest guy in the world. I'll never love anyone as much as Craig. He was the world to me.'

'I'm so sorry, Jasmine,' said Colton.

Absent-mindedly, he glanced at the newspapers and magazines on the floor. 'Do you have any idea who might have done this terrible thing?' he asked. 'Do you agree with the police that it might have been someone with mental health problems?'

'I don't know what to think. I suppose the police theory is possible. I really hope they catch this person.'

His eyes drifted round the room as he sought a way of asking his next question tactfully. 'Jasmine, do you know of anyone who might have wished to harm Craig?'

'No. I know what you're thinking, Nick. You know I was about to leave my husband and move in here with Craig.' She paused before adding, 'It's true that Alex found out about Craig and has made threats against him. It's also true that Alex has been violent towards me at times and that I was planning to leave him. I'm still planning to. But I can't believe he'd push a man under a train. In any case, he was at his mother's care home in Croydon all morning yesterday and there's no way he could have been in Brixton at lunchtime.' She tugged a paper tissue from the pocket of her jeans and blew her nose.

He shrugged. In his mind, Alex Smart had a strong motive for wishing to dispose of Craig Arnold. He had to be considered a prime suspect. But, if he was eight miles away in Croydon at the time of the death, then he could be ruled out. Therefore, he decided, the possibility that the bogus plumber had struck a second time couldn't be discounted.

He gazed back at Jasmine. 'Can you think of anyone else who might have wished Craig harm? Had he fallen out with anyone?'

She paused for a moment. 'There was a fellow at work. Don't know his name. Craig was always moaning about him. He was forever putting Craig down. He made a complaint to his manager about the guy, who was hauled up in front of the managing director and given a warning. But I hardly think–'

'Jasmine, have you been in touch with Craig's family?'

'Yes. I came round here at the crack of dawn this morning. I found a phone number for his brother, Jason, and called him. The cops had already broken the news to him and Craig's mother…'

Her cheeks by now were strained with tears. 'Listen, I have to go to the bathroom…' She left the room and climbed the stairs to the bathroom. Colton heard the sound of running water and sensed she was rinsing her face. Then she returned.

'I'm sorry. I was telling you about the cops. They came round at ten o'clock. They searched the house and took some documents and letters away. They also took his address book and mobile phone.'

He interrupted to ask, 'Have we got any pictures of Craig I can borrow for a day or two? I'll make sure you get them back.'

'Definitely. I'll email some over when I'm feeling up to it.'

As he finished his drink, he recognised that, as he couldn't quote Jasmine by name for his story, he'd need to obtain a statement from one of Craig's relatives.

'Do you think Craig's brother would speak to me?' he asked.

Jasmine shook her head. 'I'm not sure. I don't know Jason very well. I've only spoken to him twice before today. Of course, the family are absolutely devastated, like me. They've told the cops they don't want to be hassled by the press.'

'Could you give him a call and try? He might change his mind. You can explain that you know me and that I don't bite.'

'All I can do is try.'

Over the next hour, Colton was able to convince Jason Arnold to speak with him and he eventually called the journalist back with the most heart-rending statement.

> *Craig, who's been so cruelly taken from us, was the kindest, sweetest man you could ever wish to meet. He leaves behind his heartbroken mother, brother, sister and niece who all loved him dearly, as well as dozens of friends. We are appealing as a family to the public to help the police find the monster who committed this evil act.*

Chapter 23

'You're home early, darling,' said Greta as her husband turned his key in the lock and stepped inside his home. She planted a kiss on his cheek. 'What's the matter? You have a haunted look.'

'You remember the ginger-haired guy who swapped tickets with David? He's been murdered.'

It was as though a bomb had exploded in her face. 'Dio Santo! You must be joking.' He followed her into the living room where they both sat down.

'I'm not joking. Craig Arnold is dead.'

'That's the man you went to see in Dulwich on Saturday, isn't it?'

He nodded. 'Yes. Pushed in front of a train yesterday lunchtime.'

'Where?'

'Brixton. It's a Tube station close to his home in Dulwich.'

'Did anyone see who did this?'

'Police are hoping to find images of the killer on the station's CCTV. But the man ran off before anyone could catch him.' He paused before adding, 'The body's in the mortuary and police are expected to release details shortly. Where are the children?'

'Playing upstairs.'

She twiddled with a lock of her long, dark hair as she contemplated her husband's news. 'If it's not been officially confirmed by police yet, how do you know it's him?'

'I've just been over to the Dulwich house again. Jasmine, his girlfriend, was there. She confirmed it and I've got a statement from the family. The office are going to run the story tomorrow.'

'Nick, I'm thinking maybe people are going to start wondering about you. First the guy sitting next to you at the concert gets shot. Then the guy you visit in Dulwich is in a train crash. Maybe your friends are going to start avoiding you.'

He ignored her comments, which were made half-jokingly.

'Greta, I'm realizing now the two deaths might be connected. It's possible David Barron was killed in error and Arnold was the target all along.'

'Yes, Nick. That's definitely something the police should be considering. I feel sorry for Jasmine and the family.'

He nodded. She bowed her head and stared at the floor, as if a solution to the riddle of the double murders could be found there.

A sudden thought occurred to him. 'The whole situation is so bizarre. Two men swap concert tickets and they both end up dead. So, here's a possible theory. Could Craig Arnold have been in league with the gunman in some way? Do you think he was sent into the hall to find Barron and point him out to the gunman? The ticket exchange could have been to ensure Barron was sitting closer to the doorway and an easier target. Then a week later, the gunman kills Arnold and thereby eliminates the person who can identify the killer.'

Greta tutted. 'No. That sounds like nonsense, Nick. The way it looks to me is that Jasmine and her boyfriend were in love and longing for an evening out together. The gunman – maybe the angry husband – comes looking for them. He shoots David by mistake. A week goes by. He makes up for his mistake by pushing the boyfriend under the train.'

He nodded. 'I can see the logic in what you're saying.'

* * *

Later that evening, after he'd had supper with his family and read both children a bedtime story, Colton's mobile phone rang. From the gruff tones of the caller's opening remarks, he could tell it was his night news editor. He smiled.

'Nick, this ex-army guy's phoned again. He's desperate to speak to you about Barron. Didn't you get the message I left Clemmie?'

Colton's smile vanished as quickly as a teenager's first wage packet.

'I'm sorry, mate. I tried him earlier, but his phone went to voicemail. Then it passed out of my mind. I'll call him now.'

'Good man.'

He dialled the number immediately and found himself listening to the mellow, educated voice of a former soldier using the name Ryan.

'I tried you earlier, but your phone seemed to be off,' Colton explained.

'That's all right. I've got some information that you might find useful. It's about David Barron.'

'What exactly is it you've got?'

'Well, did you know he was in the army with the Worcestershire and Sherwood Foresters twenty years ago? And that he once got into some deep trouble?'

'No. Sounds like we ought to meet up and have a chat about it. Are you free? Whereabouts are you?'

'Blackheath.'

'That's cool. I'm only a few miles away. Do you know the Princess of Wales on the heath? I'll meet you there at eight o'clock. I'll be wearing a grey suit.'

After telling Greta he needed to meet a contact, he drove up the hill and across the vast open common until he reached the historic, stone-built pub.

The air was filled with the sound of clinking glasses, loud voices and revelry as he parked by the pond and approached the main doors. A few old men were sitting and drinking on a cluster of tables outside. Across the road, on the edge of the heath, customers were relaxing with drinks on the grass as the sun began to sink towards the horizon.

'You Nick Colton?' asked a man crouched beneath a black umbrella by the entrance. An empty beer glass stood on the small round table beside him.

He nodded and shook his hand. 'Ryan? Pleased to meet you.' He was a tall, burly man who was balding and had a bushy, brown beard. He was wearing dark glasses.

Colton wondered if they could find a quiet corner inside to hold their conversation, but Ryan shook his head.

'The place is packed. We'll have to manage here,' he said.

After buying two pints of lager at the bar, Colton joined him at the table. 'So you were saying you knew David Barron in his army days?' he asked in a low voice.

'That's right. By the way, I was going to ask you, is there any money in this? I wasn't thinking for me. I don't need money. But maybe for Help for Heroes?'

Colton frowned. 'That's a good charity, but I have to tell you. People hear about huge sums paid by newspapers to celebrities and think every story brings a payday, but it's not the case. We usually only pay out for really big exclusives. I tell you what. I don't mind making a small donation for your assistance.'

'That would be great.'

'What's your surname, by the way?'

'Don't want to go into that. Listen, in the 1990s David Barron and me were officer trainees together and joined the Foresters as second lieutenants. David was a great man to have around when things got tough. Reliable guy. But in 1995, when he was about twenty-two, he was involved in a night-time training exercise in Scotland which ended tragically. One of the lads was shot by mistake and David was the guy who pulled the trigger.'

Colton, who was taking notes, raised an eyebrow. 'Was the lad killed?'

'Critically injured in his lower back and spinal cord. Left paralysed from the waist down.'

'Oh God.'

'There was a disciplinary hearing. David was charged with negligently performing a duty. But he got off after army top brass admitted there'd been several failings prior to the exercise. They said the risks of such a tragedy happening hadn't been recognised by the fire team, the supervising officers or the battalion leadership.'

Colton sipped his beer before glancing across at the ex-soldier. 'That's interesting. I might be able to find reports about this in the news archives.'

'I'm not sure you will. The army hushed it up. They wanted to preserve David's career. They saw him as a promising young officer. But he was devastated, of course. He told me his heart wasn't in the army anymore and he left a year later. I imagine he tried to forget it and get on with his life, but the family of the injured private didn't forget.'

'What was his name?'

'Aron Gentle. His wife left him afterwards. She couldn't cope with a husband in a wheelchair and his life fell apart. He's spent years struggling, living on benefits. The top brass kept promising to help him, but their help turned out to be just that – promises.'

Colton stroked his chin. 'So the family can't have been too happy when David Barron left the army in one piece and became the wealthy boss of an accountancy firm?'

'Dead right, Nick. They were livid – particularly Aron's brother. I've got a relative in the Midlands who read a newspaper article about the family's campaign for justice. The brother, Riggs Gentle, was quite scathing about the unnamed officer he blamed for Aron's plight.'

Colton closed his notebook and put his pen away. 'Well, thank you, Ryan, for filling me in on this.'

‘I haven’t explained the main reason I phoned you. You know your story on the front page last Friday about the gunman? Tall, piercing blue eyes, a short goatee beard and black hair? It immediately put me in mind of Aron’s brother.’

Chapter 24

DCI Harry Haynes stepped out of the police station lift and made his way, panting and perspiring, to his office. He greeted two of the staff who passed him with a brusque ‘good morning’ but his attention was elsewhere. He was anxious to find his sergeant.

He eventually spotted her leaning against a whiteboard, rapt in conversation with a young trainee detective.

‘DS Khan!’ he bawled. ‘My office, please.’

After retrieving her black notebook from her desk, she brushed her long, dark hair and hurried to his room.

‘Morning, sir,’ she said. Her boss was settled behind his desk with the morning newspapers. ‘Sir, have you seen the front page of *The Post* this morning?’

‘Yes, I glanced at it. They’ve been foisting more startling revelations upon their poor, unsuspecting readers. They’re linking the Barron shooting with that terrible train death in Brixton.’

She nodded as she settled herself into a chair. ‘Do you think it’s simply a coincidence that the two men who swapped seats were killed just days apart?’

‘I have to look at the basic facts as I see them, Sergeant. Craig Arnold’s death was very different from Barron’s in its execution – no pun intended. To me, the Brixton incident smacks of wrong place, wrong time. Someone mentally disturbed was out searching for a victim and poor old Craig Arnold wandered into his line of sight as a train approached. Sadly, these incidents happen from time to time. But just to cover ourselves, can you liaise with our friends at the BTP? Make them aware of the possible connection to our case, if they're not conscious of it already, and see if they've got anything that might help us.'

'Yes, sir. Sir, I've been waiting to tell you what happened at the Diamonds' bungalow.'

'I gather Vinny Diamond's wife and son went berserk.'

Khan nodded. 'So Mr Diamond had failed to tell his family we were likely to be searching their bungalow and it was the day after Mr Barron's funeral.'

'We couldn't do much about it. You had a warrant, and police business has to go on,' Haynes said.

'Yes,' she agreed. 'What an amazing place they've got.'

'Six bedrooms, I've heard.'

'That's right. It's set in huge grounds.'

'Find anything?'

'Two mobile phones. I got one from Alma, Diamond's wife. She handed it over with great reluctance. Later, we found a second phone in the living room. She claimed she didn't know who owned that one. Suggested it might be her husband's old phone which he no longer used, but then the son, Mickey Diamond, admitted it was his. He wanted us to examine it in front of him and hand it back, but I insisted we had to remove it from the premises.'

'Good. So you didn't find Mickey's other phones?'

'No, sir.'

'And are both seized phones with forensics now?'

'Yes, sir.'

'Any interesting contacts on the phones that you could see?'

Khan shook her head. 'I flicked through the contacts on both. Nothing stood out.'

'All right. We'll have to wait and see what forensics come up with.'

'We also took away three sacks of documents that someone will have to sort through.'

Haynes chuckled. 'That'll probably be you.'

'I thought you might say that. It'll take an eternity.'

'Don't worry. I'll get some of your colleagues to help. Bank statements will be especially useful. We need to see whether old Vinny paid money to anyone around 27 June.'

'Don't you think, if the actual killer was a hitman, he'd have been paid in cash?'

'More than likely, but we can't rule anything out. Any large cash withdrawal around that time and we need to know about it.'

Haynes raised his gold-rimmed glasses so that they rested on top of his head. 'How did you get on at Barron & Partners?'

She beamed. 'They were far more helpful. Our team spent several hours round there yesterday. Mostly, we were in David Barron's private office, examining documents in his desk and on top of his desk. We've removed his computer. We're also checking cameras in the street outside.'

He smiled. 'That's good. We also had a successful haul from Vinny Diamond's Bethnal Green office. I decided to go back and introduced myself to several of his staff – some of whom were very helpful. I've impounded his phone and removed some of his paperwork, which I've been checking through. I've also introduced myself to several of his gang – some of whom you really wouldn't want to meet in a dark alley without armed back-up.

'There's Freddie Valmar, who's got a record as long as the A1. A nasty piece of work. He's Diamond's enforcer. Alongside him is Cliff Martin, the West Indian guy who let us into Diamond's office. He's the muscle. Been inside God knows how many times – mainly for GBH. Hard as nails.

'We mustn't forget Mickey, whom you had the misfortune to meet at the Diamonds' bungalow in

Winchmore Hill. He's thirty-eight, brother of Deborah but very different from his sister. Made very much in his father's mould, but with far fewer brains.'

Haynes leaned back in his chair. 'Trouble is, Sergeant, we're still a long way from collaring the gunman. As we've discussed before, we're possibly looking at a professional contract killer. But we also know that someone – maybe one of the pathetic specimens of humanity we've met over the past week – settled the bill. So, I suggest we've got to find the motive first and then identify who might have paid them.

'I'm happy to take care of that side of the case. What I'd like you to do, Sergeant, is to focus on the hitman. Have a word with some of our colleagues in the Met – I'll give you some contacts – and at the National Crime Agency. I want to see if you can create a list of potential suspects. A man or woman who, for the right price, will take on a job like this one at a public venue, pull the trigger and slip away into the night.'

Khan nodded. 'I'd be pleased to do that, sir.'

'Good. My present thoughts are that Vinny Diamond was probably the paymaster. He has a clear motive for wanting Barron out of the way and an uncanny knack for eliminating his adversaries. I'm convinced he's up to his Gregory in it.'

'Gregory, sir?'

'Gregory Peck. He's up to his neck in it.'

'I follow what you're saying.'

'There's no apparent link at all that we can currently find between the gunman and his victim. There probably isn't one. He was sent here on a mission and once he's accomplished it, he's fled the scene and possibly fled the country.'

The sergeant frowned. 'Have you been involved before in cases that present so many demands?'

'Dozens of them. I usually catch the bastards in the end, but this one appears exceptionally challenging. We haven't got the weapon and, as time passes, it looks less and less likely we're going to find it. We suspect the gun was a Beretta, judging by the shell cases dropped on the carpet. But we've no idea what kind of Beretta. We've got a grey thread that caught on the doorframe around the time the gun was fired. It may have come from the gunman's clothing, but there's no DNA.

'We got nothing from the car because it seems he probably wore gloves and cleaned the vehicle thoroughly.'

The sergeant gazed into her boss's eyes. 'So you're coming round to the idea that the gunman was the guy in the Porsche seen by Nick Colton?'

'That appears more likely now. But, unfortunately for us, the CCTV of both the suspects identified by Colton and the stage door attendant are hazy and inconclusive.'

'Sir, it again suggests the killer was quite cunning.'

She studied the open page of her notebook. 'I forgot to mention that Mickey Diamond came up with the same story as his father – that they were at the Curry Palace on 27 June. Last night I called in at the restaurant and the owner, Ashok Gupta, confirmed the father and son dined there that evening. They arrived at seven thirty. But what's interesting is that Vinny Diamond was on the phone a lot between eight and half past eight.'

Haynes frowned before swivelling round in his chair and staring out of the window. 'How could this Mr Gupta be so sure?'

'After their starters, the Diamonds asked them to delay the main course until the calls had been made.'

He swung his chair back and gazed at her. 'Don't suppose he's got a clue what was being discussed?'

'Bit of a language barrier, sir. He didn't seem to understand the question, although I asked him that several times.'

'Funny that, isn't it? As soon as we come to the vital question, his language skills fail him. We'll have to check the phone records. As far as the Diamonds are concerned,

I'm pretty certain neither of them nor their cronies pulled the trigger that ended Barron's life. But it wouldn't surprise me to learn they paid the gunman and I wouldn't mind betting those phone calls were made to him.'

Chapter 25

'Fiona, did you get round to doing the laundry?' The voice echoed round the spacious living room.

A few seconds passed before Deborah Barron received her reply from somewhere along the corridor.

'Yes. Sorry, Deborah. Everything should be dry by now.'

Fiona Blake put her head round the door. 'Was there anything you wanted in particular?'

'I need a couple of fresh pillowcases on the bed.'

'No problem. I'll go sort that out.'

'Thank you. You're an absolute treasure.'

Ten minutes later, Fiona reappeared. 'Are you feeling better today, Deborah?'

The older woman was reclining in her usual place on the white leather sofa. 'Yes, now we've got the funeral out of the way, I can try and get back into more of a normal routine.'

'Your family treated me very kindly. Your mother explained all the niceties of a Jewish service.'

'Thank you for helping me cover the mirrors and prepare the food, Fiona.'

'Pleasure.'

Deborah pointed towards the array of sympathy cards on the marble mantelpiece. 'Everyone's been so kind.'

Deborah watched, in envy of her housekeeper's trim figure, as Fiona stepped into the room and sat on the brown sofa. Her employee had an attractive face and twinkling blue eyes. There were tattoos of small birds on both arms.

'Who was that young guy about my age?' Fiona asked as she grinned and crossed her legs.

'Black-framed glasses, dark suit?'

'Yes.'

'My stepson, Raymond. Didn't you get a moment to chat to him? He's an extremely nice guy. I get on very well with him.'

'I didn't get a chance. Your mother and aunt snatched me away and told me David's life story.'

Deborah laughed. 'Sorry about that. That's my mother and Aunt Rebecca all over.'

'Your dad was nice.'

'Didn't he and my mum look elegant? He hides it very well, but Dad's got a lot of worries. One of his work colleagues is a bit of a maverick and another's been informing on the family.'

Fiona smiled sympathetically. 'All those stories in the papers can't have helped – you know, those ones suggesting he'd been courting bad company.'

'Dad's had a lot to contend with. This isn't the first time the press have made him and Mickey out to be successors to the Kray twins and the Richardsons. I don't understand why. He's no angel, I know. He's done time, but that was a long way back. He's trying to build an honest business and David was helping him.

'My grandad didn't make life easy for Dad. He left the family home when Dad was only fifteen and my grandmother wasn't well. He had to go out and earn a living. He did very well until he got into trouble and now he's trying to build up the business properly. He's got a nice home, but he's always had to work for it. Nothing's ever been given to him on a plate.'

'Who was the big guy? He was standing outside before the service and was still there when we came out.'

'That was Clifford. He works for Dad. He drove Mum and Dad to the funeral.'

Fiona mentioned she had noticed the *Barnet Borough Times* on the kitchen table and saw a report about her father, Vince Diamond.

Deborah frowned. 'It was obvious they were going to copy what the national press did. It's so embarrassing – all the neighbours reading about my dad and thinking he's got a reputation. I wish I hadn't spoken so freely to that journalist now. What was he called?'

'Nick Colton.'

'Yes, Nick Colton. Most of the papers have followed up *The Post* story and there's been family pictures popping up all over the place.' She paused. 'I'm so glad you've moved in, Fiona. You've come to me at the right time – my hour of need.'

'Don't be silly. Being a housekeeper and home-help suited me down to the ground. It's just so sad that a few months after I arrived, David's life should be taken so tragically. By the way, I'm a little bit worried about my mother.'

Deborah's eyes lit up. 'Oh yes, I was going to ask. You received an email from her. How is she?'

Fiona shrugged. 'Not very well. I'm desperate to get her away for a holiday somewhere – anywhere. The place she's in just isn't suitable.'

'Well, I suppose she could always come and stay for a while in the annexe. You know, once I've sorted David's things out.'

Fiona beamed at her. 'Really? Oh, that would be brilliant. Thank you so much, Deborah. That's really put my mind at rest. I'll email her straight away.'

'As I say, it couldn't be immediately. I've got to pack up all David's things. Oh Fiona, there's so much to do after someone's life ends. David's things; probate; selling his car; and God knows what I'm going to do about his business. I've got no experience of running an accountancy firm.'

Deborah hoisted herself into a sitting position. 'Do you know, Fiona, I've been doing a lot of thinking since the funeral. I'm thinking that maybe I should have told the chief inspector about Joe.'

'Remind me who he is.'

'I'm sure I mentioned him before. Joe Marsh. You know, manager of David's Tottenham branch.'

Fiona's eyes twinkled. 'The guy that was sacked?'

'Yes. My head's been all over the place since David's death, so I forgot to mention it to the chief inspector. I think I should have told him.'

Fiona stifled a yawn. 'You don't think he had anything to do with David's death, do you?'

Deborah shrugged. 'I just don't know. But, when he left the firm, there was a lot of bad feeling.'

'Was he sacked without notice?'

'That's right. He'd been office manager for fifteen years. They nearly lost a major client because Joe failed to warn them of the size of their tax liability. David was inclined to let things lie, but the other directors made a song and dance and he felt he had to act. Joe took it very badly and sent David an extremely nasty letter.'

Fiona released a sigh. 'Did you know Joe yourself?'

'Yes, but I knew his wife more. I felt very bad about it. She's not speaking to me, so I've lost a friend.'

'These things happen when you run a business.'

'I suppose so.'

'Deborah, I really think you should mention this man to the police. If he had a strong grievance and knew David would be at the Albert Hall to see Loretta Kay… well, you never know.'

Deborah nodded. 'What happened to that note with the chief inspector's name and number?'

Fiona strolled over to the mantelpiece. 'Here you are, Deborah.'

Deborah reached forward and took her mobile phone from the glass table in front of her as Fiona sat beside her. She held up the note with the number so that Deborah could see it while she dialled.

'Hello. Is that Kensington CID? I need to speak to DCI Haynes.'

* * *

Inside the main bedroom of her parents' sprawling bungalow a mobile phone was ringing. Vinny Diamond had been sleeping fitfully, worrying about the shipment that was due that morning.

As the ringing tone continued unabated, he was eventually roused. He clambered from his bed and groped in the darkness for his handset.

'Yeah?' he said.

A Scottish accent pierced the silence of the morning. 'Vinny, it's Kevin Campbell. I've picked up the trailer with my tractor unit and I'm heading to town.'

Diamond hauled himself to his feet, as he glanced down at his wife Alma, snoring beside him. He walked across the room and perched himself on a chair by her dressing table.

'More important, have you got the gear?'

'Aye.'

'Thank God for that. What time is it?'

'Nearly six o'clock.'

'God, it feels like the middle of the night.'

'I did like you said. I took the gear out of all the kayak hatches. Then I stashed it in a false compartment in the trailer's floor. After I hooked up the tractor unit, I went into the back to check and the gear's still safely where I hid it.'

The businessman smiled. 'Good. Do you think they checked the kayaks?'

'Aye, I know they did. Two of the hatches had been opened and not properly closed.'

Diamond frowned. 'Just as I expected. But at least I know who our informant is now. So where are you now?'

'Just outside Grays. At this time of the morning, I should be at your premises in under an hour.'

'You've got to cover about twenty-two miles, haven't you?'

'Aye, about that.'

'That's great, Kevin. Another brilliant job. I'll let Mickey know.'

'Och, that's nae bother.'

'If you call into see me tomorrow or on Friday, I'll make sure I've got a wad of cash for you.'

'Aye, that'll be grand.'

Diamond was still half asleep. After ending the call, he had to remind himself how to find his phone contacts. But, within a few minutes, he'd dialled Mickey's number.

'Dad. All right?' his son's croaky voice responded.

'Yeah, Mickey. The job's a good'un and the gear's safe on the trailer. Just had a call from Kevin Campbell. He's on his way and should be with you in an hour or so.'

'So around seven or eight?'

'Probably.'

'Don't worry, Dad. Cliff, Freddie and me are all set.'

'Okay. Good. Border Force searched the kayaks, but Kevin had moved them to a different hiding place – so they never found nothing.'

'How do you know they searched the kayaks?'

'Two of the hatches had been opened and not shut properly.' Diamond noticed Alma turning over in the bed as he was speaking and lowered his voice.

'You know what that means, Dad?'

'Yeah. I know that it means. But don't worry about that for now. That's for another day. Today we've got to sort out the gear.'

Chapter 26

Just before eight o'clock on that cloudy Wednesday morning, Kevin Campbell's blue articulated lorry thundered into Nazarin Street. The cobbled lane was deserted.

Campbell stopped his vehicle opposite the grey, shuttered goods entrance of Diamond Enterprises. Leaving the engine running, he darted across the street. Almost at once, alerted by the sound of the engine's roar, Mickey Diamond emerged from a side door.

The boss's son beamed at him. 'All right, mate? You've made good time. I'll just open up.'

Mickey ducked back inside and, moments later, the giant shutters clattered open. His heart was beating as he switched on the overhead lighting.

Campbell, a brawny, dark-haired, six-foot-tall Scotsman with tattooed arms, was met by a team of men as he drove the lorry inside – among them Clifford Martin and Freddie Valmar. Martin clambered onto a forklift truck. After the blue curtain had been hauled aside, he began unloading the boxes of toys. As he toiled, the sun emerged from behind the clouds and bathed the lorry bay in light.

Mickey Diamond brushed his dark-brown hair out of his eyes – small, alert eyes that darted around, suggesting a duplicitous nature. He was unconcerned about the toys. His priority was to lay his hands on the sixty kilos of cocaine that, according to his father, lay concealed in the trailer's floor. On the street, the value of the consignment was estimated at five million pounds.

Thus he was on edge as, assisted by Campbell, he climbed on board the forty-five-foot-long trailer and watched as the driver raised the wooden board covering the secret hatch.

Campbell grinned as he drew out the first plastic bag. Then his smile faded.

Mickey sensed a problem. 'What's the matter, Kevin?'

As Campbell gazed through the transparent plastic covering, the parcel in his hand should have been a grubby white in colour. Instead, it was red. Brick red.

'We've been rumbled, Mickey. Those Border Force bastards have switched the packets.'

He pulled two more out. Wrapped tightly in plastic, his secret stash amounted to an assortment of house-bricks.

Mickey's face turned as red as the bricks. 'You bloody clown. My dad's going to go mental. He said you'd checked the load.'

'I did. But I wasn't careful enough. I know they examined the kayaks so I thought they wouldn't examine the lorry floor. I thought I'd put them off the scent. When I checked in here, everything seemed untouched. But they must have removed the gear and put these bricks in their place.'

Mickey jumped to the ground and wandered round in a circle with his head in his hands.

Valmar stopped unloading boxes of toys. He'd overheard the conversation. He strode to the rear of the trailer where Mickey was standing, gazing up at the driver.

'It's no good holding a bloody inquest,' Valmar stormed. 'The cops will be here faster than a plague of rats. Get all the bricks out and hide them. Then, when they check the hatch, they'll find nothing and that might – just might – screw up part of their evidence. Then we'd better get the hell out of here.'

Mickey and Campbell followed his advice and pulled twelve bricks out of the compartment and hid them inside the warehouse before they prepared to flee. Martin, Valmar and their two other associates had already taken to their heels and were heading towards the door beside the shutters. But, as Martin flung it open, he was confronted by an array of police vehicles arriving on the far side of the street.

'It's too late,' he yelled as he stepped back inside and slammed the door. 'The cops are here.'

Valmar chose the clearest pane he could find in the grimy window beside the door. He peered out into the bright July morning. At least ten officers were crouched behind the line of cars and vans.

Heckler & Koch G36 semi-automatic carbines wielded by members of Scotland Yard's elite firearms team, SCO19, glinted in the sunlight.

A chief superintendent with a loud hailer called out, 'The place is surrounded. Give yourselves up.'

Mickey and Campbell joined their four associates behind the shuttered doors after doing their best to hide the bricks they'd found. For the moment, all six remained silent, unsure of their next move.

'Come on,' hollered the police chief. 'One at a time.' Then, as he put the megaphone down, they heard him add, 'Don't all rush at once,' to the amusement of his joint team from the Met Police and the National Crime Agency.

Valmar had already decided he wouldn't hang around. He wasn't enamoured by the prospect of a further stretch behind bars. Somehow he had to get away.

Without confiding in his companions, he crept away from the lorry bays and mounted the wooden stairs to Vince's office.

Then he climbed the next set of stairs to the top floor and stepped out onto the flat roof, where he was greeted by dazzling sunlight. Fearing he might be seen by police, he avoided venturing too close to the rear edge of the three-storey building. Instead he headed away from the Nazarin Street side and towards Fetterlock Lane.

As he crossed the asphalt roof, he recalled there was a gated community of privately owned flats next door to the Diamonds' building. For some reason, he remembered a drainpipe which clung to the wall behind the flat owners' high, wrought-iron gates.

With luck and a little skill, he gauged that he could use it to aid his escape. Feeling more of a sense of thrill than anxiety, he gripped the top of the gutter with his right hand and manoeuvred his legs down.

'Let's hope it holds my bloody weight,' he moaned as his heart began pounding.

Within seconds, he was lowering himself slowly down the black pipe.

He noticed there had been a sharp decline in his physical fitness as he went. By the time his feet touched the gravel within the residential complex, he was out of breath.

He gazed around at the three-storey flats with balconies. None of the residents of this modern-day mews development seemed to have noticed his arrival in their world. But he faced a fresh dilemma. There were locked double gates at each end of the private street.

One set, a few feet away from him, led directly into Fetterlock Lane, where the police might be waiting. The other set, a hundred metres to the north, led to a wide alley, named Falklands Walk. He had to make his way there and, somehow, get to his Jaguar, which was parked on the other side of the main Bethnal Green Road.

Within a couple of minutes, he reached the far gates. He was just contemplating whether to try to climb over them when his luck held again. A nearby car engine started and the vehicle approached. The gates sprang open and, for fear of missing his chance, he darted out in front of the car.

'Watch out! You'll get yourself killed!' the irate driver hollered.

'Toerag!' Valmar shouted back.

Once in Falklands Walk, Valmar weaved his way through the maze of alleys stretching across one of the borough's vast housing estates – all the while unaware the other gang members had given themselves up.

He eventually reached the main road and approached his car, parked in St Matthew's Row, close to the Kray twins' former family church.

Then Valmar's luck ran out. Charlie Allen, a sergeant from Bethnal Green CID, had been drafted in to help the National Crime Agency with the drugs bust because of his local knowledge. He and a uniformed constable were returning to their station, just off the Roman Road. Glancing around as they travelled, the sergeant spotted a head of dark hair and a pair of wire-framed glasses that he recognised.

'Hold on!' he shouted. 'I've just seen Freddie Valmar.'

'Freddie the Fish?'

'Yeah. He's just got into that blue Jag. He's wanted for two cases involving violence and we missed him at the Diamonds' place. We'll have to follow him. Watch which way he goes.'

Valmar turned east along the Bethnal Green Road and followed heavy traffic towards Cambridge Heath Road. Allen's driver tried to keep close behind in their marked vehicle, but two other cars had managed to manoeuvre their way between them. Their siren began to wail and their blue lights flashed as Allen's driver overtook the two cars. Using his car radio, the driver called his control room.

'Suspect vehicle making off. Failing to stop for Met officers. Speed four zero miles per hour.'

He explained they'd been involved in the Fetterlock Lane drugs raid and that they were pursuing Valmar, whom they believed had fled the premises. He gave details of the three-litre Jaguar as well as their location and requested armed back-up.

Valmar turned left at the Salmon and Ball pub.

'Looks like he's heading to Hackney, an area he probably knows bloody well,' said Allen, as they passed a used car sales centre on the left.

The driver frowned. 'He's picking up speed. Shall I put my foot down?'

Allen nodded. The driver flicked his radio on again.

'Suspect vehicle heading north towards Mare Street in Hackney. Any mobiles in that vicinity?' A period of radio silence followed before Allen admitted, 'Guess we're on our own.'

Chapter 27

Freddie Valmar's heart was beating fast as he sped through Hackney. He was overtaking, where he could. He was taking risks, where he could.

'There's no way I'm going back inside' were the words he kept repeating like a mantra.

His Jaguar, now travelling at speeds of up to sixty miles an hour, hurtled through red traffic lights at the junction with Morning Lane, forcing a van driver to pull up sharply. The two policemen had been gaining ground, but were obliged to let the van go through in front, costing precious seconds.

Valmar careered round the corner into Amhurst Road. His car then ploughed round the Dalston Lane roundabout into Pembury Road in Lower Clapton.

'Those bastards aren't far behind,' he complained as he drew up on the edge of the Pembury Estate, a collection of red-brick council blocks built in the 1930s. He leaped out and dashed down a narrow lane between two of the five-storey Victorian buildings.

A sign on a block that was immediately ahead of him read 'Midfield House'. The front doors to the higher flats were accessible via long balconies with an enclosed stairway in the centre. There were two parked cars in the yard beneath.

Valmar climbed the stairs two at a time until he reached the third floor. His heart was pounding again. His hands were clammy, his mouth dry. His breaths were coming in short bursts.

Then, fearing his pursuers may have already entered the courtyard below, he fell to his knees and crawled until he reached flat forty-three. Stretching up with his right hand, he pressed the buzzer on the door and waited.

Within seconds, it was opened by a shapely blonde woman in her late thirties in a pink top and jeans. She laughed heartily. 'Freddie Valmar, what the heck are you doing down there?'

'Let me in, for God's sake,' he whispered as he crept onto her red, patterned hallway carpet. Then, as the woman closed the door, he rose to his feet and, without another word, darted into the kitchen, leaned over the sink and peered through the net curtains at the balcony and yard outside.

She stood bewildered in the hallway. 'Whatever's got into you?'

'I'm sorry, Marilyn. I'm being chased by the cops. I think they saw me come onto the estate, but hopefully they won't realize I'm here.'

He turned as she entered the room and kissed his right cheek. She fondled his neck and chest. 'Whatever have you done this time, you naughty boy?'

He pulled her hand away. 'Not now, Marilyn. They think I'm tied up in a job for the Diamonds, so they followed me all the way from Fetterlock.'

'Oh Freddie, you're not still involved with that Vinny Diamond, are you?'

'I ask myself that sometimes. This time we were grassed up and it's all Vinny's fault. He told one person too many what he'd got planned. It's time I took over the business.'

'Freddie, I wish you'd give it all up.'

'Not now, Marilyn. I've got to think of a way out of here. This place will be running with cops quicker than a greyhound with his bum on fire.' He cast his eyes through the curtain again but saw no police activity.

* * *

Meanwhile, DS Charlie Allen and his colleague had been thwarted in their pursuit for a second time. Their car had been forced to a halt by an oncoming bus at the roundabout – despite their siren continually blaring – and lost valuable time. But, on entering Pembury Road, they were encouraged to find Valmar's car, abandoned by the side of the road.

They peered inside before dashing down the same alley he'd raced along a few minutes earlier. Two young mothers, accompanied by three children, were pushing prams. Allen ran up to them.

'Seen a man in a hurry?' he asked.

'Yes,' said one. 'He went through that doorway.' The sergeant followed their eyes to an open doorway across the yard with grey, concrete steps behind.

'Thanks,' he replied before darting off into the courtyard.

While his colleague spoke to the women, Allen cast his eyes over Midfield House for any sign of movement. He was hoping to see Valmar scurrying along one of the balconies but nothing stirred. Then he noticed an open front door on the third floor and a fleeting glimpse of a blonde woman's head.

Without a second thought, the detective dashed through the main doorway and rushed up the steps.

Then, at the third floor, he poked his head round the brickwork, unsure of what he might find. The walkway was empty except for two black tubs filled with red petunias halfway along. He couldn't be certain but believed they were positioned outside the blonde woman's door.

Allen crept along the balcony, peering into residents' windows as he passed. Valmar was close by. He was more certain by the second. He could almost smell the villain. He reached the petunias and knocked loudly on the door.

'Police! Open up!' he demanded. At first, there was no response.

Then the door was drawn back and the woman he'd seen minutes earlier appeared.

'What do you want?' she asked angrily.

'I've reason to believe there's a wanted man in here.'

She shook her head. 'Only me,' she stammered.

Allen barged past into her drab hallway, peering around him as he went. He ventured into the living room at the end of the passageway and ducked his head into both bedrooms as the woman stood in the hallway, protesting. All rooms in the council flat were empty.

'Come on out!' he shouted, peering around him. 'I know you're here.' In the dark silence of the hallway, he waited. The blonde tenant shook her head. 'You're wasting your time. There's no one here except me.'

He was standing by a cupboard as she spoke. Was it his imagination or could he hear breathing?

He snatched back the door. A hand appeared wielding a Glock 43 pistol. Allen made a grab for the weapon and caught the man's arm just as a shot rang out that shattered the peace of the morning. The sergeant toppled over backwards. Blood trickled onto the carpet.

Chapter 28

'What you done, Freddie?' demanded the shrill voice of Marilyn Harris. 'I think you've killed him.'

Valmar peered at the blood-spattered sergeant as he lay unconscious on the floor. 'Nah. He'll be all right. We'll just have to get him outside – otherwise you'll land up in trouble.'

He seized the sergeant's arms from behind and hauled him out through the open door. Marilyn tried to help by making a grab for his legs, but failed. After dragging the detective a few metres along the balcony towards the stairwell, he released his grip and let the sergeant slump onto the balcony floor. Then he strolled back to the doorway, where she was standing.

He tugged her arm. 'Get inside and get the door closed. I've got to work out what to do. His pals could be here in seconds. Sorry to lay this on you, Marilyn.'

'Have you seen the state of my carpet?'

'That's a point. Bit of a giveaway, blood on the carpet.' He got down on his hands and knees and pulled up the middle section. Then he rolled it up and stored it in the cupboard where he'd been hiding.

He shrugged his shoulders. 'Don't worry. When I've got myself straightened out, I'll buy you a beautiful new carpet.'

'It's all right for you to say that, Freddie, but I've got to live here.'

He kissed her on the cheek. 'Stop worrying.'

'What do you want me to tell them?'

'Just say you heard a shot. You ran out and saw the poor beggar on the deck. You haven't seen me. Right?'

Valmar, with his Glock pistol in one trouser pocket and his ammunition in the other, kissed her again. Then he opened her front door a fraction, gazed out and hurried towards the stairwell, stepping over DS Allen as he passed.

Hearing footsteps ahead, he slowed his pace and tapped his trouser pocket, quietly reassuring himself the pistol was still there.

He sensed that one of the sergeant's colleagues, unsure where the gunshot had come from, was quietly moving up the stairs. His footsteps told Valmar the officer was stopping at every level, checking each balcony in a search for his companion.

While the officer was exploring the first-floor balcony, Valmar slipped down the steps unseen and fled across the yard. He dared not return to the Jaguar. His precious car was no doubt already in the hands of the police, who'd almost certainly be wanting to examine it for forensic clues. What a shame he hadn't had time to thoroughly clean the interior.

As he negotiated his way through the alleys and lanes of the estate where he'd grown up in the 1980s, he realized he couldn't go home. Not yet anyway.

There was only one place he could go – his half-sister's place in Hackney. She'd take care of him while police searched his known haunts. She'd only recently come back into his life and he was certain they had no knowledge of her address. She'd never turn him away and he could lie low there until all the fuss had died down.

* * *

As soon as the young policeman reached the third floor, he peered over the balcony and witnessed the gunman's flight. But, at exactly the same moment, he noticed the wounded detective, who'd regained consciousness and was writhing in agony on the floor. His white shirt and part of his brown trousers were soaked in blood. The sergeant's plight took precedence.

'Charlie, you all right?' he cried as he dashed towards the sergeant. A blonde woman had stripped off his white shirt and was tending to him. 'He's in a bad way,' she said. 'He's still with us but he needs a doctor.'

The constable summoned an ambulance on his police radio while the woman pressed hard on the shoulder wound with a towel.

Then he bent down beside the patient. 'Charlie, you OK?'

Allen's eyelids flickered and he groaned. 'Yeah, I think so, but my bloody shoulder hurts like hell.'

'Don't worry, Sarge. An ambulance is on its way.'

The constable glanced at the woman with the towel. 'He's a policeman like me. Plain clothes. You live just here, do you?'

'Yeah, I'm Marilyn Harris. I heard a loud noise. Then I found this guy'd been shot. It's funny. We never get no trouble round here. Who do you think did this?'

'We've got a pretty good idea who it was. One of the local toerags. Here, let me take over.'

The policeman took off his peaked cap and placed it on the floor. Then he spent the next few minutes holding the towel in place to stem the flow of blood before asking, 'Could you get a glass of water for him?'

As she went inside her flat, Allen faced his colleague. 'He shot me inside her flat,' he whispered.

By the time Marilyn returned with the water and helped Allen take a sip, the paramedics were arriving downstairs. The constable waved to them.

A few minutes later, they took charge of the patient. Marilyn walked back to her flat's open doorway where, for a few minutes, she leaned on the doorframe beside her tubs of flowers and watched the ambulance crew making the patient comfortable and preparing a stretcher.

The constable moved further along the balcony, seeking a moment of privacy so he could hold a discussion with an officer in his control room.

Then he joined her, taking a notebook from his pocket.

'I'd better take some details from you,' he said. 'Marilyn Harris, you say?'

'Yes.'

'Do you mind if I come inside?'

'It's a bit inconvenient.'

He eyed her sternly. 'This won't take long.'

Albeit reluctantly, she let the officer into her two-bedroom flat and shut the door.

'Thanks very much, by the way, for what you've done, Mrs Harris. Quick action like that can sometimes make all the difference between life and death.'

She nodded. 'I've never done any first aid. I just did what I could.'

He followed her down the long, narrow hallway, past the kitchen, bathroom and bedrooms to the living room at the end. It was a bright room with light yellow wallpaper. There were blue floral-patterned curtains at each side of the large sash window at the far end. The only views from the windows were of other flats and parked cars.

The policeman made himself comfortable on a grey three-seater settee while Marilyn settled down opposite him in a matching armchair.

A photograph of a young couple in a silver frame on top of the television in the corner by the window caught his eye. 'Who's that in the photo?'

'Me and me late husband. He was killed in a car crash.'

He stood up. 'Really? Can I take a peek?'

'Be my guest.'

'How old were you there?'

'Twenty-two.'

'You were a fine young woman.'

'Thank you.'

The constable removed a notebook from his pocket. 'What did he tell you in the short time he was here?'

'Who do you mean?'

He tutted. 'Freddie Valmar.'

She turned bright red. 'I don't know who you're talking about.'

'Charlie's just told me Freddie was in your flat and I've just discovered Freddie's an old friend of yours. You've been in trouble in the past for fencing goods. So I'll ask you again, what did he tell you?'

'Honest. I don't know what you mean. I was in here watching telly. I heard a loud bang that sounded like a gun going off outside. I went to the door and there's this poor bloke lying in a pool of blood.'

The constable sighed. He was tired of her lies. 'Marilyn Harris, I'm arresting you on suspicion of assisting an offender, contrary to section four of the Criminal Law Act of 1967.' Then he recited the rest of the police caution.

Chapter 29

Nick Colton was feeling pessimistic about his chances of gaining an interview with Alex Smart's mother as he set off for Croydon on Thursday 11 July.

He had attempted to interview residents of care homes in the past and frequently been turned away. Staff zealously guarded their clients' privacy and Mrs Enid Smart would appear to have nothing to gain from speaking to him.

He had learnt of the care home's address during a phone call to Jasmine Smart the evening before in which she had also revealed that she had moved out of the family home with her children. She was now staying in a safe house provided by a charity.

'Alex has let himself go. He looks like a tramp,' she told Colton. 'I'm better off in this emergency accommodation. I'm certain Alex knew Craig. They were both Crystal Place fans and appeared in a group photo together in a fans' magazine.'

Colton had also received a message from Luke Foster to say that a stallholder at Brixton Market had called the office. He had seen the CCTV picture of the suspect in a blue hooded jacket at the station. He had earlier seen the same guy following Arnold and thought him to be a rough sleeper.

Colton tried to put all these thoughts to the back of his mind as he reached Elmfield Grange in the Croydon suburb of Shirley.

Although the entrance lay on a busy road behind a row of leylandii trees, the Grade II-listed buildings were set in grounds covering a third of an acre.

Impressed by its majestic setting, he drove up the gravel drive in the blistering heat. He began to perspire as he passed beds of red, pink and yellow roses. After reaching a sundial in the centre of a turning circle, he found a place to park.

Then, seizing from the back seat the small bouquet of pink and white carnations he'd bought earlier from a florist's, he strode across the block-paved forecourt towards the entrance.

Birdsong from nearby birch and ash trees could be heard above the thunder of traffic as he pushed open the glazed door and followed signs to the reception desk.

A slim woman in her twenties with dark hair, wearing a light-blue uniform was tapping on a computer keyboard. A sign on her curved, maple counter read 'Receptionist'.

She smiled broadly. 'Can I help?'

Colton returned her smile. 'Terrific weather.'

She nodded. 'Isn't it.'

'I just wondered if Mrs Smart was about – Enid Smart?'

'Are you related?'

'No. You could say I'm a friend of her daughter-in-law, Jasmine.' He was desperately trying to remember the name of the road where she lived. Any detail like that could help to verify he had a connection – however vague – with the woman he was seeking to visit. Woodcock Road? Woodfield Road?

Then he remembered. 'You know, Jasmine from Woodmeadow Road in South Norwood.'

A warm glow of recognition spread across her face. 'Oh yes. Jasmine Smart. It's usually Mrs Smart's son, Alex, who comes.'

'Is she free to see a visitor? I've brought these carnations.'

The girl shook her head. 'She doesn't know you, does she?'

He was forced to admit she didn't.

'We have a strict rule here. Only relatives and close friends may visit residents. But I'll happily pass on a message if you like and, of course, I'll hand her these flowers. She'll be delighted with these.'

She beckoned him forward and lowered her voice. 'You do know she's got dementia, don't you?'

'Oh I didn't know.' He was annoyed. Why hadn't Jasmine made that clear to him? All she'd said was that she 'doesn't remember everything'.

The receptionist continued at a whisper, 'Alex comes and sits with her, but he has to keep reminding her who he is.'

'That's very sad.'

He handed her the flowers. 'Tell you what. You might be able to help me any way. Do you remember, by any chance, whether Alex came to visit his mother exactly a week ago – Thursday last week?'

'That's a strange question. Why do you want to know that?'

'Well, he says he was here, but I've got feeling he wasn't.'

'Why are you asking?'

'It's complicated. Have you got a visitors' book that might tell you?'

'Well, we do, but I'm not sure…'

He persisted. 'It's a long story which I won't bore you with. But it would be extremely kind if you could check that he came that day.'

As they were talking, a young couple approached the desk. She switched her attention to them. They were asking about an aging relative. Colton studied a map of Croydon on the wall until the couple were directed along a nearby corridor.

The girl glanced up at him again. 'So I don't really think I can help you.'

Just then a woman in her forties with brown, curly hair emerged from a back room. He guessed she was the manageress and that she might have overheard the conversation.

She grinned at him. 'I'll deal with this, Lucille.'

While the receptionist got up and went to greet a new visitor, the manageress said, 'What is it exactly that you want?'

'Just a peek in your visitors' book. It's a rather delicate matter. I was speaking to Jasmine yesterday. Her husband's told her he was here with Mrs Smart all morning last Thursday, 4 July. I just need to be certain.'

The manageress stroked her chin. 'A bit of a strange request, but our visitors' book is on display here all the time. I don't suppose there's any harm in me letting you take a quick peek.'

She pointed to a white book on the far end of the counter which Colton had failed to notice. He smiled at her. 'That's very kind of you.'

Then he darted to the book before she could change her mind.

He quickly thumbed through the pages until he reached the one relating to the previous week. He ran his finger down the columns and found an entry saying, 'The fourth of July. Alex Smart. 74 Woodmeadow Rd, S. Norwood. To visit Enid Smart. Time in: 9 a.m. Time out: 9.30 a.m. Comment: Mum seemed in a brighter mood today.'

While the two staff members were distracted, he removed his mobile phone from his pocket and took a photograph of the entry before slipping out of the building.

* * *

When he returned home that evening, Colton discovered Riccardo and Ashleigh playing a computer game while their mother was cooking supper.

The family had only just finished their meal when their home phone rang. The friendly voice of DS Nadia Khan flowed softly down the phone as Colton answered.

'I hope this is a good time, Nick,' she said. 'I read your article in the paper this morning.'

'Yes. The appeal for witnesses at Brixton.'

'I thought it might be useful if we touched base. As a witness to the Barron murder and a journalist who's kept on top of the story, I feel you might have information that could prove useful to us. Conversely, we might have one or two items we could share with you. Maybe we should meet up.'

Colton was delighted at the suggestion. 'That would be really good, Miss Khan. Where do you suggest?'

'Could you come up to town this evening? I was thinking we could try The Little Drummer Boy in Kensington. Do you know it?'

'Know it very well.'

'Can we say half past six?'

'That'll suit me fine.'

Twenty minutes later, as the family were eating lasagna at the table, his phone rang again.

'Oh leave it, Nick,' Greta moaned.

'It's the office. I'd better take it,' he insisted.

As he strolled into the living room with his handset, a familiar gruff voice boomed out.

'Thought I'd better mark your card, old boy,' said the night news editor. 'The *Graphic* have got a front-page splash on Polebrook and Sadie Robinson.'

His face fell. 'What does it say, mate?'

'She's having a go at Polebrook, saying, "He had his fun, then dumped me."'

Colton groaned. 'You know I was instrumental in getting the paper to drop our investigation, don't you?'

'Yes, I'd heard. I don't blame you. If you found it didn't stack up, it didn't stack up. Would have been unsafe to run it. Just hope for the sake of the *Graphic* that they've got more evidence than we had.'

'Is Oliver Polebrook quoted?'

'He refused to comment.'

'What's the headline?'

'Minister and the make-up girl. Tory, fifty-two, bedded me in blue fireman's trunks and red braces.'

Chapter 30

A black Bentley Continental glided along the narrow London backstreet and stopped close to the pub on the corner. The driver, a well-built man dressed in black, stepped onto the road. Then he opened the nearside rear door so that Vinny Diamond could clamber out.

The side door of this quiet venue, The Foresters' Arms, creaked open and Diamond waddled in.

Three male customers sitting at the bar glanced towards him before turning away and resuming their conversation. Seconds later, Diamond was followed by his driver, who wore a stern expression.

The landlord beamed as he greeted the two customers. 'Nice to see you, Mr Diamond. What would you like?'

'Double whisky for me and a pint of your Czech lager for young Nathan here.'

He gazed round the dimly lit Stoke Newington bar with its dark oak chairs and tables, vintage sofas, gilt-framed mirrors and framed photographs of boxing stars from the past.

'It's been a long time since I was here,' he said. 'But it doesn't seem to have changed too much.'

Then his eyes rested on a hunched figure nursing a pint of bitter in the corner. Masked by a pair of sunglasses and with his greying hair tucked into a navy-blue cap was Freddie Valmar.

He sat up and pointed to the circular table and three chairs in front of him.

'Come and sit down, Vinny,' he called in a croaky voice.

Handing Nathan a twenty-pound note and asking him to collect the drinks, Diamond approached the table.

'How you doing, Freddie?'

'Not bad. You?'

'You haven't met Nathan, have you?' The driver advanced to the table carrying their drinks.

'Bloody hell,' Valmar exclaimed. 'What's your mother been feeding you on, boy? Pie and porridge?'

Nathan gave a toothy grin. 'My mum says I must be big-boned.'

Valmar stretched out his hand. 'Joking apart, pleased to meet you, Nathan.'

The chauffeur's hand was nearly twice the size of Valmar's.

Diamond laughed. 'He's a big boy, isn't he?' Diamond sat down and put his glass on the table.

'Nathan, be a good lad, will you? Go and see how many of the boxers you recognise. I need to talk to Freddie.'

Once Nathan had walked off, Diamond felt freer to speak.

'Freddie, when you said midday at the usual place, I'd forgotten how long it's been. Must be three or four years. Do you know I don't think I've crossed into Stokey in all that time?'

Valmar grinned. 'Landlord seems to know you.'

'Yeah. I know him, but he's new to this boozer.'

'Yeah. I've never seen him before and he didn't recognise me when I came in, luckily.'

Diamond frowned. 'What made you shoot the cop? It's all over this morning's papers.'

'Didn't have much choice. I was in an ex-girlfriend's flat, hiding in the cupboard.'

Diamond laughed before sipping his whisky. 'Bet that's a first, Freddie boy.'

'He opened the cupboard door. What was I expected to do? Wish him good morning and shake him by the hand? I'd be inside with the others if I hadn't. Hey, bit of a bastard, eh? The cops finding out about Kevin's cargo.'

Diamond scowled before sipping his whisky. 'Yeah. I went mental when Mickey told me what happened. He called me just before he got nicked. We were going to make a lot of money if we'd pulled it off. But we know who tipped them off, don't we? Don't ask about it, but I'm taking care of it, Freddie. So don't worry about that.'

Valmar sneered. 'Like you take care of everything, Vinny?'

'What's that supposed to mean?'

'Nothing. As you know, I didn't want to say nothing last night in case your phone's tapped, but who did they pick up yesterday?'

'Mickey, Kevin Campbell, Ronnie Medwin and Billy Jones.' He inspected his gold watch. 'They're all due at Thames Magistrates' Court round about now.'

'Any of them likely to get bail?'

Diamond shrugged. 'Who knows? You can't tell with the courts.'

Valmar picked up his glass, but before taking a sip he asked, 'And Cliff?'

Diamond glared. 'Good question. He was nicked with the others, but then released.' He paused. 'I've told you. I'm taking care of it. No one double-crosses me like this and gets away with it. Do you know the cops hauled me into the nick yesterday afternoon? Gave me a right old grilling, but they got nothing and they let me out on police bail. I told them I was expecting kayaks and toys and didn't know about nothing else. By the way, did I tell you? I'm giving those bloody kayaks to the boxing club.'

'Those lads are just about the only people who'll gain anything out of all this.'

'Yeah. The cops carried out a search of the building, but they never found the scales, mixing agents and all the rest of the clobber. I'd hidden them well.'

Diamond glanced towards Nathan, who was carefully studying a portrait of John Conteh, the former light-heavyweight champion. 'He's a good lad, that Nathan. Hey, that barmaid looks nice.'

A tall, slim blonde in her thirties, who was wiping the bar counter with a cloth, noticed their glances and smiled back.

Valmar nodded. 'Yes, very nice.'

Diamond turned towards him again. 'What's happened to your motor? Didn't see it outside.'

'The Jag? I had to leave it on the Pembury after the shooting. I'm not fussed. It costs an arm and a leg to run, so I've got myself a new little runabout. Have you heard how the cop is?'

Diamond took a sip of whisky as a group of noisy office workers arrived for a lunchtime drink.

'Still critical, it said on the news. Hang on a minute.'

He'd remembered seeing a copy of that day's *Evening Standard* on the bar counter when he came in. He got up and strolled over. Three tradesmen with the word 'Electrician' on the back of their overalls stood back to let him pass. He grabbed the paper and returned to his seat.

'Here you are,' he said, thrusting it onto the table. 'You're famous again, Freddie, "Hero cop's fight for life."'

Valmar scanned through the front-page story which was accompanied by a photograph of the injured policeman. He read it out in a low voice.

> *Courageous policeman Charlie Allen was fighting for his life in hospital today after a known criminal opened fire on him at point-blank range on a housing*

estate. The detective sergeant, who is thirty-four, was shot in the shoulder while attempting to arrest the man. As he was rushed to Homerton Hospital in Hackney, armed police launched a huge manhunt for the gunman.

The shooting happened shortly after a police drugs operation in which cocaine with an estimated street value of around five million pounds was found concealed in a lorry. A Scotland Yard spokesman said, "One of the ringleaders escaped in a blue Jaguar, but DS Allen and a uniformed constable pursued him. It turned into a high-speed chase through the streets of Hackney that went on for nearly three miles. Eventually the sergeant bravely confronted the man on the Pembury Estate in Lower Clapton, where the suspect fired at him before fleeing across the estate."

The gunman is described as about five feet nine inches tall, white, aged between forty and forty-five, of average build, with short, dark hair. He was dressed in a light turquoise shirt and dark blue trousers.

Valmar eyed him from across the table. 'The Old Bill's got the shirt colour wrong. It's blue.'

'Is the rest spot on?'

'Well, depends what you mean. As spot on as the papers ever get it.'

Diamond retrieved the newspaper from him and returned it to the bar. As he resumed his place, he gazed into his employee's eyes. 'What are you going to do now, Freddie?'

'I'm staying with someone. No one you know.'

'You got rid of the shooter?'

'Too right. Ditched it when I could. I'm staying out of sight and keeping me head down till all this blows over.'

Chapter 31

DCI Haynes hummed to himself as he checked the time on his watch. It was nearly ten o'clock on Thursday – time for his morning briefing with officers from Operation Gymkhana, the police code name for the Barron investigation.

He peered through his internal window into the main CID department. His staff were beginning to leave their desks and congregate near his door.

DS Khan, assisted by a colleague, was fixing photographs of suspects and witnesses to a whiteboard. It was time to make a start.

'Good morning, everybody,' he announced as he stepped from his room. 'Please take a seat.'

His mood was sombre. A superior officer had admonished him earlier on their failure to make any arrests. He was determined that he and his team should step up their efforts to crack the case.

He viewed the board, where his sergeant had pinned up seven photographs and scrawled names, ages and occupations beneath.

'First of all, I'd like DS Khan to tell us about the two new faces she's just added at the top of the board,' he said.

Solemnly, she began to address the team of seven detective constables, a trainee detective and two uniformed officers who'd been drafted in.

'So this first picture is Joe Marsh,' she said. 'He's the guy who until recently managed the Tottenham branch of Barron & Partners. David Barron sacked him without notice a few weeks ago.'

DC Kyle Leigh, a slim, fresh-faced constable in his late twenties, who had only recently joined Kensington CID, interrupted.

'Could I just mention, Sergeant, that I collected a copy of the letter he wrote to Mr Barron after the sacking. I've got it here. It's full of insults and abuse.'

Haynes nodded. 'Yes, thanks, DC Leigh. I think Mr Marsh was letting off steam. Doesn't necessarily point to a murderer in my book.'

'In any case,' said Khan, 'he's got a strong alibi for the night of 27 June. He and his wife were at a party celebrating their wedding anniversary.'

Haynes shrugged. 'So he's out of the picture. Who's the guy next to him?'

Khan pointed to the image of a man with short, black hair and a slightly podgy face. 'This man's got an unusual name – Riggs Gentle. He's the brother of Private Aron Gentle, the soldier whose life was ruined on a training exercise after David Barron shot him in the back by mistake. Because of what happened, this brother has held a grudge against Barron for twenty-four years and he's got a criminal record for violence and dishonesty offences.'

A blonde female detective sitting next to Leigh remarked, 'Sounds like a prime suspect to me.'

'I know, but he's got a good alibi too,' said Khan. 'He was at his local vet in Wolverhampton. His dog wasn't very well, and the vet has confirmed he was there at around 6.30 p.m. on the twenty-seventh. That wouldn't have left him enough time to drive to Kensington and pump three bullets into David Barron.'

Haynes told the meeting that this led them to an issue he'd been keen to raise.

'After all the inquiries we've made over the past two weeks, it's becoming clear this was probably a contract killing,' he said. 'We're really on the hunt for two people. One's the guy in overalls who turned up at the hall and pulled the trigger. The other's the person who organised and planned the murder.'

His colleagues mumbled in agreement. He went on, 'This means we're looking for a paymaster, who conceived the plan that Barron should be killed, and a professional assassin who carried out the instructions to kill him. We believe him to be a professional because of his brazen conduct at the hall.

'Over the past few days, I've begun concentrating my efforts on finding the paymaster. And DS Khan's taken responsibility for hunting down the assassin. She's already liaising with the National Crime Agency and Met officers who have dealt with cases featuring professional killers. As a result, the chief super's allowing me to increase our team to eighteen detectives. The extra six will be coming in a few days. Anyway, Sergeant, could you please give us a run-down on the other suspects?'

'Yes, sir,' she said. 'So this is the victim's wife, Deborah Barron. It's hard to imagine that she'd have planned her husband's death. It's actually been suggested that the pair were trying to patch up their marriage.'

Haynes interrupted. 'The husband or wife of a victim can never be totally overlooked. The starting point for so many murders has been traced back to the victim's own marital partner.'

'That's true, sir, but at the time of the death she was shopping and DC Leigh found a till receipt confirming that.'

He shrugged. 'From what I know of her, she seems the only honest and decent member of the Diamond family. DC Leigh, how are you getting on with your inquiries into Barron's will?'

Leigh, who appeared slightly uncomfortable as he lounged on top of a desk, said he hoped to have an answer by the end of the week.

'Monday at the latest,' he assured the chief inspector.

Khan tapped the next picture along. 'This slightly red-faced man with uneven teeth is Vinny or Vince Diamond, the well-known crime boss. The owner of the Curry Palace in Southgate supports his claim that he and his son Mickey – seen in the picture next to him – were having a meal there at the time of the shooting.'

Haynes interrupted again. 'But in the immediate aftermath of the killing, Vince Diamond was on the phone to someone. And he could easily have met up with the hitman later to pay him off. Crouch End, where the Porsche was found, is just four miles from Southgate.'

'Not only that, sir,' said Khan. 'There are some large payments in his bank account to some obscure payees.'

The chief inspector nodded. 'We urgently need the results of his phone analysis. Stevens, how are you getting on checking Diamond's phone?'

A stout detective constable said he hoped to have results within the next day or two.

'Good,' the chief inspector replied. 'I won't be surprised to find he's got a Continental hitman on speed-dial.'

'Sir, there's an associate of Diamond's who could have something to do with the shooting at the hall,' said DC Leigh. 'Freddie Valmar.'

Khan pointed to the image of a dark-haired man with wire-framed glasses.

'Yes, his picture's here, next to Mickey Diamond,' she said. 'Valmar is Diamond's right-hand man. As you will all know from an internal memo, he's the guy wanted by the Met for shooting a DS in Clapton yesterday.'

Haynes's eyes lit up. 'Yes, Freddie the Fish. He's definitely a person of interest for Gymkhana.'

The female officer was expressionless. 'Freddie the Fish?'

Haynes chuckled. 'No one's quite sure how he came by that name. One theory is he used to fish people's keys through letterboxes in front doors, and another's that he once swam across the River Lea to flee the cops. But the version I like most is that, as a Roman Catholic, he always eats fish on a Friday.'

A round of light-hearted murmurings swept round the team before Haynes brought them back to the matter in hand.

'Valmar partly matches the gunman's description, so we've got to keep him in mind,' Haynes continued. 'But somehow gunning down a concertgoer doesn't seem his style. Now, Sergeant, would you remind us all about the last suspect?'

'Yes sir. Alex Smart. He's the man whose wife attended the concert with her boyfriend, Craig Arnold. If you remember, you asked me to include him because he slightly resembles the bogus plumber caught on camera.'

'Yes,' said Leigh. 'And he's been mentioned as a suspect for the killing of Craig Arnold.'

Haynes frowned. 'Sadly for us, our colleagues in BTP have discounted him as a suspect in the train incident because they say he's got a firm alibi. They suspect Arnold was victim to a disturbed individual who went to the station intent on pushing someone under a train. There's a history of this in London. But we need to be sure his alibi is cast-iron.

'We certainly can't rule out Alex Smart as a suspect for the murder of Barron, mistaking him for Arnold. He's got a poor alibi – watching television. I asked him what happened in the episode of EastEnders he claimed to have been watching and he had trouble remembering.'

The sergeant interrupted to say, 'All he could recall was a row between Max and Tanya.'

'Mr Smart has a fearful temper,' said Haynes. 'He didn't want to be interviewed by us. He only agreed to speak when I threatened to bring him to the station. He's still on our radar.'

He strolled over to the whiteboard. 'To me, there's only one person here, on this list of suspects, that I believe really warrants our scrutiny.'

He slapped the board next to the picture of Diamond.

'We found some text messages on his phone, speaking angrily about Barron, claiming the man had tricked him out of money. That's why I'm going to be focussing all my attention on Vinny Diamond.'

Chapter 32

'I hope you're proud of yourself, Nick Colton,' hissed a woman's voice on Friday morning as he queued for a batch of coffees in *The Post* canteen. He spun round expecting to find the smiling features of a friendly colleague. Instead he was confronted by the infuriated face of Denise Barton-Jones who evoked an image in his mind of a deranged fishwife.

'After you got my Polebrook story spiked, Sadie skipped round to the *Graphic* office and gave the story to them. Did you see it? It was splashed all over this morning's front page. That was my story, Nick. My story that I spent three months working on.'

He was waging an inner battle to control his temper as other customers in the queue turned to watch them. 'I'm very sorry *The Post* didn't run the story, Denise. But it wasn't my decision to drop it. It was Chris Lane's, so have a go at him. I only found flaws that suggested it would have been very dangerous for us to run it.'

As the pair moved forward in the queue, she sneered. 'Very dangerous? The *Graphic* didn't find it very dangerous. They chose to run it on the front page and on pages four and five inside. It's going to supercharge their circulation and that should have been us. It's a story that's rocked the government and will be spoken about for years to come.'

'And if we'd run it and Polebrook had sued, it might have led to us having to close down,' he replied.

He was on the verge of making a further point when he realized a stern-faced young canteen assistant was asking whether he wanted coffee or tea.

'Three white coffees, please,' he informed her.

Denise was in no mood to desist. 'Sadie was really good in offering the story to us first and, because of you, they killed it.'

'Look, Denise, you're being utterly ridiculous. I found major flaws with the story. The woman's clearly a fantasist. They crop up all the time, but you haven't had the experience to recognise it.'

'Next, please,' said the canteen lady in an irritated voice.

'You've got a nerve, Nick Colton…'

'Could you move along. What's yours, love?' demanded the assistant.

'Just a coffee, please,' Denise replied quietly.

Then, as Colton paid the cashier for his coffees, Denise raised her voice again. 'You criticise me for a lack of experience, Nick, but I've been a hack for twelve years and I know this business as well as you do. There's no question that bloody story should have been in *The Post*.'

He didn't wait to hear any more of her diatribe. He headed back to the newsroom where he handed coffees to Foster and McMillen and then slumped down at his desk in silence.

McMillen immediately sensed his annoyance.

'Are you all right, Nick?'

He leaned back in his chair. 'Yes. Denise in Investigations has had another go at me. That's all.'

'She can be a cow.'

'You obviously saw the *Graphic*'s splash?'

'Yes. So what? It's just one woman's claims.'

'She's deluded, that Sadie Robinson.'

'I can see why Denise is upset. She worked hard on that story. Then you step in for a day and ker-pow! Her story's out of the window. But you checked it out, found the story unsafe and passed that knowledge onto Chris Lane. It was him who took the decision to shelve the story, not you.'

He nodded. 'I know, but Denise doesn't see it like that. Now that the *Graphic*'s run it, she believes the story must have been safe for us to run.'

McMillen said, 'Did you know Polebrook was chased down the street this morning by a reporter from *Good Morning Britain*? Labour are going to be asking questions in the House. The BBC's political editor wonders whether he's going to last the day.'

'I'm not really surprised.'

'Did you know they were talking about it in conference this morning?'

'Who were?'

'The editor, Chris Lane, Clemmie – everyone. Lane made it clear he took full responsibility. He'd discussed it with the editor, and they'd mutually agreed it was too risky to run it.'

Colton frowned. 'In spite of that, there must be some feeling that we missed a trick.'

McMillen smiled. 'That always happens when we lose out on a story and a rival paper snaps it up. But you've just got to move onto the next one.'

'Yes, you're right. Onto the next battle. Let the *Graphic* have their moment of glory, but it won't last for ever.'

However, as Colton travelled to Kensington later that day, he began to have doubts about the way he'd found fault with the Polebrook story.

Maybe he should have probed a little deeper rather than readily accepting the word of an antiques dealer. Maybe there'd been incidents involving sexual shenanigans above the shop which had escaped Raj Sharma's attention, or that he'd wanted to hide, perhaps fearing any hint of scandal might have damaged his trade.

Maybe the man had skilfully steered him away from the stark truth of what had been happening on those sultry afternoons in West Ealing.

* * *

Hanging baskets brimming with pink and purple fuchsias and begonia swayed in the summer breeze as Colton arrived at The Little Drummer Boy. He pushed the door. He was confronted by the chatter and laughter of early evening drinkers along with the clinking of glasses and the stench of stale beer.

Framed prints of dancers and horses lined the right-hand wall with a full-sized portrait of a young soldier playing a drum in the centre.

He felt a tap on the shoulder. He turned to see the smiling face of DS Khan.

'I saw you arriving and followed you in,' she said as he warmly shook her hand. 'I'm still hesitant about venturing into a pub on my own.'

'What can I get you?'

'Just an orange juice. I'm still on duty,' she said.

A few minutes later, as he returned from the bar with their drinks, he discovered she'd laid claim to a small table by the doorway.

'So this isn't the CID pub?' he remarked, sitting down and sipping his ice-cold lager. He had to raise his voice to ensure she could hear him above the hubbub.

'No, The Three Doves is where all the CID generally drink. I chose this place on purpose to avoid prying eyes.'

He chuckled. 'You didn't want to be seen in the company of a notorious hack. That's quite understandable.'

Khan blushed as another customer brushed past her. 'Not at all. But you know how it is with gossip. Nick, I hope anything I tell you will remain between us. I don't want anything I say to find its way into your paper.'

'Of course. You have my word, Miss Khan.'

'It's Nadia, by the way. Nick, the reason I wanted to speak to you is that you've kept very much on top of events since you were unfortunate enough to find yourself sitting next to the murder victim.'

'I'll never forget that night.'

She nodded. 'I can imagine how you felt afterwards. But you acted bravely in chasing the person you felt was responsible and since then I've read most of your articles. You still think the man in the overalls who sped off in the Porsche was the gunman?'

He folded his arms. 'Yes, I do. It's a pity no forensic evidence turned up in the car.'

'So we've gone through the evidence about the car again. We think the Miles Davis CD may after all have been left behind by the man you saw. We initially assumed it belonged to the car's real owner. Now it appears the man you followed left it there by mistake.'

'Perhaps his only mistake,' he observed.

'That's right,' she said. 'Nick, the article you wrote about Aron Gentle interested us.'

He adopted a serious tone. 'Yes, the soldier mistakenly shot by Barron. His family were only too happy to talk to me.'

She nodded again. 'There was something about that revelation of yours that stopped me in my tracks. It made me think. What if someone held a grudge bordering on the psychopathic against someone because of a shooting incident? Wouldn't the most appropriate way to exact revenge be to shoot them back?'

'I can see what you mean, Nadia.'

She sipped her orange juice. 'So we looked long and hard at the Gentle family. We interviewed the aggrieved brother. Everything in your article turned out to be accurate.'

He gazed into the sergeant's eyes before sipping his lager. Was she about to make some startling disclosure?

She sighed. 'However, Aron Gentle's brother was at a veterinary practice in the Midlands at six thirty on the day of Barron's murder. There's no way he could have been in the Albert Hall.'

He shrugged. 'Pity. Would have led to a neat resolution of the whole case.'

'In addition, Joe Marsh, the sacked accountant, was at a wedding anniversary party.'

'What about the stockbroker who harassed Craig at work?'

'At a pub all evening with friends.'

He put his glass down on the table. 'False alibis can be cracked. I was going to tell you that Alex Smart's alibi for the time of Craig Arnold's death in Brixton has fallen apart.'

'You know that's not our case. The transport police are dealing with that.'

He sipped his drink. 'I know, but it has a bearing on the Barron case, doesn't it?'

'The chief inspector has doubts about whether there's any link. He's about to make an arrest, but I can't tell you more just now.'

'Really? It would be good to get a heads-up when you're able to.'

'Of course. I'll try to keep you in the loop.'

'Anyway, whatever the chief inspector thinks, Alex Smart told his wife – and, presumably, the police – he was at his mother's care home in Croydon at the time of the Brixton murder. But I've been over there and he left the care home at 9.30 a.m., giving him ample time to track down Craig and follow him into the station.'

'You realize, Nick, this is a very serious allegation.'

'Of course, it puts him in the frame for the train death. And if he's crazed enough to do that, why could he not have carried out the Barron shooting?'

'Whoa, whoa, whoa! Two very different affairs. The Barron case involved a cunning, confident assailant – a brazen attacker armed with a Beretta. The Brixton case involved no skill at all. One push and it was over for poor Craig Arnold. But I think I should get an account of your inquiries from you so I can liaise with British Transport Police. Could you send me the basic details if I give you my personal email?'

'Of course, no problem. I grant you they involved a totally different modus operandi, but it strikes me the two crimes might well be connected.'

She tore a sheet of paper from her notebook and began writing. 'Nick, thank you for mentioning it, but we don't think so. However, I'm duty-bound to pass on what you know to our colleagues across the water.' She handed him the piece of paper with her email address.

He shrugged his shoulders. 'Thanks. There was another thing I was going to mention. Did David Barron leave a will?'

She smiled. 'A very timely question. We've just found out this afternoon. He was an accountant, so of course his financial affairs were fairly up to date. Everything goes to his wife, Deborah. But a few days before he was killed, he made a phone call to his solicitor and was talking about changing his will.'

Chapter 33

The driver switched off the CD player. 'I'm sorry. I can't stand any more of that Ed Sheeran. We've had half an hour of him. I think it's time for a break.'

Nathan Richards, who was sitting in the front passenger seat of the black Ford transit, was disappointed.

'Oh that's a shame. One of his best ones was about to come on. Me and my mum really love him.'

'Leave it for the moment, Nathan. We've got to find somewhere to stop.'

Clifford Martin, who was crouching uncomfortably in the back with a bearded man in a navy-blue tracksuit, was becoming increasingly uneasy.

'Why won't you tell me what this job is?' he asked. 'I need to know how long it's going to take. I told my missus I'd be home by midnight and it's already half past eleven.'

The driver sneered. 'You'll find out soon enough.'

The road was shrouded on this humid night by dense woodland on both sides. The only light came from the van's headlights and the beams of passing cars.

'This'll do,' said the driver as he slowed down and turned into a clearing in the forest. A lorry thundered past as the van proceeded across the rocky terrain amid bushes and trees.

The driver stopped the vehicle and turned off the engine. Martin was growing ever more worried. He'd been told they were going to break into a mansion. But he'd seen no signs of a mansion. They appeared to be in the middle of nowhere.

'Where's the job then lads?' he asked.

The driver ignored his question. 'Let's all get out.'

Martin opened the side door and scrambled out, along with the bearded man. They stood together on the flat, muddy ground, staring across at a line of oak trees and into the black void beyond.

As the driver walked round the van, he switched on a torch. Then he collected an item from the back and approached the two men who'd disembarked. Nathan remained inside. He was searching for a second Ed Sheeran CD.

By the time he found it and opened the passenger door, he could hear Martin screaming and watched him being attacked by the other two men.

'Leave me alone, you bastards!' Martin was shouting. 'This was never the plan.'

'This was very much the plan,' said the driver, who was striking him repeatedly with an iron bar. 'You've been shouting your mouth off, haven't you?'

'No. It wasn't me. Honest!'

Handing his torch to the man in the tracksuit, the driver struck Martin one final blow, which sent him sprawling onto the muddy ground. His head bleeding profusely, he lay writhing in agony.

The driver turned to Nathan. 'Right, make yourself useful, lad. Get the rope out of the back and tie his hands and feet.'

Martin was moaning. 'Let me go, lads. Please.'

As the driver started the engine and turned the vehicle round, Nathan tied Martin's hands together tightly. Then he turned his talents to binding his feet.

'Let me go, Nate. I'll make it worth your while,' Martin whined.

Nathan shook his head. 'Boss says you've got to learn a lesson.'

Five minutes later, the driver, who'd been sitting at the wheel smoking a cigarette, returned to check on Nathan's knot-tying skills.

'Good job, Nathan,' he assured him. 'You weren't in the scouts, were you?'

Then, without waiting for an answer, he said, 'Right, help me to empty his pockets of anything that could identify him. Don't want to make it easy for the cops, do we?'

'What about his money?' asked Nathan, who'd pulled a brown leather wallet from Martin's trouser pocket.

'We'll put the money in a charity box. No sense leaving it for some bent copper to line his pockets.'

'And his phone?'

'Give that to me as well. And give me his rings and gold medallion.' The driver hurled the phone into a nearby bush and placed the jewellery in his pocket. 'Now help me with this,' he insisted.

He rummaged about in the rear of the van, which Vinny Diamond had arranged specifically for the job. After finding some metal chains, he and Nathan looped them round their victim's feet and secured them to the vehicle's towbar.

He and his two colleagues then jumped inside and the van drew away. Their terrified victim screamed and shouted abuse as he was dragged through the grass and mud.

The van rejoined the road and headed north at an initial speed of around twenty miles an hour. As the shouting behind them became louder and more desperate, the driver raised the speed to thirty and then forty.

'Shut up! Shut up!' the driver grumbled until the noise behind them petered out.

When the van had travelled for around two miles through Epping Forest, on the north-eastern fringe of London, the driver stopped by the side of the road and unfastened the chain. Then, without even glancing at the bloodied remains of Clifford Martin, he turned the vehicle round in the middle of the road and drove back towards the capital.

* * *

Half an hour later, two Essex Police traffic officers received a call from their control room. PC Colin Minton responded. 'Go ahead, control.'

'A motorist's reported a large object in the road at Horseshoe Hill in Upshire. Could you take a look? Your car's the only one in the area. The guy thinks it may be a deer carcass, but he didn't stop to check.'

'Wilco.'

The pair, who at the time were travelling along the deserted high street in the nearby market town of Epping, set off on their three-mile journey.

Eventually, after passing secluded detached houses amid the semi-rural terrain, they came upon the narrow lane where the motorist had reported seeing an object. Sure enough, there seemed to be a bulky item in the road. From a distance, it appeared to be a bundle of clothes.

PC Minton got out and walked over to take a look. Then he turned his head away in disgust.

Chapter 34

Alma Diamond tied her grey hair behind her head and studied herself in the full-length mirror. She adjusted her hair and made sure her blue and white floral dress was hanging correctly.

Her husband, still in his pyjamas, sat up in bed and stared across the room.

'What time are you visiting Mickey?' he asked.

She turned and smiled at the husband she adored. 'Midday, but, as it's Saturday, I've got some shopping to do.'

'Good God, woman. It's still only ten to nine. You've got all day to worry about shopping.'

'I'm going over to Eve's first.'

'It's working out to be quite a day trip you've got planned there.'

She frowned. 'Mickey's my first priority, of course. Debs said she might come as well. Why don't you join us?'

He shook his head. 'I've already told you. I've got plans.'

'Are you still trying to speak to Ben Cooper?'

'Oh, sorry, darling. I forgot to mention. I managed to have a quick word with him yesterday before his office in Lincoln's Inn shut for the day. Doesn't look like there's much chance of any of them getting bail.'

'We guessed as much, didn't we?' she said as she sat on the bed.

'I wonder if Nathan's up and about yet,' he remarked. He pressed a button on a handset beside the bed and Nathan's hesitant voice resonated round the room.

'Yes, boss?'

'Nathan, how did the operation go last night?'

'The operation? Oh, the job with the transit. Sweet as a nut.'

'Good. Could you check the building? I just heard a car.'

'Yes, boss. I was going to tell you. A blue Audi and a police car have pulled up.'

'Oh shit. Can you go and see what they want while I get dressed?'

Alma panicked as the doorbell rang. 'Vinny, I'm just going to slip out the back door. I don't want to keep Eve waiting.'

As she left the room, he snatched a shirt from the wardrobe and pulled on a pair of trousers. Then he peered through the vertical blinds into his front garden. A man and woman in plain clothes were remonstrating with Nathan in front of the glazed porch while three officers in uniform were admiring the roses blooming beside his front wall.

He shuffled into the hallway and proceeded into his porch where a slim-faced man with unkempt dark hair and a wrinkled grey suit was talking to Nathan. He recognised the visitor as DCI Harry Haynes, immediately.

'What seems to be the trouble?' he asked.

Haynes frowned. 'We've got a few questions for you, Mr Diamond.'

'I've got one for you. When am I going to get my phone back?'

'I don't know, is the best answer I can give at the moment.'

'That's bloody typical of you coppers. You want me to answer your questions but you won't give a proper answer to one of mine.'

Haynes glanced at DS Khan and sighed. 'Mr Diamond, we're investigating the murder of your son-in-law. We'd like you to accompany us to the station.'

Diamond groaned. 'In Kensington? Why can't you talk to me here? You can come in, if you like. But I'll be honest. I've got a busy day planned.'

'We can do this the easy way or the hard way. It's in your interest to cooperate. Do you want to get your coat?'

Diamond stared at the floor. 'Let me think…'

Haynes scowled. 'All right. I've had enough. Vince Diamond, I'm arresting you in connection with the murder of David Barron. Sergeant, do the rest, please.'

Khan read him the police caution. 'Shall I cuff him, Chief Inspector?'

'No. I'm sure that won't be necessary.'

Diamond stroked his chin. 'Can I just phone my solicitor and ask him along?'

'You can do that when we get to the station.'

While the chief inspector watched him like an owl studying a vole, Diamond selected a dark grey jacket from his hallway cupboard. Then, after instructing Nathan to wash the car, he stepped outside and closed the front door.

'Haven't even had any breakfast,' he moaned as he slipped into the back of the Ford Focus police car and was driven away.

* * *

Vinny Diamond had seen the inside of several interview rooms during his life. He gauged the one inside Kensington custody suite was more congenial than most. A large sash window, which was barred, afforded a degree of light. The table and chairs were of light maple and appeared new.

Diamond sat down on one of the chairs by the table at just after ten thirty. The police were being unusually cordial. They'd even offered him tea or coffee, which he'd declined.

'Don't want to cosy up to the bastards,' he told himself.

He spent the next half hour wondering if there was some way of arranging bail for his son. Finally, at just after eleven o'clock, his solicitor's jaunty face appeared in the doorway in a dark blue suit. They greeted each other like long-lost relatives, slapping each other on the back and shaking hands warmly.

Silver-haired Ben Cooper, sat down beside his client and squinted at him over the top of his glasses.

'So what trouble are you in now, Vinny?'

'Well, I'm not sure,' said Diamond. 'It's something to do with David, my son-in-law who died.'

'The Albert Hall.'

'Yes. They say they just want to ask some questions. They haven't explained why. Benny, I can honestly say I've got nothing at all to do with David's death.'

He shook his head. 'Thanks again for what you did yesterday, Benny. The National Crime Agency were determined to catch me out, but you put them in their place and they crawled away like wounded animals.'

'Just doing my job, Vinny. Just doing my job.'

'I actually wanted to talk to you about Mickey.'

'Well, one thing at a time. We've got this interview to get through first and the best advice I can give is for you to say "no comment" to the chief inspector. Let's find out the strength of their case. Now you'd better give me a bit of background. To start with, tell me more about where you were on 27 June.'

* * *

Half an hour later, DCI Haynes and DS Khan arrived in the room. The chief inspector settled into a chair opposite Diamond. The sergeant sat beside him after turning on the video recording equipment.

'Right, Mr Diamond. I must remind you you're still under caution,' Haynes explained while placing a folder of documents on the table. 'First of all, I want to show you a transcript of some texts sent and received by you. This has been produced by our phone expert, who found they'd been deleted.'

He handed both Diamond and Mr Cooper some sheets of paper.

'For the recording, I'm showing the suspect a transcript of some text messages sent on 3 June this year. They were found on the suspect's Samsung phone.' He then read the messages aloud.

> Diamond: *Need to talk to you. Are you coming in?*
> Valmar: *Not sure. On my way to the Downs Tavern. Why?*
> Diamond: *Want to talk to you about Barron.*
> Valmar: *What's he done?*
> Diamond: *Think he's been nicking funds. Ten thousand has gone missing.*
> Valmar: *What do you want me to do about it?*
> Diamond: *Not sure. Want to talk to you and work out a plan.*

Mr Cooper's face was blank. 'Who's Valmar?'

'Thought you'd have known, Mr Cooper,' the chief inspector said sternly. 'He's one of your client's most trusted colleagues.'

'Wouldn't say that,' said Diamond.

'He's wanted by police in East London for gunning down a detective. Don't you read the newspapers or watch the telly, Mr Cooper?' said Haynes.

The lawyer frowned. 'Sorry. I hadn't made the association.'

Haynes and Khan exchanged glances before the chief inspector continued.

'Mr Diamond, you'd fallen out with David Barron. Text messages sent from your phone indicate you strongly suspected him of defrauding you. You had a strong motive for wishing to eliminate him. Three weeks after these texts were exchanged, your son-in-law was shot dead.'

Diamond opened his mouth to speak. Although Mr Cooper glared at him, he said, 'He was family. There's no way I'd kill a member of my own family. It's against all my principles.'

'Is it a coincidence that your son-in-law's life ends in dramatic fashion as soon as he becomes a problem for Diamond Enterprises? Or is it just, as far as you're concerned, a twist of fate?'

'No comment.'

'I don't believe his death, coming after you fell out with him, was a coincidence, Mr Diamond,' said Haynes. 'And I don't believe fate played any part.'

'No comment.'

'The simple fact of the matter is you arranged his murder, didn't you, Mr Diamond?'

'No comment.'

Chapter 35

DCI Haynes eyed his suspect coldly. He'd just accused him of master-minding the murder of his own son-in-law. The atmosphere in the interview room was laced with tension.

The detective knew by his reputation and list of past convictions that Diamond was a ruthless individual with little regard for anyone who happened to get in his way. But, as he faced him across the table, he was beginning to realize what a callous, contemptible man he truly was.

The chief inspector leaned back in his chair. 'All right. We move on. What does the name Renzo Gaudiano mean to you, Mr Diamond?'

The businessman glanced at Mr Cooper. Then he stared at the table.

'It's a name I've heard somewhere. I can't quite place it.'

Haynes turned his head towards his sergeant before his eyes switched back to Diamond. 'It's on your contacts list, on your phone.'

'Can't think why.'

'Let me continue. What do know about the name Maxim Zimyatov, Mr Diamond?'

The businessman peered at the wall behind his interviewer while he appeared to be exploring the deeper recesses of his memory. The sergeant's phone beeped. She read a message on the screen and, after mumbling an apology, left the room.

Diamond glared into the chief inspector's eyes. 'No, you've got me stumped again. Was his name on my phone?'

'Yes.'

'No, I can't think what those names would have been doing there. Unless they're suppliers. Yes, that's probably it – toy suppliers. I obviously can't have been using them very much. But I'm glad you mentioned this. It's obviously time for me to go through my contacts and delete those I don't use.'

Khan heard his explanations as she re-entered the room and resumed her seat. She peered across at their suspect and frowned. 'Don't try and be clever with us, Mr Diamond. You know who these people are as well as we do.'

Mr Cooper interrupted to say, 'Chief Inspector, it's not only my client who has no knowledge of Messrs Gaudiano and Zimyatov. I'm in the same position. Could you fill me in? Maybe we can short circuit things and bring these proceedings to a rapid conclusion.'

Haynes sighed. 'They're on a list of international contract killers. Men prepared to travel anywhere at the drop of a hat to carry out murder for money. And their names and numbers are on your client's phone.'

Diamond suppressed a yawn. 'Maybe I'm being framed. Maybe one of you put those names on my phone. Or maybe my son added their names as a joke.'

Khan shook her head. 'Not an exceptionally funny joke.'

'The National Crime Agency suspect these two men – and others on their list – of having carried out contract murders in Britain and Europe,' said Haynes. 'We believe your son-in-law may have been killed by one of these contract killers, acting on your instructions.'

'No comment.'

'All right. One moment, please.'

The two detectives moved to the side of the room where they held a brief conversation. They then returned to the table.

'DS Khan,' said the chief inspector, 'you wanted to ask our friend a question.'

She assumed a grave expression while removing a notebook from her pocket.

'Mr Diamond, you've already told us you were at the Curry Palace on the evening of Thursday 27 June,' she said. 'We've been examining your handset and found you made several calls to a pay-as-you-go phone linked to North London. Do you remember who you were speaking to?'

Diamond shook his head. 'Do you remember who you were talking to more than two weeks ago?'

'We've found a customer who remembers you and your son because of your lively conversation. She overhead part of one of your calls before you took the phone outside.'

'What's happening to freedom and privacy in this country? You can't go anywhere these days without eavesdroppers, people snooping, cameras…'

Khan retained her serious expression as she referred to a page in her notebook. 'Here's what she recalls. You were saying there'd been a change of plan and you were trying to set up a meet near to the Clockhouse Junction on the North Circular. Then you said something along the lines of, "Go and have a drink. Chat up a woman for all I care. I'll see you at ten and you'll get your money."'

Diamond grinned. 'I can't remember many of the conversations I had yesterday, young lady. How do you expect me to remember some conversation more than two weeks ago that someone from a nearby table thinks they overheard?'

Mr Cooper raised an eyebrow. 'Chief Inspector Haynes, I must protest. My client's quite right. How can he be expected to recall a conversation he had last month? He's a businessman and an extremely active one who's calling a wide variety of people all the time.'

Haynes sneered. 'I don't doubt that.'

'I'm advising my client not to comment any further and, if I may say so, all this so-called evidence appears rather circumstantial, not to say flimsy.'

Stung by this criticism, the chief inspector scowled. 'The point my sergeant's trying to make is that, less than an hour after Mr Diamond's son-in-law was killed, he was constantly on the phone and arranging a late-night rendezvous with someone in order to make a payment.'

The chief inspector brought out two sets of documents from his folder. 'Now these are copies of your bank statements for June and July, Mr Diamond. They show substantial movements of money.'

He handed copies to both Diamond and Mr Cooper. 'The item I'm going to ask you about is marked with an asterisk. It shows a bank withdrawal that you made, Mr Diamond, on Monday 24 June for ten thousand pounds.

The following day your wife, Alma, made a similar-sized withdrawal from another account, which you control jointly. If you'd care to read the second page of the document, you'll see the first payment marked there.'

The two men studied the statements. Then Diamond said, 'Well–'

Mr Cooper stopped him. 'I'd advise you to make no comment.'

Diamond shrugged. 'I was just going to say that I needed the money for a shipment of toys from China.'

'What? You pay them in cash?'

'You fellas obviously don't know much about the Chinese. They've got a traditional preference for cash. I pay the factory owner's brother in cash in London. It's a nuisance, but I get all the toys at a good discount. It's good for business. Everyone's happy.'

Haynes exchanged glances with Khan. 'Sounds highly unlikely to me.'

He gazed round in exasperation. 'Mr Diamond, you had a strong motive for wanting your son-in-law disposed of. You'd got access to the private phone numbers of at least two professional contract killers, so making the arrangements wasn't difficult.

'The only problem you encountered was finding the right time and place to arrange the murder of your relative. He was a hard man to target because he took his motor everywhere and it had bullet-resistant glass. But then you had a stroke of luck. You discovered that he'd bought a ticket to see Loretta Kay at the Royal Albert Hall. And this was where you had another card up your sleeve. One of your employees, Clifford Martin, has a sister who works at the box office. He was able to find out, by questioning her discreetly, where David Barron was going to be sitting.'

'Nonsense. Questioning discreetly? He's a useless prat. I couldn't trust him to feed my canary.'

Haynes ignored the flippant remark. He took some chewing gum from his mouth and hurled it into a waste bin.

'Mr Diamond, you had a strong motive,' he said. 'You had access to the private phone numbers of contract killers. You'd pinpointed a location for the hit. You had the money to fulfil your side of the deal. And, just after the murder was committed, you were overheard making arrangements to meet someone. Now tell me you've got a good explanation for all of that?'

Diamond glanced at his lawyer and then gazed back at the chief inspector.

'No comment.'

The sergeant removed a report from her pocket and placed it in front of her. 'Since the name Clifford Martin's come up, I thought I'd mention that his wife's reported him missing. He was sent on a job for you somewhere in London last night and never came home. So it appears we'll have to sit here a little longer while we ask you about that.'

Chapter 36

Detective Sergeant Nadia Khan fiddled with her pen nervously and took another sip of coffee. It was quite unlike her boss to be late.

She studied her watch again. It was nearly 10.30 a.m. and there was no sign of him.

DC Kyle Leigh strolled across the office, yawning and looking as though he hadn't had much sleep. His brown hair was dishevelled and his face seemed pale.

'Have you seen the chief inspector this morning?' the sergeant asked as he brushed past her desk.

Before he reached the coffee machine and dropped in a coin, he simply said, 'Haven't seen anyone this morning, apart from you.'

A few minutes later, perspiring profusely and breathing heavily, DI Haynes stomped along the corridor.

'Bloody traffic. Gets worse every day,' he declared as he unlocked his room and threw his jacket down on the desk.

Khan watched him with a concerned expression. 'Are you all right, sir?'

'Yes, nothing that a strong cup of coffee couldn't cure. You couldn't get me one, could you? Black, one sugar.'

Shortly afterwards, she presented him with a steaming cup of coffee which he accepted gratefully.

The sergeant took one of the chairs and sat down by his desk with a broad smile.

'Sir, the switchboard received a message last night from a desk sergeant at Kilburn police. An old man came in and reported he'd found a gun.'

The chief inspector, who was neatly arranging documents on his desk, stopped and raised an eyebrow. 'What sort of gun?'

'A Beretta 92S like the one used at the hall. That's not all. It was wrapped in grey clothing.'

'What kind of clothing?'

'Grey tradesman's overalls.'

His eyes lit up. 'That's a bit of a breakthrough, Sergeant.'

'There was a key in one of the pockets.'

'Where are the items right now?'

'They've all been properly packaged and taken to forensics. The man said he found them in a refuse bin in an alley.'

'Might have been rummaging around for something of value.'

'It was an industrial waste bin behind some shops and a short distance from Kilburn nick. Very public-spirited, I thought.'

The chief inspector stroked his chin. 'I think we need to get photographs taken of the gun and clothes and make a public appeal. We want to know, did anyone see a man or woman disposing of these items? And did they arrive and leave by car?'

The sergeant appeared thoughtful.

'Maybe the gunman dumped them there because he had some reason to be in Kilburn – you know, maybe he lives there or spent a night there.'

'Yes. Or was just passing through and decided a bin in an alley was a good, anonymous place to dump them. What sort of key was it?'

'An ordinary Yale key.'

'Maybe he left it in the pocket by mistake.'

'That's quite likely, sir. Maybe he's not the cunning professional we thought he was.'

He sat quietly with his head bowed. 'Sooner or later everyone makes mistakes.' He paused before adding, 'This might be the time to hold a press conference. It's been on my mind for a few days. We can try and put the family up in front of the cameras for an appeal and include these items as well. What do you think?'

'Excellent idea.'

'Can you call the media team and make the arrangements then? Maybe for eleven o'clock tomorrow? And can you put a call in to the Barron family, just to keep them in the picture?'

'Right, sir. I was wondering how the sergeant's getting on, Charlie Allen, the officer who was shot. Have you heard anything, sir?'

Haynes stood up and peered through the blinds at the slow-moving traffic in the street below.

'Funnily enough, I was just speaking to the superintendent about him last night,' said Haynes. 'Charlie's going to be OK. He's sitting up in bed and seems quite cheerful.'

She smiled. 'That's very good news, sir. Apparently, Freddie Valmar's still at large. CID at Bethnal Green have visited all his known haunts but he appears to have gone to ground.'

He shook his head. 'Won't be long before they catch him. He's too well-known. Just a matter of time. You know, I'm still not happy about us having to let Vinny Diamond go on Saturday.'

'We didn't really have any choice, sir.'

'No, all the evidence at present's circumstantial. We just need the missing piece of the jigsaw to tie him directly to the murder. He claimed at one point he wouldn't kill Barron because he's family. That's just a load of baloney. Anyway, how far did you get with checking out the two men on Diamond's phone, Gaudiano and Zimyatov?'

'So the team have made a bit of progress. Gaudiano's the more likely candidate. There've been intel reports of him being sighted in Paris. There's no evidence of him crossing the Channel, but the French capital's only six hours' travelling time away.'

Haynes walked back to his desk and sat down. 'No reports of him wandering along Kilburn High Road then?'

'No sir. The other man, Zimyatov, was last heard of in Greece.'

'Very popular with the Russians, Greece. They like the warmer weather which is so lacking in their own country. Well, I'd concentrate on Gaudiano. See if we can get the help of our Continental cousins. Who knows? Assisted by a photograph or two, we might find he pops up on the Eurostar passenger list or on a flight list from Charles de Gaulle.'

'I'll get that organised, sir, as soon as I've made arrangements for the press briefing.'

Haynes opened a folder on his desk. He informed her that the body found in Epping Forest had been positively identified as Clifford Martin from dental records. A post-mortem found he had died from multiple injuries including a brain injury that would have rendered him unconscious before his death.

He shook his head. 'I feel very sorry for the family. He had a young wife and three children. I don't know how they're going to cope.'

The sergeant stood up and made her way to the door. 'I thought Diamond's reaction was strange when we mentioned Martin's name. He seemed genuinely surprised to learn of his death,' she remarked.

Haynes rolled his eyes. 'It's all acting. I'm sure he's implicated in the death of his office assistant just as he is in the death of David Barron. With luck and a lot of detective work, I don't think it'll be too long before he's facing the full weight of justice for those crimes and probably for the many others he's been involved in.'

* * *

The Monday morning sun was masked by cloud as Nick Colton stepped off the bus at North Greenwich Station and prepared for the second part of his journey to work on the London Underground.

He was annoyed with Nadia Khan, the detective who had promised to let him know about any arrest. Several of that morning's newspapers had revealed a businessman had been arrested over David Barron's death and she had failed to give him an early tip-off about it.

Near the station entrance, he saw a newsstand promoting the *Daily Graphic*.

This annoyed him even more. That was the last newspaper he wished to read that morning. He hardly wanted to be reminded about the *Graphic*'s front-page story on Oliver Polebrook.

The whole affair had unsettled him more than he'd anticipated. All the other national newspapers had followed it up in a major way.

The Sunday papers had published photographs of Polebrook at his West London constituency office and also with his family at their Gloucestershire farm. All *The Post* had done was to publish a six-paragraph story at the foot of page two, summarizing the claims.

He almost felt now as though he had committed some kind of disservice to his newspaper colleagues by pointing out the potential flaws with their investigation into the minister's conduct.

He'd been having problems sleeping because his mind had been unable to shake off these inevitable feelings of guilt.

The O2 Arena, with its twelve yellow spars jutting from its glass-fibre fabric roof, reared up before him as he entered the Underground station. He was about to descend the escalator when his phone rang. It was Clemmie Jones.

'Nick, don't come into the office. I want you to go to the Bailey. There's a case I want you to check out – a guy who firebombed a house in south London. A woman and her two children died.'

Nick stood back from the top of the escalator. 'I remember the case.'

'It may not go ahead today but, if it does, we need someone there. I expect you're feeling chipper today.'

'Why's that?'

'You've seen the front page of today's *Graphic*, haven't you?'

'No.'

'Oliver Polebrook's suing them. He's taken on lawyers and he's going to the High Court. They've printed a grovelling apology at the foot of the front page, saying they now realize the whole story was untrue. But he's still proceeding with his legal action.'

'Good God! That's amazing.'

'Polebrook's said in a statement that he knows Sadie Robinson because she's a member of his constituency party, but he's never associated with her in any way and he can't even remember speaking to her.'

* * *

When he arrived at the office three hours later, smiling colleagues came up to him and shook his hand or slapped him on the back.

Foster left his desk and crept over. 'Good news about Polebrook, mate. I knew you were right all along,' he said. 'How was your court case?'

'It didn't go ahead. What have you been up to?'

'Just doing a piece about some bastards who tied a man to the towbar of a van and dragged him through Epping Forest. Clemmie says it might make tomorrow's splash.'

Katie McMillen peered round the side of her computer screen. 'The folk at the *Graphic* are looking like a right load of knobheads, Nick.'

He grinned. He felt vindicated. 'Of course, I knew honest reporting and thorough research would always triumph,' he said, tongue in check.

Foster raised an eyebrow. 'Yeah, right. Anyway, mate, if you're coming to the Bosun later on, I'll buy you a pint.'

* * *

At lunchtime, the three friends were sitting at a table inside the office pub, laughing and joking together.

McMillen revealed she'd been talking on the phone to *Daily Graphic* reporter Leyla Hussein.

'Leyla says the staff over there first became aware that the story might be untrue on Saturday. The desk received an anonymous call from someone who claimed to know Sadie Robinson and said she lived in a fantasy world. She was always talking about the MP, but had never met him. A few years ago she had claimed to be well acquainted with the lead singer in a famous British rock band. On that occasion, it never got to the papers. But after a few weeks her friends realized it was a bogus friendship. So there seems to be a pattern with her.'

'Quite sad really, isn't it?' Foster observed.

McMillen continued, 'The news editor of the *Graphic*'s been in a bad mood all day.'

Colton gazed out over the quayside where several blue and red narrowboats were bobbing up and down in the dark water.

'It would be a shame if he lost his job over this,' he murmured as his phone rang. The caller was a slightly breathless Jasmine Smart. It sounded as if she had been running.

'Nick, I phoned you because I've discovered something,' she said. 'I went back to the house in Woodmeadow Road this morning with an escort to collect some clothes. Alex's car wasn't there, so I knew it would be OK.

'I went upstairs to collect my clothes and noticed some receipts on the windowsill. Out of curiosity, I started browsing through them. You'll never guess what I found. A till receipt for a drink and a sandwich dating back to the night of the Loretta Kay concert. It was timed for half past eight in the evening, and it was from a petrol station in Clapham, just three miles from the Albert Hall.'

Chapter 37

Camera crews were unloading lighting equipment, tripods and cameras from liveried TV company vans as Nick Colton and Luke Foster arrived for Tuesday morning's press conference at New Scotland Yard in Westminster.

Thick black power cables snaked across the pavement outside the nine-storey, stone-fronted building and wove their way inside past a glass door that had been wedged open.

The pair followed other reporters and the trail of cables along a corridor to the ground-floor press room in the neo-classical, riverside building. They found sound and lighting crews busily setting up equipment beneath the high ceilings.

Behind the long desk and chairs on the podium, the face of murder victim David Barron smiled down from three large posters attached to the back wall. The word 'Murder' appeared above his head while details of the crime were printed beneath.

More than a dozen chairs had been arranged in rows on the floor in front of the platform. The two reporters took seats in the first row and chatted quietly for the next ten minutes. Then they heard Tommy Mundon's gruff voice as their photographer approached.

'The widow's outside,' he was saying. 'I grabbed a couple of shots before I came in.'

Colton turned round to greet him. 'Bit of an ordeal for her.'

Colton was pleased when, through the open door, he spotted Leyla Hussein walking towards them. She beamed when she entered and spotted the two *Post* reporters.

'I couldn't find anywhere to park,' she complained. 'In the end, I had to leave the car half a mile up the road on a meter.'

Foster nodded. 'We came on the Jubilee Line.'

'Couldn't help noticing the apology on your front page yesterday,' Colton remarked.

She sat down behind them. 'Yes. I expect you did. The news editor's been sent home and the lawyer's been given a bollocking.'

Leyla was clearly unaware of Colton's part in helping to prevent his own paper from publishing the story. He decided to say nothing about it. 'Who's going to be the next news editor?'

'Who knows? Barry or Jill, I suppose.'

Finally, at eleven thirty, half an hour late, DCI Haynes and DS Khan, both carrying plastic bags and envelopes containing exhibits, entered the room and stepped onto the podium. They were followed by Deborah and Raymond Barron.

As the sergeant helped the relatives to their seats, the solemn-faced chief inspector remained standing and clapped his hands like a headmaster calling school assembly to order. He seemed slightly better dressed than on the two occasions Colton had seen him. He was wearing an immaculate navy-blue suit and his dark hair was neatly combed.

Haynes tapped the microphone. 'Is this working?' Mumbled assertions from his audience assured him it was.

'Right, I'm sorry we're a little late, ladies and gentlemen. Let me introduce myself. I'm Detective Chief Inspector Harry Haynes from Kensington and Chelsea CID. Next to me is Mrs Barron, the widow of David Barron. Mr Barron's son Raymond's sitting next to her, while, at the end, is Detective Sergeant Nadia Khan.

'It's now nearly three weeks since David Barron was killed while sitting in the auditorium at the Royal Albert Hall. He was waiting patiently in his seat for a performance by the singer Loretta Kay when, out of nowhere, he sustained three bullet wounds to the head and neck.

'Detectives investigating the attack are keeping an open mind as to the motive. I'd like to assure everyone we're doing all we can to catch the person or persons responsible. The purpose of this press briefing today is to appeal to anyone with information to come forward.

'I'm pleased that we've got two members of Mr Barron's family with us today. Perhaps, Mrs Barron, you'd like a say a few words?'

The chief inspector sat down and moved the microphone across. Deborah, in a smart, dark-green summer dress that suited her, began in a hesitant manner. Colton was concerned on her behalf, worried she might not cope in front of so many onlookers. Her face was pale. She was trembling.

'Nearly three weeks ago my beloved husband, David, was taken from us. I'll never get over the loss. Every day I suffer a silent pain. I'm told that, in time, this will pass. But then the next day dawns and the pain's still there. He was an innocent man who'd been happily anticipating a relaxing evening watching his favourite singer perform the songs he loved.

'He was just forty-five years old – barely halfway through his life and brutally murdered.' She paused while she found a tissue and wiped away her tears.

'I've come here today to appeal for anyone with information about that tragic night of 27 June to come forward. It doesn't matter how trivial that information may be. It may prove significant to the police.'

Raymond placed his arm round her in an effort to console her. Then Haynes invited his sergeant to speak.

Khan stood up and glanced apprehensively round the room.

'So, one reason we planned to hold this briefing today is because we believe we've recovered certain items that the gunman may have used on the night of the murder,' she said. 'A Beretta handgun, a set of overalls and a house key. The gun has been thoroughly examined and I have it here.'

She held up a transparent bag containing the weapon.

'And we have photographs of the clothing, which is still being thoroughly tested and is therefore unavailable for us to put on display today.'

Cameras began clicking as Khan removed the large colour photographs from envelopes and held them up so the journalists could see.

'The light-grey tradesman's overalls are in a small-to-medium size with two breast pockets and an inside zip pocket.'

The chief inspector interrupted to say, 'Our press team will be releasing copies of the photographs at the end of the briefing.'

'Thank you, sir. The trousers have two large side pockets and a thigh pocket for a mobile phone or tools. There are knee pads interwoven into the trousers. The whole garment is made from polyester and cotton. The other item we'd like to show you is a door key that was in the right-hand pocket of the trousers.'

She brandished it like an auctioneer holding a medal aloft for buyers to see.

'You'll notice it's a standard Yale key, but what's of interest is the orange key fob on which someone's written the number 106.'

Colton, intrigued by her disclosures, raised his hand. 'Sergeant, could you tell us where you obtained these items?'

She nodded. 'Yes, Nick. A member of the public was looking through a rubbish bin in Kilburn. They found the gun wrapped in the clothing and took the items to the police. It's not a practice we recommend – digging about in bins – but it was fortunate for us on this occasion they did. A day or two later, Brent Council contractors were due to empty the bin and these items would have been lost forever.'

Haynes gazed across at Colton.

'Ladies and gentlemen, we've suspected from the start that we're dealing with a cunning individual. However, he's clearly not as cunning as we thought. The clothing had been thoroughly cleaned with strong bleach in an effort to destroy forensic evidence. But our forensic people are confident we will still be able to collect some DNA.

'Now, someone might remember seeing this person buying or wearing the overalls. They might even have met them in a laundrette with the overalls. So we want people to cast their minds back over the past two weeks.

'We're also keen to find out information about the key and the key fob. Is there someone whose address is associated with the number 106 and who recognises this key fob? If so, they should call us urgently at the

Operation Gymkhana incident room in Kensington or contact Crimestoppers on 0800 555111.'

After a few questions from other journalists, the meeting drew to a close. Colton slipped outside in the hope of catching a word with Deborah Barron. However, other reporters had a similar idea and a scrum formed round the police car being used to whisk her and Raymond away.

But as Deborah was about to take her place on the back seat, she noticed Colton's face in the crowd.

'I need to speak to you, Nick,' she yelled. 'I'll call you.' Then the vehicle pulled away.

As he watched the car head along the Victoria Embankment towards Charing Cross, he received a call from Katie McMillen, back at the office.

'Nick, I thought you'd like to know that a man's been arrested over the Brixton murder.'

Chapter 38

The sky darkened overhead as Freddie Valmar left his sister's flat at midday on Friday 19 July and began walking towards the nearby shops. He hadn't prepared himself for bad weather. In fact, he couldn't remember the last time it had rained, but as he reached the busy Hackney thoroughfare, the heavens opened.

He removed his peaked cap and pulled his blue jacket over his head. Then he sprinted the final few metres to the door of the street-corner bookmakers.

'Bit sudden, John,' he remarked as he passed through the shop door and was confronted by the bank of illuminated screens on the right-hand wall. They always reminded Valmar of a high-tech control room or perhaps the flight deck of a plane – a flight deck of dreams that could raise your hopes to the sky or send them crashing down to earth.

The voice of a racing tipster could be heard from a large-screen television fixed to the far wall, telling viewers in an excited voice about the runners and riders.

'Oh, is it raining, Mr V?' said the manager, a stout, white-haired man in his mid-forties.

Valmar peered at him over his sunglasses.

'Only just started, John. Bloody quiet in here, ain't it?'

Three men sitting on stools were studying newspapers on the wall for race details and form. Money was clattering from a betting terminal in a far corner where one gambler on a lucky streak was reaping his rewards.

'Still early. It's barely gone eleven. Usually gets busy about twelve.'

'Listen, John. I fancy a flutter on Midday Passion in the one o'clock at Newbury. I'll just look at the prices and I'll be over.'

When he was ready, he strolled to the counter and placed a ten-pound bet on the horse at odds of forty to one.

John the bookmaker leaned forward so his mouth was close to the plastic protective screen. 'Thanks for all the help you've given us lately, Mr V,' he said quietly.

'Don't mention it, John.'

'I know you've–'

'Been in the paper? That's right. That's why I haven't been around much.'

'You can sit in my room at the back if you want to. There's a telly in there.'

'No, thanks, John. I'll be fine here. No one who knows me will say a word. Anyway that business over the Pembury – it was all a huge mix-up. The cop hurt himself, but they've got me in their sights for some reason. Today's the first time I've been out of the house in days, but there's only so much time you can spend staring at four walls.'

'You still working near Brick Lane?'

'Off and on, mate. Off and on.'

Valmar then settled down on a stool in the middle of the shop to listen to a television commentator discussing the day's racing prospects.

When the door opened and a man in his twenties in a red T-shirt and brown trousers strolled in, Valmar hardly glanced at him. He was focussed on the television screen. The newcomer, who was tall and with receding brown hair, went to the counter to collect some winnings from the day before. Then he sat in a corner, reviewing the starting prices.

A few minutes later, Valmar noticed the man in the red T-shirt was no longer in the corner. Perhaps he'd only been sheltering from the rain, he thought. Maybe, after collecting his money, he'd gone to have some lunch.

The manager strode over. 'Would you like a drink, Mr V?'

'What have you got?'

'Tea, coffee, soft drinks. Or, if you fancied something stronger, I could serve you a whisky in my back room.'

'Too early. I'll have a tea, thanks.'

Twenty minutes later, Valmar was sipping his piping hot tea and when wailing sirens emerged in the distance, he ignored them. They were a common sound on the streets around this part of London.

But the whining noise grew closer. It became deafening. The racket was resonating around the street outside. His eyes travelled past the banners in the window advertising 'More ways to win'. He could see the street outside was overrun with police cars.

The manager rushed over with a horrified expression. 'Quick, Mr V. Perhaps you'd like to use the back door.'

A voice outside bellowed, 'Armed police. Stand clear of the doors.'

John hurried his customer out seconds before two burly policemen stormed through the door in blue helmets, wielding G36 Heckler & Koch rifles. The five customers studying form spun round with shocked expressions.

The first officer confronted one of them, an old man in his eighties. 'Where's Valmar?' he demanded.

The old man raised his hands in a sign of ignorance before the two officers crept round the room, their eyes darting everywhere.

Valmar himself was meanwhile scurrying down a passageway at the rear.

'Cheers, John,' he shouted as he passed through two glazed doors and entered the rain-soaked yard outside, which lay in the shadow of a five-storey office building.

No sooner had he burst into the open air than he was confronted by two constables in helmets, toting rifles.

'That's him,' yelled one of the officers, who dashed forward and pressed the muzzle of his gun into Valmar's stomach.

Anger welled up inside him. He knew someone must have given him away, but there was no point trying to argue with a loaded rifle. His spell on the run was over after nine days.

'On the ground!' the lawman barked. As Valmar crouched on the damp tarmac and then lay down, the officer knelt on his back and handcuffed him.

'Frederick Valmar, you're under arrest for the attempted murder of Detective Sergeant Charles Allen.'

* * *

At the time of Freddie Valmar's arrest, Nick Colton was sitting at his office desk. It had been a morning of high drama.

There had been a scuffle in the dock at Croydon magistates' court when Alex Smart had appeared, charged with Craig Arnold's murder. On being remanded in custody, he had screamed abuse and struggled with one of the court security officers.

Closer to home, details had emerged about how the *Daily Graphic*'s news editor had been sacked.

Katie McMillen and Luke Foster were fired up about the dismissal.

'It's shaken everyone over there. People said he was destined to edit the paper one day,' said McMillen.

Foster laughed. 'It's one of the sharpest reversals in fortunes since the great escape artist Harry Houdini got trapped in the toilet.'

Colton was about to contribute a joke of his own when his mobile phone rang. He stepped away from his colleagues before answering. The gentle, engaging tones of Deborah Barron flowed out of the handset.

'Nick, I wanted to catch you after the Scotland Yard meeting and thank you for the publicity your paper's given to the murder.'

He smiled. 'It's been a pleasure to help,' he said. 'Partly I was just doing my job but, of course, there was a personal dimension as well – since the shooting happened in front of my eyes.'

'You've given a lot of prominence today to the gun, the overalls and the key found in the bin.'

He pressed the phone firmly to his ear as two reporters swept past, talking noisily like excited children. 'Yes. Let's hope the police are swamped with calls,' he said.

'Nick, I've been wanting to talk to you, but life's been so hectic. This is the first chance I've been able to call. I need to ask your advice. You seem to be a knowledgeable guy. I'm considering legal action against the Royal Albert Hall.'

'On what grounds?'

'On the grounds that they let an armed person into the building without checking them. I want to seek redress for their negligence. Their security staff failed to stop the gunman entering through the stage door and then failed to confine him.'

Colton looked blank. 'Well, I'm not a lawyer but I can make some inquiries about this. And obviously I can make sure you receive publicity for your legal case.'

Deborah was sounding excited. 'This guy comes swanning in off the street in his grey outfit, gaudy boots with red laces and swinging a tool bag. He makes up some story about a leak in the toilets. They let him pass without so much as a by-your-leave and, less than twenty minutes later, David's dead. Their security is a joke.'

He nodded. 'From the little I know, I think you've probably got a good case.'

'I think I've got a brilliant case. Of course, I'm not interested in the money. That would go to charity. It's the principle. Nick, is there any chance you could call round to see me? Are you free on Wednesday?'

'Wednesday's fine. Ten o'clock?'

'That's perfect.'

'I'll try and find out the legal position by then,' he said while ending the call.

Afterwards, he sat at his desk stroking his chin. McMillen peered round the side of her screen. 'You all right, Nick? You've gone rather quiet.'

He smiled back. 'Just puzzled by something she said. She knew the gunman was wearing flashy work-boots with red laces.'

'Well, wasn't he?'

'Yes, of course. I'm just wondering how she knew. I certainly haven't told her, and it hasn't been in any of the press reports.'

Chapter 39

Nick Colton stirred in his sleep. Was that irritating noise his phone? Had he forgotten to switch it off?

Taking care not to disturb his sleeping wife, he seized the handset from his dressing table and ran into the bathroom. After turning the light on, he pressed the answer key.

'Hello?' he whispered.

'Hope I haven't woken you up,' said the caller, DS Khan.

He struggled to open his eyes as he perched on the edge of the bath. 'Er, no. What's the time, Nadia?'

'Seven o'clock.'

'Don't worry. I was due to get up anyway. We've got to get the kids ready for school.'

'So the reason I'm calling so early is I wanted to tip you off about something before I go into the office. You've helped us regarding the Gentle family, whom we've now spoken to. I reckoned we owed you a favour.'

'Kind of you to think of it like that,' he said as he became increasingly uncomfortable in his sitting position.

'Nick, following our appeal on Tuesday, a witness has come forward with some important information that's helped to move our inquiries forward.'

'Someone who recognised the door key?'

'Yes. The woman's name is Bridget Walsh,' said Khan. 'She runs a guest house off the Kilburn High Road, and we spent most of Saturday morning taking a statement from her.

'A guy stayed for one night and failed to hand in the key after paying. She recognised it straight away as her missing key and called our incident room. My boss is going to pass the details on to the media team in a few hours, but I thought I'd give you a heads up.'

'Very thoughtful. Thank you, Nadia,' he said as he stood up and peered at his pale, unshaven face in the mirror.

He raced back to the bedroom to find some paper and a pen. Then he sat on the stairs. 'Do you want to give me the address?'

'Yes, it's the Three Crowns Guesthouse, Wiltshire Road, Kilburn. The boss is encouraging her to speak to the press. He thinks it might encourage other witnesses to come forward.'

He grinned and quietly suspected the chief inspector had warned the woman about what to tell the press and what to conceal from them.

'By the way, my friend with the BTP asked me to thank you for the tip-off about Smart's flawed alibi,' said Khan. 'It helped enormously. When they raided his house, they found a blue hooded top, grey slacks and a white scarf hidden in a corner of the attic. They also found a pay-as-you-go phone which proved he'd been in Brixton at the time of Arnold's death.'

Nick grinned. 'Glad I could help. That's great. I'll have to let the news desk know so they can cover that in tomorrow's paper. Nadia, getting back to Mrs Walsh, do you know if she's at the guest house today?'

'I really don't know, Nick. Look, I'd better go. And remember, you didn't get it from me.'

After she'd hung up, he dressed hurriedly and phoned the picture desk, who, in turn, alerted Tommy Mundon. Then he got Riccardo and Ashleigh washed and dressed and roused Greta before leaving for Kilburn.

Bridget Walsh's guest house was at the end of a terrace of large, three-storey Victorian houses on a busy bus route. The premises were partly shrouded from the noise of traffic by two horse chestnut trees and a high hedge.

Lorries and cars roared by as Colton parked in a side turning just before half past ten and waited on the street corner for Tommy Mundon to join him. Five minutes later, he caught sight of the photographer's BMW and watched as he parked.

'You pick 'em, young man,' Mundon moaned as he lumbered towards him, laden with cameras. 'It's taken me two hours from the office. Let's hope she doesn't slam the door in our faces.'

They waited for a lorry to pass and then crossed the street.

The period, red-brick house with bay windows and an off-street parking space for two cars was immaculately presented. A wooden tub on each side of the entrance porch was overflowing with red, purple, and white petunias and a freshly painted sign saying 'Three Crowns Guesthouse' hung above the front door.

Mrs Walsh was a short, amiable woman in her early sixties with greying hair. Colton gazed at her somewhat apprehensively as she held the door open. Looking prim in a navy-blue dress with a white cardigan, she had a smile that could light up a darkened room.

'Mrs Walsh?'

The woman nodded.

'We're from *The Post*.'

Mundon interrupted to say, 'We're here about your door key.'

They both presented their press cards. 'I'm Nick. This is Tommy.'

The woman frowned. 'I'm sorry. I've been having a little think. I'm not sure I want to talk about what happened.'

Colton folded his arms. 'We've got something in common, Mrs Walsh.'

'And what might that be?'

'We both came face to face with the murder suspect.'

'You met him? How come?'

'I witnessed the shooting and I followed the gunman through the building after the incident, and out onto the street.'

'You'd better come in.'

The pair followed her along a bright, narrow hallway until they reached the foot of her stairs, where she hesitated.

'I think you'd best come into the front room,' she said.

She led them into a sumptuous room with a stone fireplace, bespoke white shutters around the bay, and a large chandelier. Paintings of Dublin street scenes were displayed around the walls.

She moved some scatter cushions aside so her visitors could sit down. Mundon placed his cameras on the solid-oak floor.

'I still don't know if I should talk about it,' she continued. 'What's to stop him coming after me?'

Mundon cast his eyes towards her. 'If I can speak frankly, Mrs Walsh, Chummy's got much more to worry about than a guest house keeper in Kilburn.'

She stared directly into his eyes. 'You think I've got nothing to worry about?'

Colton interrupted. 'Nothing at all. He must have realized you might be approached by the police. He'll have taken that into account in his calculations.'

She raised her hands to her face. 'My mind's been a complete muddle since I saw my key on the television. I've had two detectives – a man and a woman – round here interviewing me and then, for five hours, the people in white suits were examining the top room.'

'So you recognised your key straight away, Mrs Walsh?'

'From the orange key fob and my house number.'

Colton decided against taking out his pen and notebook for the moment, fearing that it might jolt her into silence.

'What did the man call himself, Mrs Walsh?'

She leaned against the fireplace.

'He told me his name was Boyle.'

'No first name?'

'No. Just Boyle.'

'Almost certainly not his real name.'

'He said he was from County Meath. He was about fifty with short, dark hair, clean shaven, and he was about five foot five in height.'

Colton was puzzled. 'He wasn't tall with a beard?'

'No.'

'That's strange. That doesn't match up with the man I saw at all. How did this Mr Boyle make contact with you?'

'He sent me an email ten days before, asking to stay one night.'

'He booked for 27 June?'

'That's right. I told him all I'd left was a single backroom on the first floor and a twin room on the top floor that faces the road. For some reason, he wanted the top floor room. I told him the rate for bed and breakfast would be seventy-five pounds. He booked it straight away and said he'd call round on the twenty-seventh at about three o'clock to leave his case. I thought that was a little early, but when he said he was coming all the way from County Meath, I said I was sure that would be all right.'

Colton leaned forward. 'So he came at three o'clock?'

'Just after three. He was smartly dressed in a suit. Very nice gentleman, I thought. I told him I'd fond memories of visiting Trim Castle, which he knew. He told me I must go back there.'

'So he lives near the castle?'

'No. He moved from there as a child. He wouldn't tell me where he lives now.'

Mundon wanted to move the conversation on.

'So he turns up at three and dumps his gear?'

'Yes. He said it was a very nice room.'

Colton had covertly removed his notebook and was now jotting down some of her observations. 'Did he come by car?'

'No. He took a train from Euston to Kilburn High Road – or that's what he told me. I'm not sure what I believe now. Ten minutes after arriving he was gone and he wasn't back until just gone 9 p.m.'

'Did you see him when he returned?'

'No. I heard him come in and go straight to his room. I didn't see him until the next morning. He'd asked if he could have his breakfast left for him on the landing outside, but I explained that wouldn't be possible. So he came down early for his breakfast at half past seven on the Friday morning. He paid me in cash and he was gone by eight.'

Colton looked up from his note-taking. 'Did he speak to any other guests over breakfast?'

'He was the only one in the dining room at that time.'

'And how did he seem, Mrs Walsh?'

She sat down on an armchair. 'Slightly agitated is the best phrase I can think of. A man with a lot on his mind. He didn't want to become involved in conversation.'

Colton stroked his chin slowly. He failed to understand how her visitor had been such a short man and clean shaven.

'Mrs Walsh, this might sound a strange question but is it possible you had two guests that night rather than one?'

'How do you mean?'

'Your door key was found in a waste bin along with a gun believed to have been used in the Albert Hall shooting. But the gunman that I saw at the hall was tall with a small beard. You mention your Mr Boyle was keen to have the room with twin beds. Is it possible Mr Boyle let a second man into the house after you'd gone to bed – you know, so the second man would have somewhere to lay his head?'

Mrs Walsh stared down at the floor. Then she gave her interviewer the kind of frosty expression a mother might reserve for a child that's scored poorly in their exams.

'I keep a very orderly house and would never allow my guests to invite strangers in.'

Mundon sat back on the settee with a broad smile. 'You've got a good reputation and you want to keep it.'

'Yes. That's right.'

Colton smiled at her. 'Please forgive me for raising the issue, but it's surely possible that someone might have sneaked in without your knowledge, Mrs Walsh?'

'Well, I suppose it's possible, but I'm a light sleeper. I'm sure I would have heard the main door.'

'Is it possible for us to see the room?'

'The police told me not to show it to the press.'

'All right,' said Colton. 'Fair enough. There are a few other questions. When did you first contact the police?'

'Immediately after the evening news on Tuesday of last week.'

'So nearly three weeks have passed since Mr Boyle's visit. Presumably, that top room's been used by several other guests since?'

'Yes, some builders have been working nearby and the room's been in constant use ever since.'

Colton shook his head. 'So it's highly likely any DNA evidence will have been lost.'

'I don't know anything about any DNA.'

'Can you give us Mr Boyle's email address and phone number?'

'The police asked me not to. His number's not working anymore in any case.'

The photographer had been quietly considering his colleague's suggestion that two men might have secretly shared the room.

'Mrs Walsh,' said Mundon. 'You've no doubt at all that only one man used the top room that night?'

'Well, you've both got me thinking now. I must admit the duvet cover on the second bed was a little creased when I inspected the room afterwards. But I just assumed Mr Boyle had been lounging around on it.'

The two men exchanged glances.

At that moment, someone knocked loudly on the front door.

'Sounds like someone's desperate to find a room, Mrs Walsh,' Mundon suggested.

She peeked through the shutters. 'It looks like one of your friends from the press.'

'If it's all right, I'll take some snaps of you by the window,' Mundon said. 'It's nice and light there.'

'Oh, I'm not keen.'

He raised the smaller of his two cameras to his face, made some quick adjustments and then the device flashed. The knocking resumed.

'Lovely job,' he declared before repeating the action.

'I haven't had a chance to do my hair.'

'You look lovely, darling,' Mundon assured her.

'I must answer the door,' Mrs Walsh insisted.

Colton nodded. 'Time we were going anyway.' He held out his hand and she shook it warmly.

'Thank you so much for your time.'

'You're welcome – both of you,' she said with a smile before heading off into the hallway.

As the pair strolled out of the house, Colton vaguely recognised the face of the visitor standing expectantly on the threshold.

'Mrs Walsh? I'm from the Press Association,' the woman was saying.

* * *

Nick Colton stopped at a pub in Kilburn to write his report while Mundon headed back to the office.

As he sipped his pint of lager, he composed his story about the mysterious Irishman 'Mr Boyle' on his small laptop and then sent it to the news desk.

Chapter 40

A stream of mourners moved solemnly along the pavement towards St Matthew's Church at half past ten on Tuesday morning. They passed flowerbeds brimming with blue delphiniums and red dahlias before entering the huge red-brick Victorian church for Craig Arnold's funeral.

Forecasters had promised it would be one of the hottest days of the year with temperatures expected to climb to thirty degrees Celsius. Rail chiefs had warned that train tracks would be at risk of buckling in the heat. Fierce storms were predicted for that night.

Nick Colton and Greta were among the first to arrive. They chose a seat near the back so the journalist, dressed sombrely in a dark-blue suit, would be able to watch the congregation and more readily catch a word with anyone leaving early.

The organist was playing Bach's *Sheep May Safely Graze* as Colton took his pew. He and Greta watched Jasmine and her children pass through the church door, followed by a man he suspected was Craig Arnold's brother, Jason. He was helping an elderly lady who walked with a stick.

Colton gave a brief wave to DS Nadia Khan and *Daily Graphic* reporter Leyla Hussein, who seemed to arrive together.

He assumed that, among others who'd come to pay their respects, there would be work colleagues from the city and representatives from London Underground and Transport for London. Altogether, he estimated there were sixty people present.

Before the service began, DS Khan strolled over, and Colton introduced her to Greta.

'Stifling out there, but it's lovely and cool in the church, isn't it?' the sergeant remarked. 'I do hope this doesn't go on too long. There's not much fun in funerals.'

He nodded. 'No fun at all, apart from the first three letters.'

After a few more minutes, the pallbearers brought in Craig's coffin, which was draped in the claret-and-blue Crystal Palace football club colours.

During the service, Craig's manager from the firm Springfield Mead gave a moving address in which he praised Craig for his hard work, ingenuity and sense of humour. He also deplored the manner of his death.

'His death underscores the fragility of human life,' he declared. 'He was taken from us so swiftly. We just turned around and he was gone.'

Colton was touched by the man's words. He cast his mind back to the last weekend in June when he'd visited Craig's house. He recalled the stockbroker had been friendly and unpretentious. A lump formed in his throat.

After a rousing rendition of *Amazing Grace*, the mourners began filing out of the church. Once outside, the Coltons stood by while some of the visitors offered condolences to Jasmine.

They were about to approach her and express their sympathies when the woman with the walking stick they'd seen earlier began shouting.

'My Craig would still be alive if it weren't for you,' she screamed.

Colton moved nearer so he could catch the conversation. Jasmine was cowering against the wall.

'I don't know what he was doing with a married woman, I really don't. You two were courting trouble. My son deserved better than this.'

Silver-haired parish priest, Father Michael, dashed to Mrs Arnold's side and did his best to calm her down while Jason tried to console Jasmine.

Greta clasped her husband's hand. 'It's not good when families fall out but it's so bad when it's happening at the funeral,' she concluded. 'Where you going now?'

Colton had walked a few paces away and was dialling a number on his phone.

'I'm just going to send a short piece over about the funeral,' he whispered.

'Oh Nick!' she cried. 'This is meant to be your day off.'

* * *

The Coltons were able to park right outside their house when they returned from the church service. It was lunchtime and there were plenty of spaces in the street since many neighbours had gone to work.

'It's so nice for us to have some time together, Nick,' said Greta, while admiring the blue clematis flowers and mauve asters still blossoming by the front door.

'Yes, it's been a hectic month,' he admitted.

As Greta prepared a light lunch, he relaxed on the settee and read through the latest news reports on *The Post*'s website.

The report he'd filed on Craig Arnold's funeral had been reduced to a caption beneath a photograph of the coffin being borne into the church by the six pallbearers. The headline read 'Funeral of train death stockbroker'.

Then he noticed a report that Luke Foster had written about the dead body found in Epping Forest ten days before. He clicked on the headline, which said, 'Father dragged to death may have been target of gang revenge hit.' The report read,

> *A father of two who died from catastrophic injuries in Epping Forest may have been targeted by members of a criminal gang. The man's body is understood to have been dragged behind a vehicle for several miles. Essex Police confirmed the victim was missing Hackney man Clifford Martin, aged twenty-nine. A post-mortem found Mr Martin, who was found by police in the early hours of 13 July, died from multiple injuries, including a severe brain injury. His wife Hope, twenty-seven, said, "He went off to work on the Friday night and it's devastating to learn he will never be coming home." Police said dental records had to be used to identify Mr Martin, who worked as a security assistant for a wholesale business in Bethnal Green.*

He viewed other online reports about Mr Martin and gradually realized he must have worked – either in the past or recently – for notorious gang leader Vinny Diamond.

As he and Greta ate their lunch, he couldn't stop thinking about the surname Martin. Hadn't he come across someone with the same surname over the previous weeks?

'You're quiet, darling,' Greta remarked. 'Still thinking about poor Craig Arnold?'

'No, there's something else on my mind,' he replied. And then he remembered. Children in sunhats enjoying the sun outside the Royal Albert Hall. The queue for the Elgar Room. The brightly lit box office. And the welcoming smile of the sales assistant whose name-badge read 'Liz Martin'.

Chapter 41

A phone call to the box office at the Royal Albert Hall established that Liz Martin would be working that evening until 9 p.m.

So, eager to speak to her as soon as possible, Nick Colton left his house at six o'clock and set off for West London. He'd intended to take his car, but was annoyed to find he had a flat battery when he went to start it.

As a result, he travelled by train to Cannon Street and then by Underground to South Kensington. His journey ended with a ten-minute walk along Exhibition Road.

While he strolled past the Victoria and Albert Museum and five-storey blocks of white, stucco-fronted period houses, he was quietly pleased with himself. He'd found out through online family history research that Clifford Jermaine Martin was born in Hackney in 1990 and that his mother's maiden name was Thomas. It took him just a few minutes to find his older sister, Elizabeth Evelyn Martin, born in Hackney in 1987. The family link was confirmed because her mother's maiden name was also Thomas.

Further research revealed a marriage between Eustace Martin and Nellie Thomas in Tower Hamlets in 1986.

He was confident the sales assistant would have been in a position to pass on details of seating arrangements if her brother had requested them. But he was also aware that she would be upset at the loss of her brother and he would have to frame his questions delicately.

Concertgoers were milling round outside and in the foyer when he arrived at the hall. He had to weave his way through the crowds before reaching the box office.

Then he had to wait for several minutes as Miss Martin, wearing the same name-badge as before, was assisting a customer. When he finally approached her, she recognised him at once.

'You came in at the end of last month, didn't you, sir? You were the one inquiring about a woman in a black dress and a man with ginger hair.'

His smile faded. 'How did you remember that?'

'We don't get many obscure questions like that from our customers. It's the sort of thing you remember. Plus I had to bother the manager about it. Did you find them?'

'Yes, I did, actually. To be honest, I'm a little surprised you're in work. I believed there'd been a sad event in the family.'

Now it was her turn to show surprise. 'How did you know that?'

'Long story.'

'Yes, my brother's died rather tragically. I've only just come back after time off. Did you know Clifford?'

Colton shook his head. 'No. Just read about his death.'

'It was awful.' She looked extremely distressed and made an effort to change the subject. 'Anyway do you want some tickets?'

He shook his head. 'I'll be straight with you. I was the last person to speak to David Barron the night he died and I'm on a mission to find out what happened. David was mixed up with the same ruthless people your brother Clifford was involved with.'

She scowled. 'It's not my place to comment. The whole family are devastated about what happened, but we want to leave it to the police to investigate.'

He shrugged his shoulders. He'd been expecting that kind of response.

'I suppose you're not going to confirm it was you who tipped off your brother about where David Barron would be sitting?'

She looked aghast. 'I think you'd better go or I'll call the manager.'

'It *was* you, wasn't it?'

'I'm warning you. I'll call the manager.'

'All right. I'm going.'

* * *

Greta was sitting up in bed in a white nightdress, reading an Italian romance novel, when Colton arrived home just before ten o'clock.

She swept her brown hair out of her eyes as she gazed up and smiled at him. He reached down to kiss her.

'The damn car wouldn't start,' he moaned. 'I think it might be the battery.'

'What are you going to do?'

'I'll call the garage in the morning.'

She closed her book and placed it on a bedside cabinet. 'Were your suspicions proved right, Nick?'

He nodded. 'Yes. The box office woman is Clifford Martin's sister but I couldn't get her to admit she passed on information about the seat number.'

She put down her book. 'No surprise, Nick. No one's going to admit to something like that – passing on confidential information to a mafioso. So where does that leave the hunt for the assassin?'

He sat down on the side of the bed. A cloak of fatigue wrapped itself around him. 'Everything points towards

David Barron's killer being someone from Vinny Diamond's gang.'

'Have you got any of their names?'

'Well, there's Vinny himself. He's in his sixties. Then there's his son, Mickey, who's been remanded in custody on drugs charges. There's a guy called Freddie Valmar, who's just been arrested after shooting a copper.'

Greta began combing her fine, brown hair. 'And there's Deborah. You mustn't forget her.'

'Of course. There's also Clifford Martin, the man whose body was found in Epping Forest. There must have been at least three people involved in the Barron murder. There was the gunman, who was presumably hired. There is the "Mr Boyle" character I was telling you about. I'd call him the "enabler" or "facilitator". He probably provided the gun and the car and found the guest house and disposed of the gun and clothing. And finally, there's the client who had the motive and must have hired the other two.'

Greta put down her comb. 'Nick. It's clear as daylight. Alex Smart's the killer. I don't know why you can't see that. He so closely resembles the man I saw before the shooting. He was looking for Craig Arnold. But he didn't know what the man looked like. He'd seen the ticket number, L97, and shot the man who was sitting in that seat. Then, when he realized his mistake, he found out where Craig lived, followed him and pushed him under the train.'

Her husband peeled off his shirt and began preparing for bed. 'There's plenty of reasons why Smart couldn't have been the gunman,' he insisted. 'Smart was clean-shaven at the end of June, but the gunman had a beard. Also, if Smart was the gunman, how do you explain where he got the Porsche? Jasmine doesn't think he knows how to break into cars. She told me she wasn't even sure he could break into a conversation.

'But more important than that are the gun and clothing. They, along with the door key, were found in Kilburn. Smart was at his home fifteen miles from Kilburn when Jasmine got back from the concert. She's never seen any grey overalls in the house and doesn't think he'd know one end of a Beretta from the other. He's certainly never had the kind of training required to fire such a gun with accuracy.'

'What about the bill from the shop that Jasmine found? That showed Smart was only three miles away from the concert in Clapham at half past eight – just an hour after the murder.'

He muffled a yawn. 'Maybe just a coincidence,' he said. 'He got bored at home and went out for a drive.'

But ten minutes later, as he lay his head on the pillow, he cast his mind back to the night of the shooting. Smart was a ruthless individual whom the police held responsible for Craig's death. Was he being too swift in discounting him as a suspect in David Barron's murder?

Chapter 42

'This blessed heat's getting too much again,' Detective Chief Inspector Harry Haynes moaned as he opened his office window.

His sergeant, who was sitting on a chair by the door clutching some black and white photographs, agreed.

'They're expecting it to be cooler this weekend,' DS Khan assured him.

He loosened his tie. 'I wonder if the top brass will get the ventilation system working properly before I retire. How have you been getting on with our friends in the Gardaí?'

'So we've made a bit of progress. I've been studying the CCTV pictures they've sent to us of passengers arriving at the ferry port in Dublin.'

She stood up and placed three photographs on the chief inspector's desk.

'This man stood out. He's aged about forty, tall and slim with a dark jacket and blue jeans. As you can see, he's carrying a brown rucksack.'

He frowned. 'That's a description that could probably apply to dozens of passengers.'

'I know, sir, but you can see his face in one of the pictures.'

The chief inspector held up one of the photographs. 'This one?'

'Yes, sir. He's clearly got a goatee beard as well as distinctive eyes.'

'I see what you mean. But our witnesses spoke about a mop of black hair. This guy's got short, dark hair.'

Khan shrugged her shoulders. 'Maybe he was wearing a wig when he shot Barron. These pictures were taken at just after 6 p.m. If this is our man, it means he caught the 2.30 p.m. ferry from Holyhead.

'I've spoken to the ferry company. They've been checking through the passenger lists, but they've got hundreds of single passengers and many of them are about the same age.'

The chief inspector frowned. 'We may have to send you over to Dublin if we don't have any success soon. Anyway, now we know there's this Irish connection, how are we getting on with our inquiries into Irish criminals with form for contract killing?'

Khan took out her black notebook. 'There's several potential suspects.'

'Didn't realize it was such a thriving business on the Emerald Isle,' he said.

'Two of them stand out – Patrick Gaughan and Brendan Maguire. Gaughan served in the British Army, while Maguire's worked as a mercenary. They're both sharpshooters with known form for criminal violence. Of the two, Maguire looked like the most interesting one. So the Gardaí showed his photograph to some of the members of the Irish Ferries crew.

'One of them thinks he recognised him as a passenger on the two-thirty boat. We went back to the passenger lists and there was no Maguire. But there was a man listed as Dan Kelly, and they believe that might be him.'

Haynes stroked his chin thoughtfully as the sergeant went on, 'Dan could be short for Brendan. The credit card he used to pay with links to an address at a village in County Louth, to the north of Dublin. The Gardaí have checked it out and it's a smallholding where no one's lived for years.'

The chief inspector scratched his head. 'A false address?'

'Yes, sir. The place is all boarded up.'

He grinned. 'Ah well. All in a day's work for an honest copper, Sergeant. But we mustn't be defeatist. We're within touching distance now. I'll be getting onto Interpol regarding Gaughan and Maguire. By the way, did I tell you the ballistics report's come back on the gun?'

She leaned forward, agog with interest.

'Our forensic department has examined the Beretta found in the waste bin and the bullets fired in the hall,' he said. 'They concluded that it definitely *was* the gun that killed Barron. They also confirm the gunman was standing by the door at the entrance to Block L and the strand of grey thread caught on the doorframe came from the grey trousers found in the bin.'

The sergeant sighed and sat back. 'Just confirmed what we thought. Anyway, sir, I need to tell you about my visit to Belmarsh yesterday.'

'Yes, how was our friend Mr Valmar?'

'Not so cocky, sir. He's resigned to spending at least ten years behind bars.'

The chief inspector smiled. 'Good. Did they let you take him into the interview room?'

'Yes. He says he was at the bookies in Mare Street, Hackney on the evening of the Barron shooting. I've spoken to the manager on the phone. They've confirmed Valmar left just before the shop closed at ten.'

Haynes stood up and walked towards the window. He stared through the blinds into the bustling street below.

'The Diamonds have got a protection racket going on round there and the bookie might be involved,' he said. 'He might be vouching for Valmar as a favour. So I'll ask Kyle Leigh to go and see if any of the punters remember whether Valmar was in there that night.'

He turned to face her. 'The Irish connection's strong and maybe the Diamonds were calling the shots. Or maybe the Irish link is a red herring and one of the Diamond gang pulled the trigger. Vinny Diamond had a grudge against Barron and, as his close confidant, Valmar could have sorted out that grudge. Remember what he did to Charlie Allen.'

Khan nodded. 'I hear Allen's making a good recovery.'

'He is, thank God.'

'There's talk that Valmar might get off the attempted murder charge relating to Allen. His solicitor's claiming the evidence isn't that strong. Allen hasn't got a complete memory of the shooting on the Pembury Estate and the constable with him didn't get a close look at Valmar.'

'That's right, Sergeant,' said Haynes. 'But there's clear evidence linking Valmar to the drugs on the lorry. So he'll be copping a fair stretch for that.'

Khan's eyes followed her boss as he walked back to his desk and sat down.

'Freddie Valmar has at least had some luck in the field of romance,' she said. 'The arresting officer told me he's been boasting about a new girlfriend.'

'Lucky fellow.'

'She ran over to the dock and kissed him at the start of his remand hearing.'

'Soon summer will be gone, Sergeant, and he'll need someone to send him long letters to read during those cold winter nights in his prison cell.'

'Otherwise he hasn't had much luck,' Khan observed. 'A friend in Central East Command say they were tipped off that Valmar was in a bookie's by a man whose brother had been roughed up by him. He'd just put a tenner on Midday Passion when he was arrested.'

'Don't tell me. It came in last.'

'No. It fell at the first fence.'

Chapter 43

When he arrived at Whetstone Underground station on Wednesday 24 July, Nick Colton was remembering his previous visit to Orchard House.

He hadn't appreciated it at the time, but he now believed he'd been suffering then from a form of delayed shock after witnessing the murder of David Barron.

Furthermore, he then had to face the heart-breaking task of interviewing a distressed widow just hours after her husband's life had been snatched away.

Now, as he left the station and climbed the hill towards Totteridge village, he felt more at ease with himself. He hoped Deborah Barron would have recovered some of her previous fortitude and confidence. She was talking now of launching a legal action. That surely indicated she was beginning to come to terms with her loss.

After a twenty-minute walk, he arrived, perspiring a little, outside the black wooden gates of Deborah's home. He pressed the intercom button on the wall and waited. But when a voice spoke, it wasn't Deborah's self-assured, educated voice, but a slightly deeper woman's tone.

'Who is it?'

'Nick Colton from *The Post*. Deborah's expecting me.'

'Really? She didn't mention anything to me. I suppose you'd better come in.'

He followed the gravel drive to the front door, noticing as he walked that the door to the annexe on the right was partly open. David Barron's red Ferrari, which had so impressed him and Tommy Mundon on their first visit at the end of June, was no longer on display. The black Mercedes was also missing but a gleaming silver Toyota Corolla hatchback was parked in the Ferrari's place beside the front door.

Fiona Blake, the housekeeper, looked dispirited as she came out of the front door to meet him. She was more casually dressed than before in a yellow T-shirt and blue jeans. Her spiky hair now boasted shades of dark brown and natural black.

'I can't find Debs at the moment. What time did she arrange to see you?'

'Ten o'clock.'

'It's strange. She didn't mention it to me, although I know she said something about wanting to see you. Her phone's off. Do you want to come back another time?'

His face fell. 'It's Fiona, isn't it? Fiona, I've travelled all the way from Greenwich.'

She sighed. 'Well, if you don't mind waiting. I expect she's only gone to the shops. You haven't chosen a brilliant time really – I'm seeing to my mother in the annexe.'

'I don't mind waiting.'

She led him through the hallway and along the passage to the living room. He noticed the landscape paintings and photographs of singers had been replaced by colourful rustic scenes.

The Regency table and chairs had gone and the sofas, still arranged at right angles to each other, were now closer to the French doors.

He headed towards the white sofa, but the housekeeper tutted in disapproval.

'Would you mind sitting on the brown one?' she remarked. 'We keep the brown one for visitors.'

She herself sat on the white sofa and peered at the screen of a black laptop, which was resting on a coffee table. For the first time, he detected that she had a faint accent. Did she originally hail from America? he wondered.

A faint female voice could be heard calling from some distance away – possibly from the annexe. Fiona scowled. 'Oh damn! It's mother,' she muttered. 'I'll be back in a minute.' Then she pushed the laptop lid down and left the room.

He gazed around. The room was tidier than before. Bottles of wine and spirits had been lined up neatly on a small oak sideboard in the corner. The sympathy cards on the mantlepiece had gone.

For some reason, he noticed the housekeeper hadn't fully closed her laptop. A white light at the side remained on. Glancing over his shoulder to make sure he was alone, he crept over to the white settee and raised the lid. It was still logged into Fiona's email inbox with Yahoo.

The latest message, dated that morning, was headed, 'Mum's birthday.'

'I shouldn't be doing this,' he told himself. 'It's personal information.' But, just as he was about to press the lid down, his eyes fell upon an email which was dated 13 June. The headline 'Night of the concert' drew his attention.

Gingerly, he opened the email and was astounded by what he read.

> *Dear F,*
> *I can confirm your booking for 27 June. All you have to do is to pay the first instalment of the agreed fee as stipulated into our Dublin account.*
> *Regards, B.*

A bank account number and sort code followed. The name of the account was given as 'Miles Davis Jazz Appreciation Society'. The journalist leaned back on the leather sofa where, moments earlier, he'd been dissuaded from sitting. The message was brief and succinct. It also left a sinister impression.

All his previous concerns about invading a person's private realm were swept away. It felt as though he had witnessed an explosion and all his previous ideas and theories about the shooting of David Barron had been sent cascading into the air.

Had he misunderstood the words? Could the email have an innocent explanation? No. He was forced to the inescapable conclusion that Fiona Blake might have had a hand in David Barron's murder.

She was being asked to pay money into an Irish bank account for an unspecified service carried out on 27 June. That much was clear. And the beneficiary was concealing their true identity behind the letter *B* and behind a bizarre alias.

'What the hell do you think you're doing?' a female voice at the door demanded. The cry jolted him back into the present. He stood up, but it was too late. Fiona had spotted the open laptop.

As he sidled back towards the brown sofa, she marched across the room in a fury and examined the screen. There in plain text before her eyes was the guilty secret that she'd no doubt forgotten to delete. The guilty secret that she'd believed was safe from the eyes of the world. The guilty secret that could never be laid bare. And should certainly never be imparted to a journalist.

He shrugged his shoulders. 'I'm sorry. You left your laptop on. I was concerned you might be wasting the battery.'

She sneered. 'Don't try and get round me. I can see exactly what you were doing. You've been sneaking a look at my emails.' She snapped the lid down shut.

He tried to calm her. 'I was just trying to find the start button and shut it down for you.'

Their conversation was disturbed by the hum of a car engine. The pair stood in silence for a moment as the engine spluttered to a halt and a car door slammed. Fiona took a few steps towards the door.

Then Deborah's voice could be heard calling from the hallway. 'Fiona, darling. Have you missed me?'

Fiona glanced at him before replying with a yell, 'I'm in the living room, Deborah. Nick Colton's here.'

Appearing flustered, Deborah stepped into the room in a peach-coloured summer dress holding a shopping bag which she promptly dumped on a chair.

'Nick, what are you doing here?' she asked. 'I'd got it in my mind you weren't coming until this afternoon. I hope you haven't been waiting long.'

He beamed across at her. 'I'd written ten o'clock in my diary.'

'I didn't see a car outside.'

'I came on the Tube.'

Fiona interrupted. 'Debs, I'm afraid you've arrived in the middle of an argument. I've just caught your journalist friend prying into my emails.'

Deborah advanced into the room, her blonde hair swaying from side to side as she moved.

'I'm sure there must be an innocent–'

'No. When I came in, he was reading one of my emails.'

Colton frowned. 'Deborah, I think you should know I saw something very concerning. It was an email headed "Night of the concert". It was asking Fiona to pay money into a Dublin–'

Fiona interrupted after sitting down on the white sofa beside her laptop. 'This is nonsense, Debs.'

'I'm sure there must be a simple explanation,' said Deborah.

'Don't you remember the flowers and chocolates I bought you?' Fiona continued. 'It was a payment for them.'

Colton, who was standing by the French doors, rolled his eyes. 'You've taken to buying bouquets from a florist three hundred and fifty miles away in Dublin?'

'No, of course not,' she snapped. 'The florists are in London. It's just that the head office is in Ireland.'

Deborah walked to the coffee table. Her eyes rested on the black laptop. She touched Fiona's hand and then sat down next to her.

'I'll tell you something else,' he said. 'Bit of a strange name for a florist – Miles Davis Jazz Appreciation Society. You'd expect the outfit to be called Flowerbox or Pretty Petals. Or the Floral Appreciation Society.'

Fiona's face reddened. 'This is all nonsense. I asked the retailer to use a different name as I wanted the gifts to be a surprise for you, Debs. Her husband was away having a night out, Mr Colton, and I wanted to cheer her up.'

Deborah whispered to Fiona, 'We'll have a chat about this later.'

Colton frowned. 'I'm sorry, Deborah. I think it's probably best I leave.'

Fiona sneered as she walked towards the sideboard. 'I think that's a bloody good idea.'

He noticed her open a drawer and slip something black and metallic inside her handbag. He couldn't see what it was.

'Don't be harsh on our friend, Fiona,' said Deborah as the journalist edged his way towards the door. 'I'm sure he meant no harm.'

Fiona said quietly, 'I'll see him out.'

Colton stopped by the door and turned round.

'Deborah, I'm sorry this incident happened. Listen, I did actually have a word with our lawyer at the office. He said you can sue the concert hall for negligence. You'd have to prove that security on the night in question wasn't adequate. But he said you'd have a good case.'

* * *

Colton left the room without another word, but, as he stepped along the corridor towards the hallway, he became aware that Fiona Blake was close behind him.

He glanced round as they reached the front door. Then he saw she'd got a small Remington pistol in her hand.

'I'm sorry, Mr Colton. You've placed me in an extremely difficult situation.'

He shrugged. 'I'm sorry you think that. I wasn't going through your emails, if that's what's on your mind.'

'One of my emails was on the bloody screen,' she barked. 'It wasn't on the screen when you first walked in here. You'll do as I say now or I'll have to shoot you.'

He sneered. 'You're being a bit melodramatic.'

'I've got cousins who were in the IRA and they taught me a little about guns, Mr Colton. There's a magazine in this pistol and I know how to use it. Walk out of the front door and make your way over to the annexe,' she ordered. 'And don't do anything stupid.'

It appeared pointless to argue with the woman, who he now realized hailed from Ireland. She'd got a gun. She was angry. She was probably desperate to save her neck. And she might be foolish enough to fire it.

He thought of calling out to Deborah, but he was probably out of her range of hearing and, in any case, Fiona might shoot him if he tried to alert her.

After stepping outside, he turned left and headed towards the red-brick annexe, which was the size of a large bungalow and partly shrouded from the main house by trees. The half-glazed front door was now wide open.

He turned and stared into her eyes. 'What now?'

She glared at him. 'Walk straight ahead along the corridor and go into the last room on the left.'

He peeked inside a spacious living room on his right where an old lady was sitting in an armchair with her back to him watching television. He assumed that room had formerly served as David Barron's main living area.

After passing several other doors, he came to the last room, which had a solid grey metal door. He strolled inside and was disappointed to find it was a dim storeroom with light-green walls. There was little natural light. It could have only measured six by five metres. There were just two small windows close to the ceiling.

As he came to terms with his new surroundings, Fiona reached in and switched on a light which filled the room with an orange glow. She scowled at him.

'Give me your phone,' she demanded.

After he'd handed it over, she pointed to a dining chair in the corner.

'I'm afraid I'm going to have to lock you in while I try and decide what to do.'

'My news editor knows I was coming to see Deborah. If she doesn't hear from me soon, they may send someone up here to look for me. Or they may call the police.'

'We'd have to tell anyone that asks that you left. Oh and don't bother shouting for help. It's only my mother here and she's totally deaf.'

Then she slammed the door and turned the key.

Chapter 44

Nick Colton glanced at his watch. It was twenty past ten on Wednesday morning and he was a prisoner.

He cast his eyes around. Half the room comprised two rows of grey metal shelves filled with dusty accounts ledgers.

The other half was cluttered with an assortment of household articles. He guessed they were David Barron's unwanted possessions: two metal garment racks containing men's clothes; a fifty-five-inch smart television; books about foreign travel and accounting; and, inevitably, Loretta Kay memorabilia.

He was shocked and confused. His mind was swirling with thoughts about his discovery of the disturbing email on Fiona Blake's laptop, her feeble explanations and Deborah's well-meaning attempts to make sense of the whole incident.

To add to his bewilderment, so soon after the death of Deborah's husband, the two women appeared to have embarked on a relationship together. He was reminded of the words he spotted on Deborah's laptop when he first visited her home: *'I'm so glad we met. We seemed to click instantly. So looking forward to seeing you again.'*

Maybe this was part of an email from Fiona relating to her application to become a housekeeper. Maybe Fiona had been intent on wheedling her way into Deborah's affections from the moment she came for her first interview for the position.

But his primary concern now was to escape. His best course of action would be to contact DS Khan. However, he didn't have his phone, so how could he get a message to her?

He sat on the chair and racked his brains. Perhaps one of David's old phones had been dumped in the room. He spent ten minutes rummaging through the dead man's belongings to no avail.

In any case, any phone he came across would need to have a current, working SIM card – and that was unlikely.

He was disturbed by the sound of a female voice. Fiona was speaking on the phone to someone in the nearby corridor. He thought he caught the name 'Mr Boyle'.

He crept to the door. He was desperate to hear what was being said, and managed to catch quite a bit: 'I know you told me not to call you, but this is an emergency … I've had a journalist snooping around looking at my emails… I left him alone for just ten minutes. I couldn't have shut my laptop down properly … There was an email about Miles Davis on the screen when I got back to the laptop … Yes, I think so … Yes, I've got a gun but I really don't want to have to use it. For the moment, I've locked him in the storeroom … You're going to call me back shortly? OK.'

Colton knew he had to think hard. Fiona had been handling her pistol as though she knew how to use it. Perhaps she'd had some target practice in Ireland.

Worried she was planning his execution, he had to find a way of alerting Khan. But how? And then, as he gazed round the room, the idea came to him. He'd try to use the television to send her an email.

He found the TV remote on the floor close by. Then he plugged in the Samsung television and it burst into life. Quickly he reduced the volume to zero – fearing that any noise might alert Fiona to his intentions.

He was delighted to find David Barron must have used the online services at some point during the weeks before he died – because he had no problem finding an internet connection and no Wi-Fi password was needed.

Then he crouched on the red patterned carpet and began the laborious process of writing an email, using the TV remote to input letters on the screen's keyboard. After twenty minutes, he'd written, *'Sounds crazy, but Fiona Blake is holding me prisoner at Orchard House annexe. Found email asking her to pay into a Dublin account on 27 June. No phone. Get me out! Nick Colton.'*

After logging onto his personal email account, he found in his diary a note of DS Khan's email address, which he'd copied from the scrap of paper she'd given him twelve days earlier. Then he entered it in the address line and sent it.

At first, nothing appeared to happen. His heart was pounding as if it would burst from his shirt. Then a message flashed up on the screen, saying, 'Email sent successfully'.

After switching the TV off, he returned to the dining chair and slumped down, relieved to know there was nothing else to do except wait.

To fill in time, he peered across the room at the shelves heaving with ledgers. He got up and pulled one volume out, blowing off the dust as he did so. The accounts related to a shop in Tottenham. Then a fresh thought occurred to him. Perhaps the financial secrets of London's notorious crime family, the Diamonds, might be lurking there – right under his nose.

It took him a while but he eventually realized David Barron's system of stacking the ledgers loosely followed an alphabetical sequence. But, confusingly, some volumes had been removed and randomly put back in the wrong place.

There were dozens of green ledgers relating to 'Diamond Enterprises' but there was nothing recent. The most up-to-date account book he could find was for 2002 and he surmised that they must have done the accounts online since. As he turned the pages of the firm's final paper ledger, he began to learn that the Diamonds' activities amounted to big business. He was astonished by the huge sums of money listed under income and expenditure. They ran up huge bar and hotel bills in Barbados. They hired yachts in Venezuela. Nearer to home, they hired boats in Salcombe, Devon and Poole, Dorset. They rented lock-up garages in Southend, Essex and a farm in Hertfordshire.

The rewards were significant too. As he turned the pages, he found the Diamonds had bought a series of villas in Spain in September 2002 and a two-million-pound yacht in December of that year. Vinny Diamond even had a box at Royal Ascot.

Then, in the distance, he thought he could hear a phone ringing and a woman's voice penetrated the stillness. He hurried to the door and pressed his ear against it. He could detect Fiona's Irish lilt. She was saying, 'I'm not sure I can do it.' There was a brief pause. Then she said, 'I haven't got any more money.'

He had the impression the caller was Mr Boyle again.

After a longer pause, she said, 'If I kill him, I'll have to get rid of the body.' Then he heard her say, 'Yes, we're not far from the countryside. I'll have to hunt in the garden shed for a spade. I suppose I'll just have to kill him … You're right. I must be strong.'

He at once felt as though he was locked in a nightmare with his eyes wide open. He had to sit down because his legs were shaking like those of a new-born calf. Surely the sergeant had received his message? Surely help would come soon?

He checked his watch again. It had turned midday. He thought he heard a noise. It sounded like a door being slammed far away. Then a woman's shouts. There were footsteps in the corridor. They were coming closer. He could hear keys rattling. Was Fiona coming to finish him off?

He could hear his heart beating in the cold tranquillity of the storeroom. The key turned in the lock. Would this be his final moment on earth?

Chapter 45

As the door of the storeroom creaked open, Nick Colton was greeted by the smiling face of a policeman. He couldn't recall being so delighted to see an officer of the law.

'You all right, sir?' he asked. 'We received a message that you'd got yourself trapped.'

'You got it slightly wrong. A mad woman locked me up,' he retorted. 'But I'm a hell of a lot better for seeing you.'

As he followed the constable back along the corridor, he complained that the housekeeper had kept him under key for nearly three hours.

The quiet, unassuming officer glanced over his shoulder at the slightly dishevelled journalist. Colton had got dust both on his shirt from the ledgers and on his trousers after crawling on the carpet.

'Looks like you might need a clean-up, sir,' the officer said in a low voice.

Colton didn't care what he looked like.

'I'm really so grateful to you, officer,' he said.

'Pleased to be of help, sir.'

'Do you work with DS Khan?'

'No, sir. We're from Barnet Police.'

Colton glanced into the living room as they passed. One of the policeman's colleagues was engrossed in a conversation inside with Fiona and her mother. Colton was tempted to burst through the door and harangue Fiona, but thought better of it for the time being.

At the forefront of his mind was a strong desire to escape the building and taste the fresh air of freedom.

As he emerged in the bright sunlight, he remembered Fiona Blake had taken his phone. He tapped the constable on the shoulder. 'Could you get me my mobile? The woman who locked me up took it from me.'

'I'll see what I can do, sir,' he said, stepping back inside the annexe.

Five minutes later, as he was pacing around on the lawn, the officer returned with his handset and passed it to him.

'Thanks. How did we ever manage without them?' the journalist asked. Just then a convoy of police vehicles with sirens blaring and blue lights flashing arrived in the road.

Here and there, curtains were twitching as curious neighbours peered out at the vehicles lined up beside the pavement.

After alerting Deborah via the intercom, the gates opened and DCI Haynes's Audi swept in. As the constable went to rejoin his colleague who was interviewing Fiona, DS Khan jumped out of her boss's car. She'd spotted Colton, who was standing by some rose bushes, and headed straight towards him.

'Are you all right, Nick?' she asked in concern at his shabby appearance.

'Yes. I'm absolutely fine. Thank God you got my email.'

'Well, it came as a bit of a surprise.'

'It was bloody awful, but I'll survive.'

'What happened?'

'I came over here to see Deborah. She wanted to discuss suing the Albert Hall. But there was some kind of mix-up over the time. She wasn't here. So Fiona Blake let me in. Nadia, I've got a feeling Fiona could have something to do with the shooting.'

'You said in your email she'd been asked to pay some money into a Dublin bank account.'

'Yes, that's right. Around the time of the Loretta Kay concert.'

'This is the housekeeper you're talking about? The woman who comes from Dunboyne?'

'I didn't know she was from Dunboyne, but yes – the housekeeper,' he replied.

'How do you know this?'

'I got to see one of her emails. Someone was asking for money to be paid into a Dublin bank account in relation to the evening of the shooting. The message was headed "Night of the concert".'

'Bloody hell, Nick. I wondered what you meant in your email. Have you got a copy?'

'No, but I can remember it exactly.' He recited the details to her, word for word.

'So the sender signed off with "Regards, B". Did you take a note of their email address, Nick?'

'Sorry, Nadia. That's the one thing I haven't got. I only got a sneak look while Fiona was out of the room. She came back and caught me with her laptop.'

'What was her reaction?'

'She went mental. She pulled a gun on me and locked me in the storeroom.'

'You've done a great job, Nick, but it's a shame you don't have a copy of that crucial email.'

'I know. I just didn't have time.'

'What surprises me, Nick, is, if it was so important, why didn't she delete it before anyone else had a chance to see it?'

'I wondered about that. Perhaps she kept it for the bank details.'

'Maybe.'

'I just hope she hasn't deleted it since I saw it,' he said.

'Don't worry. The Met have computer experts who can find things. All right. I'll go and explain all that to the chief inspector. It's highly likely we'll need a search warrant so we can collect the evidence properly.'

'There's one other thing I should mention,' said Colton. 'Deborah and Fiona seem to be involved in some sort of relationship.'

'That's no surprise, Nick. I thought that might be the case. Oh, we'll need a statement from you later on. The DCI's a stickler for doing things by the book.'

* * *

Colton's eyes followed as she walked to the Audi and reported back to her boss. Then he sat down on a wooden bench beneath a cherry tree and witnessed how quickly the chief inspector took charge of proceedings.

First of all, Colton overheard him phoning DC Leigh, who had remained behind in Kensington, and asked him to obtain a search warrant from Westminster magistrates. Then he ordered his sergeant to fetch the housekeeper from the annexe and bring her to the main house for questioning.

Colton wasn't a man to gloat, but he felt an intense sense of satisfaction as Fiona Blake was led from the annexe in handcuffs. She sneered at him as she passed but not a word was spoken.

While sitting in the sun, he called his news desk and described the morning's dramatic events to Clemmie Jones. She said she would immediately brief a team of reporters to start researching the housekeeper's background. She also urged him to send over a full account as soon as possible and then head back to the office.

Colton was stepping towards the gates when he noticed Deborah had opened a front window. She was waving at him.

'Nick, I thought you'd gone. Why the hell did you call the police?'

He wasn't sure what to say. 'Fiona took me into the annexe.'

'I know. She told me.'

'She told you?'

'Yes, she wanted to explain to you what the email was about. She worried that you'd jumped to the wrong conclusions.'

'You know what really happened in the annexe, don't you?'

'No.'

'I've spent the past three hours trapped in the storeroom.'

'Don't be ridiculous. How could that happen? She told me she took you to the annexe for a brief discussion and then watched you leave. Nick, she's very protective of me and didn't want you making any false assumptions.'

He said guardedly, 'I hear what you're saying.'

'I don't know how open-minded you are, Nick.'

'I'm a journalist. I've seen life from all sides.'

'You may have detected that Fiona and I have formed an attachment. It didn't begin until after David's passing. I want to assure you of that. At first she provided a shoulder to cry on. Now it's become a real closeness. It's a feeling I've never really experienced before. I do hope you understand.'

'Of course I do.'

She glanced over her shoulder.

'I'm going to have to go in a minute. The police are with Fiona right now, but they want to interview me as well. Fiona's frantic with worry. She thinks you're confused and believe the email was somehow connected with David's death.

'I've read the email myself and heard her account. It's obvious the email's nothing ominous. It really was connected with the wonderful presents she gave me. I don't know if you remember, Nick, but I think there were flowers and chocolates here when you first visited. Do you remember? It was the day after David's death.'

'Yes, I remember them. There were several vases arranged about your living room and there were some hand-made chocolates on your glass table.'

'That's right. So you're not going to write a story about this, are you, Nick?'

He shrugged on hearing her request and replied with a question of his own.

'Deborah, what if that email isn't about an order for flowers and chocolates? What if it's something else?'

'How do you mean?'

'It looks like a request for payment for a service due to be carried out on the night of the concert. It's couched in a secretive way, using initial letters instead of names, and has a cryptic account name.'

'Nick, I know all that.'

'On top of that, the account's in Dublin and police have found a clear Irish connection to your husband's death. You had a call on your intercom from a man with an Irish accent in May. And the gunman's clothing and pistol were left in a bin by an Irishman who rented a room in Kilburn on the night of the concert.'

'I know all that too. The police have kept me fully informed or I've learnt about it from the papers or TV. But you don't think for a minute that Fiona's involved in David's death in any way, do you? She wanted to buy the best gifts and must have spent something like eighty or ninety pounds on me. It was very sweet of her. The money she spent was absolutely nothing to do with David.'

'You're sure about that?'

'Yes, I've got total faith in her and you should too. I know words were exchanged between the two of you, but she raised her voice through frustration because you didn't seem to believe her. You can't think there's anything suspicious about the email now, can you?'

He began to walk away from the house and then turned back.

'So why did she pull a gun on me and lock me in the storeroom?' he asked.

Deborah became silent. She didn't have an answer for that.

Chapter 46

After Nick Colton had left Orchard House, Deborah Barron decided to confront the chief inspector in the hallway. She was determined to find out exactly why police were there. She interrupted the two detectives, who were questioning the housekeeper in her large Poggenpohl oak kitchen.

'Look, why have you been searching the annexe and why are you interrogating Fiona?' she demanded. 'I think it's time you explained.'

The chief inspector, who was flanked by several male and female constables, stood up and glared at her.

'Mrs Barron, everything will be revealed in due course,' he insisted.

She appeared bewildered.

'I really don't understand. Fiona's done nothing wrong.'

The chief inspector folded his arms.

'I'm afraid I'll be the judge of that. We've received information that might lead us further forward in our investigation into your husband's death. If you'd like to remain in the living room, Mrs Barron, as I suggested, I'll have a chat with you in a moment. First, I need to finish speaking to Miss Blake.'

As Deborah reluctantly returned to the living room, Haynes assigned a female officer to accompany her.

Then he resumed the interview with the housekeeper, who was looking shocked and distressed.

The chief inspector raised an eyebrow and scowled at Fiona as he sat down on a wooden chair beside his sergeant.

'Let's go through this again. We've reason to believe that you were asked to make a payment into a Dublin bank account,' he said. 'It was round about the time of Mr Barron's death, so it's a matter we've got to look into.'

Fiona shook her head. 'This is what happens if you allow yourself to make friends with the press.'

He stared into the housekeeper's cold eyes.

'We understand you've got a laptop. Where is it?' he demanded.

'It's upstairs in our bedroom. I'll just go and get it,' she replied.

'No, thank you. We'll fetch it ourselves.' He assigned his sergeant to climb the stairs and search the main bedroom.

'There are seven bedrooms, sir,' said Khan. 'Do you happen to know which is the main one?'

'Of course, not. Perhaps you'd like to tell us, Miss Blake?'

Fiona was gazing at the floor. She glanced up. 'It's the big room above the living room.'

After fifteen minutes, Khan returned with a pale purple laptop, which she handed to the chief inspector.

He frowned at Fiona. 'Our information leads us to understand that you own a black laptop. Where is it?'

Stony-faced, she replied, 'No. You're mistaken. I've got a mauve laptop, a small black tablet and a smart phone.'

Haynes was becoming impatient. 'All right. You've tested our patience for long enough. Fiona Blake, I'm arresting you in connection with the murder of David Howard Barron on 27 June in Kensington.' He then read out the rest of the police caution.

'This is totally absurd.'

Khan returned to the bedroom to collect Fiona's jacket before the suspect was driven away in a police car.

* * *

The chief inspector found Deborah sitting on the white settee in the living room shortly afterwards. Her sad demeanour reminded him of the day he interviewed her just after the loss of her husband. She was tearful, dabbing her eyes with a tissue like an orphaned child.

She glanced across at him when he stepped into the room.

'Where are you taking Fiona?' she demanded.

'Just need to ask her a few questions down at the police station in Kensington,' he explained. 'If it's all right with you, Mrs Barron, I'm afraid we're going to have to conduct a thorough search of the house.'

Deborah gazed anxiously at him while pouring herself a glass of white wine. 'Have you got a warrant?'

'One of our detective constables has gone to court to get one.'

Deborah glowered.

'You're making a huge mistake, Chief Inspector,' she said. 'When can I go and visit Fiona?'

'I don't know how long we'll be speaking to her.'

'I'd like to arrange a lawyer for her.'

'She has a right to a lawyer, of course,' he said, settling himself down on the brown settee without being invited. 'Mrs Barron, when I first met you, I promised I'd do everything in my power to bring your husband's killer to justice. I still believe we'll achieve that objective. Now I need to ask you something important. Did you yourself see the email that referred to a payment being made into a Dublin account?'

'Yes, she showed it to me. She got me flowers and chocolates around the time of the concert to cheer me up. She says the email was about the payment and delivery.'

The chief inspector leaned back.

'We're going to be examining all of Miss Blake's computers. Do you know any of her passwords?'

'No, I'm sorry. I don't.'

'Or where she kept them?'

'I don't have the faintest idea.'

'I've been wondering, Mrs Barron. Did you ever suspect Miss Blake of wishing to cause harm to your husband?'

'Never. She's been the kindest, most caring person you could imagine.'

The chief inspector frowned. 'How did she seem in the months before the shooting?'

'Just the same as now – helpful, sympathetic and incredibly loyal.'

He stood up. 'Any idea what's happened to her black laptop?'

'No. Probably in the house somewhere.'

Haynes smiled. 'So she has got one?'

'Of course.'

'It's just that, a few minutes ago, she denied having a black one.'

Deborah was struck dumb for a moment.

Haynes continued to speak. 'You've got a very big house, Mrs Barron,' he said. 'It's probably going to take us a good few hours to conduct our search.'

She shrugged. 'Take as long as you like, Chief Inspector. But I'm extremely confident you'll find no evidence that Fiona had anything at all to do with David's death.'

* * *

Two hours later, DC Leigh arrived at Orchard House with the search warrant. Forensic staff, who had been waiting in the street outside, embarked on a thorough inspection of the house and annexe.

The sergeant took her boss aside and told him she recalled seeing some household bins next to the gates.

'I think it's worth a peek, sir,' she suggested. 'Might find the black laptop there.'

'All right. Take one of the forensic team with you,' he replied.

Khan strode down the drive and raised the lid of a black bin containing general waste. Her phone rang while she was rummaging unsuccessfully around among some grocery packaging. She answered with a brisk, 'DS Khan.'

'Nadia, it's Nick Colton. I just wondered if the police have made any progress.'

'Well, we've made an arrest. That's all I can say at this moment.'

'Fiona Blake?'

'Sorry, Nick. The boss is around and things are a little delicate. I'm in the middle of doing something. Sorry.' She then hung up.

Over the next hour, the forensic team continued their search. Phones and computer equipment were seized and loaded into a white van.

Haynes beckoned his sergeant to accompany him into the garden.

'I hope this lead from that interfering journalist isn't going to turn out to be a load of hogwash,' Haynes told her. 'Neither of us has set eyes on this bloody email from Dublin that he told us about.'

Khan shook her head. 'Sir, I'm sure his concern about the email was genuine. In any case, Fiona must have had a reason for holding him up at gunpoint and locking him up. Once we've handed the computers over to the cybercrime department, I'm sure we'll find the email and possibly other incriminating material.'

'Well, where's the bloody laptop he told you about?'

'Blake must have disposed of it,' she replied. 'Anyway we know it's a Yahoo email account and we can access that from any device, sir.'

'That's a good point, but that missing laptop's still bugging me. Points to there being something else on it that's suspicious – some other document perhaps. Get the team to search the garage and the garden shed. I'll have another word with Mrs Barron.'

Chapter 47

Fiona Blake had only been in a police station three times before. Once, as a young girl living with her parents in Dunboyne, County Meath, to report her family's missing dog. Once to show her driving documents after being stopped on a country road for speeding. And once because of a late-night dispute in Dublin with an ex-girlfriend that had led to her being cautioned.

So she remained concerned about what might happen as they drew up outside the custody suite in Kensington just after 4 p.m.

She had to hand over all personal items as she was booked in by a crotchety desk sergeant. Then, after learning Deborah had arranged a solicitor for her, the handcuffs were removed and she was led tearfully into an interview room. She was handed some magazines and warned to expect a long wait.

Nearly an hour passed before she heard a conversation outside and the policewoman on duty opened the door to admit her smartly dressed lawyer.

'Miss Blake? Ben Cooper,' he said, shaking her hand and grinning. 'Deborah Barron asked me to drop by. I gather you're in a spot of trouble.'

She tried to smile. 'It certainly seems that way.'

'I've acted in the past for Mrs Barron and her father. Are you willing for me to represent you?'

'Yes, of course.'

'I've been told the police want to talk to you about the incident at the Royal Albert Hall – the night Mr Barron was shot. Is that right?'

She leaned forward on the table and placed her head in her hands. 'Yes. The police have got it firmly fixed in their heads that I might have had something to do with it. They've taken my phone, laptop and tablet.'

He placed his hand on her shoulder. 'Don't worry. I'm here to help. You've been cautioned, I take it?'

'At the house.'

He peered at her over his glasses. 'Good. Well, it'll be best for you to make no comment until we've learnt the strength of their case. Now, Miss Blake, perhaps you can help me by telling me what happened at Orchard House today. Deborah's told me a little, but I'd like to hear it in your own words.'

* * *

At a quarter to five, DCI Haynes and DS Khan arrived. The sergeant, who was carrying Fiona's mauve laptop, went to the corner to switch on the video equipment before taking a chair opposite Mr Cooper.

Haynes looked unusually solemn as he sat opposite Fiona. 'Right, let me introduce myself for the purposes of the tape. I'm DCI Haynes. This is DS Khan. We're here to conduct an interview with Fiona Blake in the presence of Mr Cooper. Now, I must remind you that you're still under caution.'

Blake's eyes glazed over.

The chief inspector continued, 'We're very interested in the email we discussed earlier. If we pass over the laptop you gave us, do you think you could find it for us? Then you can explain who sent it and what it was all about.'

Blake shook her head. 'I'm sorry. I don't have the password. It's at home. I've just changed it and I can't remember it.'

Haynes tutted. 'What about the pin and password for your account with the Allied Irish Bank?'

'No, sorry. A friend advised me to update all my passwords and now they're long, full of capitals and lower-case letters and impossible to memorise.'

'It'd make life a lot easier for us all if you could just try and remember the ones for your emails and bank account.'

She paused while she gazed down at the light maple desk. Then she stared into his eyes. 'Sorry, I can't remember any of them off hand.'

'Well, that's unfortunate. I'm sorry, Mr Cooper. This means we'll have a slightly longer wait. I'm confident we'll be able to go through the evidence in a short while. It's just that, if your client had been able to provide the passwords right now, it would have speeded things up.'

Mr Cooper looked blank. 'Do we take it that someone's in the process of examining my client's phone and computers?'

Haynes nodded. 'That's right. I'm afraid Miss Blake hasn't been as fully cooperative as we'd have liked.'

'How do you mean, Chief Inspector?'

'We received a phone call this morning from someone who'd visited Orchard House.'

'Nick Colton, the journalist,' mumbled Blake.

'We're not divulging the person's name. He shouldn't really have been prying into Miss Blake's emails, but the fact is that he did and, in time, we might be grateful for that. He's told us the laptop was black. We've carried out an exhaustive search of the house and annexe but can't trace it. Can you help us with that, Miss Blake?'

She glanced at the chief inspector and then averted her gaze. 'I don't know what you're talking about. I don't have a black laptop. That's what happens if you put your faith in journalists. The facts come out wrong.'

He shook his head. 'On this occasion, I trust his powers of observation, not least because what he said has been supported by your employer. Now let's talk about the email he found, which was headed "Night of the concert". In this email, you were asked to pay some money into a Dublin bank with the account name "Miles Davis Jazz Appreciation Society."'

Blake scowled. 'There's a simple explanation which I've already given. I was paying for gifts.'

Khan peered across the table. 'Seems unlikely.'

'It's the truth. There's nothing suspicious about it at all.'

At that moment, there was a knock on the door. The sergeant scurried across the room. A uniformed officer handed her a folder of papers and whispered in her ear. Then the sergeant brought the papers back to the table and exchanged glances with the chief inspector.

'Could we take a break?' Haynes suggested. 'We've just received some fresh information.'

* * *

Leaving Fiona Blake with her solicitor, DCI Haynes led his sergeant along the corridor until they reached the stairs, where he stopped. She handed him the folder.

'I need a few minutes to read through these,' he told her.

She took a few steps down the stairs.

'Sir, the team working in the annexe have found the black laptop. It was hidden under some floorboards – directly beneath the armchair where Blake's mother was sitting.'

'Oh that's great work. What a wonderful team of people we've got working for us, Sergeant. Where are you off to now?'

'I've just received a message from reception. I'm needed downstairs.'

The chief inspector nodded. 'See you in a minute, Sergeant. I'll be in my office.'

* * *

Luke Foster was sitting in the station reception area when DS Khan came down the stairs. He got up and stepped towards her.

'This is the young man who wanted a word with you,' the constable behind reception explained.

Foster grinned and shook her hand. 'I'm Luke from *The Post*. Just wondered if there was any update?'

She gestured towards the entrance door. 'Shall we go outside?'

He followed her until they were standing next to the station's bicycle stand, beneath the station's blue light.

'You're working with Nick, are you? So all I can tell you is one person's assisting with inquiries.'

'Is it Fiona Blake?'

'I can't tell you any more at this stage. You'll have to get onto Press Bureau.'

Foster grinned. 'They haven't even told us someone's assisting. Is it a woman? A neighbour in Pine Tree

Avenue's told us a woman was in the back of one of the police cars that left Orchard House earlier.'

'I can confirm we're speaking to a woman.' The sergeant sighed. 'It *is* Fiona Blake, but you didn't get that from me.' Then she re-entered the building and headed straight for her chief inspector's office.

'I'd better show you this,' said Haynes as she knocked and walked in. She studied the document he handed to her. It was an itemised bill for the landline phone at Orchard House, which one of the detectives had obtained from British Telecom.

'What am I meant to be looking at?' she asked.

'The Dublin call, of course. Twenty-five minutes on 11 June. Made from Orchard House. Mrs Barron and Fiona Blake both deny making the call.'

Khan sat down on the edge of a chair, still studying the statement. 'The only other possibility is that David Barron made the call,' she said.

Haynes scowled. 'Don't be stupid, Sergeant. It must have been made by Miss Blake. It was the exact time she was organising the hit. It's one more point we'll have to ask her about, along with her banking history.'

* * *

At ten minutes past five, the two detectives returned to the interview room and took their seats. Khan was carrying a black laptop, which she placed on the table with a flourish. Blake flinched before regaining her composure.

The chief inspector, who was clutching a sheaf of documents, gazed across the table.

'I was disappointed by your failure to engage with us over your email passwords, Miss Blake, but all's not lost. We found a list of several passwords in one of the bedrooms at Orchard House.'

The suspect appeared crestfallen as he drew open the folder and picked out the top document.

He then proudly raised it in the air.

'For the tape, I'm holding a list of Miss Blake's passwords. Our sharp-eyed young detective, DC Leigh, found it in a bedroom. It was glued to the underside of the top drawer of a desk you've been using. A very neat hiding place, I must say. And, thanks to this list, we've been able to gain access to your Yahoo emails and bank account.'

Mr Cooper frowned as he looked the chief inspector in the eye. 'I gather you served a warrant upon Mrs Barron.'

'Yes, we've complied with all the evidence rules. To the letter,' the chief inspector replied while perusing papers in his folder. He handed copies of a document to both the suspect and Mr Cooper.

'The first document shows the Orchard House landline phone bill with an item marked with an asterisk. It's a phone call to Dublin on 11 June. You made that call, didn't you, Miss Blake?'

She shook her head. 'No, definitely not.'

'How do you know?'

'I was shopping at Brent Cross shopping centre, so I was more than five miles away.'

The chief inspector glared. 'All right. We'll leave that for the moment. Now, here are copies of the email that's at the heart of the evidence, together with a printout of Miss Blake's June bank statement.'

He pushed the documents across the table.

'You'll see the items on the bank statement that have caught our attention. Three payments to the Miles Davis Jazz Appreciation Society. Altogether they totalled thirty thousand pounds.'

Khan stared across at Blake, who was trembling. Her face displayed signs of shock and despair. She slumped forward with her head in her hands.

'Rather a lot of money to pay for a bouquet of flowers and a box of chocolates,' the sergeant said.

Chapter 48

Above the clatter of fingers striking keyboards and the buzz of conversation, Katie McMillen could hear a voice bellowing across the newsroom. Clemmie Jones was calling for her.

Collecting her notebook and pen, the blonde-haired reporter strode across to the news desk. Jones was rushing to attend an editorial conference.

'Katie, a woman's been arrested over the Barron murder, and we've just had it confirmed she's called Fiona Blake. We hope to go to press tonight with a big story, provided she's not charged in the meantime,' said Jones.

McMillen's eyes lit up. 'Isn't that the Barrons' housekeeper? Nick was telling me something about that half an hour ago.'

'That's right. Nick's in with the editor at the moment. Katie, this woman's twenty-six and comes from a small town near Dublin called Dunboyne. We need to know all about her – parents, brothers and sisters, school friends, boyfriends. All that sort of thing. This could be tomorrow's splash. Also have a word with pictures. We desperately need a snap of her.'

McMillen began to walk away but Jones called her back.

'Katie, can you also check with the cops every hour to make sure this Blake woman isn't charged? Because, if she's charged tonight, we'll be very limited on what we can say.'

McMillen agreed before heading to the nearby picture desk and attempting to speak to the picture editor. But he was on the phone with two calls waiting and brushed her away.

So she returned to her desk and searched in vain for any online information about the housekeeper. She then searched for details of all local newspapers serving Dunboyne and began phoning the editorial department of each one in turn. She acted discreetly, saying she wanted information about a woman named Fiona Blake who had recently come to work in London. She omitted to mention the Barron case for fear they would publish a story about the arrest themselves.

After his meeting with the editor, Colton appeared back in the newsroom ready to re-write his story about Fiona Blake's arrest.

Katie smiled at him. 'I've been asked to find a snap of this woman and do some background.'

He smiled back. 'Half the office must be working on this story. Luke's outside Kensington nick, keeping up with events down there.'

McMillen continued to spend nearly an hour phoning the news editors or chief reporters of the local newspapers in Blake's hometown. Eventually she struck lucky. The chief reporter of one of the weekly papers searched their news archive and found two reports about a woman called Fiona Blake, who appeared to be around the same age as the housekeeper in question.

'This is from five years ago,' he said.

> *Woman charged with assault in Dunboyne. A twenty-one-year-old woman appeared at Trim District Court today charged with assault. Fiona Blake, who gave an address in Station Road, Dunboyne, was charged with striking a woman on the head with a bottle of wine.*
>
> *Judge Patrick O'Farrell remanded the accused on one hundred euros bail to Trim District Court on 10 December. The judge directed that the accused have no contact with the alleged victim, and that she sign in with police between 9 a.m. and 9 p.m. on Monday, Wednesday and Friday at Dunboyne Garda Station and that she be contactable by phone.*

'Then there's a note that the case was discontinued and the young lady was given a caution by the Gardaí. That probably means the victim withdrew their statement.'

McMillen took a careful note of the details. 'You mentioned a second report?'

'Yes. Evidently, Fiona Blake was a volunteer at an animal rescue centre in County Meath when she was eighteen. They were appealing for financial help and we used a picture of her. She's quite a lovely girl with short, brown hair. She's got tattoos on her arms and she's holding a Jack Russell terrier.'

McMillen was delighted.

'Could you email the picture over? I'll make sure you get paid well,' she said.

'That would be no problem at all.'

Colton, meanwhile, had sent his main story to Clemmie Jones. He was now in the middle of writing a second report, outlining how he discovered the crucial email.

His desk phone rang. The caller had an Irish accent and he remembered that the news desk had commissioned a freelance journalist from Dublin to search for Blake's relatives in an exclusive arrangement for *The Post*.

'Nick, it's Eamon Kelly,' the caller said. 'How are you doing, mate? I've found Blake's brother.'

'That's cool, mate. Well done.'

'Well, it wasn't so good to start with. He slammed his front door in my face.'

'Expect you're used to that,' said Colton with a smile. 'We're all used to that in our game. Then you speak to the neighbours who gabble away and tell you nothing of any value. There's an unwritten rule: the knowers don't talk and the talkers don't know.'

'I know that one well enough,' Kelly admitted. 'But listen, I went back an hour later and I finally got him to agree to talk.'

'Excellent.'

'He's still living in a flat a short distance from the old family home where the girl was brought up. The father's dead and the mother's now living in London.'

'That's right. She's in Totteridge, being cared for by Blake. Have you got the parents' names?'

'Ronan and Siobhan. He was fifty-three when he died five years ago and she's sixty-two. I thought I'd better have a word with you before I filed anything.'

'That's good of you, mate.'

'Nick, the brother eventually opened up to me. He was devastated when I told him Blake was being questioned about a murder in London. He claimed she'd never been in trouble with the law. He thought she'd found her feet when she secured her job with the Barrons a few months ago.'

'So you got some nice quotes then?'

'Yeah. Nick, I tried for pick-up pictures but he wasn't having any of it. He wanted to hold onto them and, when I persisted, he slammed the door on me.'

'Never mind. Sounds like you did your best.'

'That's only part of it, Nick. There was something in the back of my mind about the father. When I got home, I went through my files and, sure enough, I was right. He was a well-known character who was murdered in 2014 amid accusations he was a police informer. He was found in a gutter in Dublin, shot in the head. They never caught anyone for it.'

* * *

An hour later, Colton was on the point of leaving the office when he decided to call home. Greta answered after just three rings.

'Nick, how did your meeting with Deborah Barron go?'

He lowered his voice. 'It was more dramatic than expected, Greta. It looks as though her housekeeper arranged David's murder.'

'Is that the young woman you told me about?'

'Exactly. Anyway the woman's been arrested and the editor's talking about running the story on the front tomorrow. So it looks as though, four weeks after David was murdered, the culprit's finally been unmasked.'

'So it's down to you, Nick?'

'I played a small role. But it's not all cut and dried. The woman hasn't been charged with anything yet and the whole case against her could fall apart.'

Greta broke off to settle an argument between the children, who'd just returned from school. Then they resumed their conversation.

'Nick, what did that woman hope to gain by the murder of David?'

'I've no idea, except that she and Deborah are now involved in a lesbian relationship.'

'The two women are in love? Maybe she wanted David out of the way so she and Deborah can live together in happiness. I thought I read in your newspaper that the Barrons were trying to patch up their marriage. Perhaps Blake was thinking David would spoil her plans.'

He scratched his head. 'I hadn't thought of that. What you're saying has got a certain ring of truth about it. But I should point out that Deborah doesn't seem to have been involved in any way at all in arranging the murder.'

Greta paused for a moment. Then she said, 'Nick, I'm so sorry for Mrs Barron. First she loses her husband. Now she stands to lose her lover.'

Chapter 49

Most of the early evening drinkers had wandered off into the night as Nick Colton entered the bar of the Little Drummer Boy the following night. Three female office workers, slurring their words and giggling, were huddled round a bottle of wine at a corner table.

A group of middle-aged men were exchanging light-hearted banter about football managers while standing at the bar. Some customers were peering at a television screen on the far wall which was tuned to the BBC News channel.

After buying a pint of cold lager, he sat down at a table beneath the portrait of the blond-haired army drummer and gazed around. On the next table, lying almost forgotten among crisp packets and empty glasses, was that day's edition of *The Post*. As he reached across to take it, he felt a hand on his back.

'Nick, you haven't been waiting long, have you?' asked a smiling DS Khan. 'It's only just gone half past eight.'

'I've only been here a few minutes,' he replied, standing and shaking her hand. 'Thanks very much for agreeing to see me at short notice. What can I get you?'

'I'll just have a small white wine as I'm driving.'

A few minutes later, he presented her with her glass and sat down. She took a gulp. 'Thanks. I needed that.'

He sipped his lager. 'Hasn't the weather been tremendous? Did you know it was the hottest day of the year today? It reached nearly thirty-nine Celsius in Cambridge.'

She smiled. 'Really? Listen, I've just been reading your story, Nick. How on earth did you find the picture of Blake holding the puppy?'

'We just did a trawl of the local newspapers in her hometown.'

'She was a pretty girl with a nice smile,' said Khan. 'Her hair was very short, even those days.'

She pointed to the front page of the paper he'd just picked up. It bore the banner headline 'Housekeeper held in hall murder probe.' A brief, down-page report revealed 'How *The Post* helped police.'

'So on this story, Nick, I have to say you've done a good job,' she said. 'We saw the details about her father's death and we're interested in that. The DCI hadn't picked up on it and we're talking to the Gardaí about it.

'Luckily, you haven't imperilled the ongoing investigation with your story. The chief inspector and I are determined to complete things and bring Fiona Blake to trial. We didn't want anything to prejudice that and you haven't done.'

'I'm at one with you on that. I want justice for David Barron. So Blake's been charged now?'

'Yes, soliciting to murder. She's appearing tomorrow at Westminster Court. This is strictly off the record, Nick, but she's talking about pleading guilty. It changed everything when we revealed we'd seen her bank statement and the three payments totalling thirty thousand pounds.'

He drew a quick breath. 'Thirty grand? That's a lot of money. How could she have afforded that?'

'I can't discuss everything, obviously. We don't want to release details that could help her defence. I haven't told the chief inspector that I'm seeing you. As you know, he's no fan of the press.'

'Except when he wants our help,' he said, sipping his lager.

She nodded and, for a moment, he detected a faint sign of embarrassment in her facial expression.

'Nick, Blake had power of attorney for her mother after the house sale. I won't say any more about that, but you can probably work it out for yourself that she was hoping to marry Deborah. By the way, we think we know who the hitman is – a guy called Brendan Maguire. He fits the description you gave us, although we haven't tracked him down yet. Nor the elusive Mr Boyle who booked the room.'

Colton shrugged his shoulders.

'Any idea how she went about finding Maguire?' he asked.

She sipped her wine. 'So we think she made contact with him through a friend of Maguire's cousin. But a close inspection of her deleted internet history by our cybercrime department showed she'd been researching contract killings for some weeks. The only time we doubted ourselves was when we asked about a landline call to Dublin made from Orchard House. Her mobile phone signal showed she'd been at Brent Cross at the time. But then we realized she'd cunningly got someone to take her phone there to lead us off the scent.'

He beamed. 'That's ingenious – using your phone signal to support an alibi. But why do you think Blake wanted to have David killed in the first place?'

The sergeant took a sip from her drink before continuing.

'Blake had fallen in love with her employer. But was devastated when Deborah happened to tell her she was thinking of rekindling her marriage and inviting David to move back to the main house. It was a fatal admission because, from that point, Blake began devising her evil plan.'

He said nothing for a moment and gazed across the room as he digested her words. He was wondering how a woman of just twenty-six could steal the life of a kind human being in the interests of her own selfish love.

Then he turned to Khan. 'Do you know, Nadia, there's one thing that's really been puzzling me for a while. How did the gunman know where David was sitting at the concert?'

'That's simple to explain. Blake overheard David booking his ticket and remembered him saying out loud that his ticket was for seat J50. We think it was at that moment that she saw an opportunity for him to be shot there. So, after Maguire set his price, she sent him photographs and a video of David. She gave him a full description and stressed that, from behind, he should keep an eye open for David's ponytail.'

'A ruthless woman.'

'Definitely.'

He thought for a moment.

'But he didn't sit in the seat he booked, did he?' said Colton.

'No, but he wasn't too far away and the description was so accurate, the killer had no problem finding his intended target.'

Colton emptied his glass.

'Do you want another one, Nadia?'

'Just a small orange juice this time, please.'

He bought the drinks and returned to the table.

'Nadia,' he said. 'There's something else I've been wondering about. Deborah Barron knew the gunman was wearing black boots with red laces, but that fact wasn't released to the public. So how on earth did she know that?'

'I believe I must have mentioned that to her in passing.'

He smiled. 'That explains it then.'

'At one stage, Deborah was a suspect but we began switching our attention to Blake when aspects of her earlier statement didn't ring true.'

He was surprised by those words, but made no comment. 'One more thing. What can you tell me about this fellow Maguire?' he asked.

'Not a lot. He's not been caught, so I can't say much for operational reasons. The Gardaí are on the case. We've had another word with the owner of the Porsche, and he's now confirmed the Miles Davis CD found in the glovebox isn't his – so it could have been left behind by Maguire.'

'I vaguely remember seeing a jazz CD at Orchard House the day after the murder,' said Colton.

She nodded. 'Maybe Blake and the hitman had a shared love of jazz. We'll definitely catch him, eventually. It's just a matter of time.'

Chapter 50

County Louth, three months later

'You know this is the second time I've been called out on this, don't you?' said Pat O'Sullivan as the Ford Transit van sped along the main road out of Drogheda. 'It's old Ronan O'Reilly's place. He's been dead for fifteen years.'

'Doesn't matter,' said the driver, Sergeant Bronagh Doyle. 'We've still got to check the place over.'

'This is all to do with Dan Kelly, isn't it?'

Doyle nodded. 'Yes.'

'Tell me again,' said O'Sullivan. 'The superintendent wants us to go back because of some copper's theory over in London?'

'That's right,' said Doyle. 'You remember Kelly's been on the run for that double shooting in Dublin six years ago? This English DCI reckons he could also be behind the murder of a guy called David Barron, who was gunned down at the Royal Albert Hall.'

'I remember reading about it,' said O'Sullivan. 'But we've spent years looking for Kelly. If you ask me, this is just another waste of time.'

After they had followed country roads north of Drogheda for a few miles, Doyle turned left into a narrow lane. They continued for ten minutes past small, detached houses, smallholdings and ramshackle farm buildings until they finally came to a sign saying 'Blackbridge.'

Doyle turned through the farm gate and drew the vehicle to a halt outside a small derelict farmhouse. The sergeant got out and stretched his legs. Then he strolled over to inspect the boarded-up windows.

His companion strode across the dusty yard to join him.

'What time did that British girl say she'd meet us?' O'Sullivan asked.

Doyle glanced at his watch. 'Round about now,' he said.

He found the interruption a distraction. He was examining a square board that had been nailed across the farmhouse door.

As he peered closely at the timber, a dark-blue Renault Megane estate glided down the hill, swept past the hedgerows and turned into the gateway.

DS Nadia Khan parked beside the white van and jumped out, eager to meet her counterparts from the Garda National Surveillance Unit for the first time.

'Sergeant Doyle?' she asked as the stocky sergeant broke off from his observations and stepped towards her.

'Yes,' he said with a smile. He shook her hand.

'DS Khan,' she said.

'My colleague, Garda O'Sullivan,' he explained. 'How's it going?'

'Not too well, Sergeant,' she admitted. 'I've been called back to London. I've been over here for a month and haven't made any progress at all. The guy seems to have gone to ground. I've spent the past week checking out old addresses in Dublin and got nowhere.'

'Well, I think you might be interested in this,' said Doyle, beckoning her over to the farmhouse door. 'As you can see, some pieces of wood covering have been removed from the lower part of the door – including a piece that covered the letter-box. What's more, there's two loose bricks at the side, look.'

Doyle lay down flat on the ground. After slowly easing the bricks away, he was able to reach round with his arm to the base of the door internally and collect some mail that had been posted through the flap.

He stood up, smiling in triumph as he brandished the two letters in his right hand.

'Here you are, Sarge,' he said, brushing dust off his trousers. 'All part of the service.'

She stared at the two letters as she grasped them. One was addressed to Dan Kelly and bore a Dublin postmark. The other was intended for Brendan Maguire and postmarked County Wexford. They were both addressed to The Old Farmhouse, Blackbridge, County Louth.

'This is encouraging, Sergeant,' said Khan, folding both letters in two and stuffing them into her trouser pocket. 'You've done well. The guy must still be around here somewhere.'

'To be sure,' he said, crouching down to replace the bricks.

Khan stroked her chin. 'I think it's time to take a look around,' she said.

She strolled round the building, eyeing the blocked windows as she passed. Every now and then, she would tap the wood to ensure it was secure. Then, when she had finished, she glanced around at the entire site.

The farm was situated at the foot of a wooded hill. There were open fields on each side of the farmhouse, but no other farm buildings. They appeared to have been razed from the ground years before.

Behind the farmhouse, a quarter of a mile away, was a wood consisting mainly of ash, birch and hazel trees.

The two Gardaí officers joined her.

'You two must know this area so much better than me,' she said. 'Can you tell me something? Is that some kind of shelter or bird-watching hide over there?'

She pointed towards a timber structure in the centre of the wood. It blended in so well with its surroundings that a less keen eye might have struggled to see it.

Doyle and O'Sullivan shielded their eyes from the sun as they peered out towards the woods in the direction in which she was looking.

'Some kind of cabin, Sergeant,' said Doyle. 'I think we need to take a closer look.'

They locked both vehicles and set off across the leaf-strewn field. Doyle led the way, warning Khan from time to time of any marshy or uneven ground.

Eventually, the detectives found themselves at the beginning of the wood and realized they were a short distance from a small bungalow, partly concealed by trees and bushes. A lazy feather of smoke was drifting from a chimney perched on the edge of the pitched roof.

As they stepped closer, mournful jazz notes floated over the morning air.

Khan glanced into the faces of her colleagues.

'Have either of you got a gun?' she whispered.

'I have,' replied Doyle, tapping a pocket inside his jacket.

'Good. We might need it,' she said. 'All I've got is my taser, which I've only used before in training.'

'We're not going to wait for armed back-up then?' asked O'Sullivan.

The two sergeants glanced at each other. They made no reply. The Garda guessed neither of them was in any mood for waiting.

'I think it's time to interrupt the concert,' said Khan, advancing into a morass of bracken, bushes, branches and brambles.

The building, which had two high windows facing towards the farmhouse, was entirely made of wood and painted dark green. A front door stood on the left-hand side.

Khan allowed her fingers to trace the outline of the taser device on her hip as a boost for her confidence. Then she rapped on the door.

There was no reply. The distinctive jazz track featuring Miles Davis on trumpet continued without interruption.

Khan glanced into the anxious faces of her colleagues before turning the handle. The door creaked open.

She found herself in a quaint room with a bed in the centre and a roaring log burner at the far end. To the left was a kitchenette, shower room and toilet. Music was blaring from a hi-fi which stood on a box at the foot of the bed. A black and white cat was curled up on a rug beside the fire.

As the three officers stepped further into the cabin, they were suddenly aware of a presence behind them by the door.

Before they could react, a tall man in dark clothing clutching an AK47-style machine gun darted out of the building and fled.

'After him!' shouted Khan, dashing through the door and searching desperately beneath the trees to see which way he had gone.

Within seconds, her eyes picked out the dark figure, who had a short, dark goatee beard and short, black hair.

The three of them pursued the man for several minutes through the trees until she felt certain they were gaining on him. She could make out his head, bobbing up and down as he raced along a woodland path and, occasionally, vaulted over branches.

Then, as they hurried behind, their hopes of a positive result quickly faded and were replaced by short-term fear. A hail of bullets was dislodged in their direction.

All three pursuers ducked to the ground as their quarry continued to release his succession of bullets. Then the shooting stopped, and the man took to his heels again.

Finally, when the suspect had nearly reached the far edge of the wood, Khan observed him tripping on a tree branch and toppling hard onto the ground. His weapon flew out of his hands and landed on a pile of leaves.

As the three detectives rushed to the scene, Doyle was ready to jump onto the man's back and handcuff him. But the suspect was by now writhing on the ground in agony. His ankle was broken or sprained. He would not be sprinting off again for a while, Khan told herself.

She stooped to pick up the rifle.

'Dan Kelly, also known as Brendan Maguire,' Sergeant Doyle announced, 'I'm arresting you in connection with an armed incident in Ronanstown six years ago. You're also required for questioning by the Metropolitan Police regarding the murder of David Howard Barron on 27 June in Kensington, West London.'

He read out the rest of a police caution before asking if he wished to make any reply. The suspect glanced up with an anguished expression.

'Can someone look after my cat?' he asked.

* * *

A few days later, DS Khan was climbing the stairs at Kensington Police Station when she heard the sound of heavy footsteps behind her.

When she reached the third-floor landing, she paused and waited. Sure enough, the crumpled suit of her boss, DCI Haynes, emerged round the corner of the stairs.

'You did an excellent job over in Ireland, Sergeant,' he said.

He paused to catch his breath before he began negotiating the final steps.

'That guy could have been hiding anywhere and you find him living like a hermit in the wood,' he said. 'Remarkable!'

She laughed.

'Yes, sir. It was as much of a surprise to me as to anyone. It was a relief to find him after all the wasted time I spent knocking on doors in Dublin.'

Haynes leaned against the wall while he stared across the landing towards her.

'We've started the extradition process,' he said. 'All being well, Kelly should be handed over to us by the New Year.'

'How did Blake get on before the bench this morning?' he continued. 'Was it a straight up and down, Sergeant?'

'Yes, sir. But you should have seen her face when it was disclosed an arrest had been made over there. It was quite a picture.'

THE END

If you enjoyed this book, please let others know by leaving a quick review on Amazon. Also, if you spot anything untoward in the paperback, get in touch. We strive for the best quality and appreciate reader feedback.

editor@thebookfolks.com

www.thebookfolks.com

Also by Tony Bassett

The Detectives Roy and Roscoe crime fiction series

MURDER ON OXFORD LANE (Book 1)

A budding chorister doesn't return home from practice but his wife doesn't appear concerned. DS Sunita Roy becomes convinced he has been murdered but she has her own problems in the form of an ex-boyfriend who won't take no for an answer. Will she keep her eye on the ball when all expect her to fail?

THE CROSSBOW STALKER (Book 2)

When a serial killer armed with a crossbow terrorises the West Midlands, Chief Inspector Gavin Roscoe suspects a motive of jealousy and revenge. But as the number of victims increases, the connection initially established between them wears thin. DS Sunita Roy has a different theory and resolves to pursue her own instincts, come what may.

MURDER OF A DOCTOR (Book 3)

Police search for the identities of people seen near the scene of a doctor's murder. And it seems like an open and shut case when a father with a grievance against him can be placed nearby. But Detective Sergeant Sunita Roy wants to dig deeper, and with an internal affairs investigation ongoing, she'll have to tread carefully.

OUT FOR REVENGE (Book 4)

A dangerous prisoner is killed shortly after his release when the Heart of England police mount an undercover operation to investigate corrupt cops who were in cahoots with him. Who wanted the drug lord dead? And whose fury will detectives face when they expose the truth behind the murder?

All FREE with Kindle Unlimited and available in paperback!

Other titles of interest

THE NAME ON THE BULLET
by John Dean

When a cop taking part in a reality TV show is shot dead, it makes the police look pretty bad. DCI John Blizzard, no media darling himself, sets to finding the killer. This leads him to lock horns with a renowned gangster who acts like he is above the law. Yet as Blizzard tries to balance the scales of justice, he is thrown a curve ball.

FREE with Kindle Unlimited and available in paperback!

MURDER ON A YORKSHIRE MOOR
by Ric Brady

Ex-detective Henry Ward is settling awkwardly into retirement in a quiet corner of Yorkshire when during a walk on the moor he stumbles upon the body of a young man. Suspecting foul play and somewhat relishing the return to a bit of detective work, he resolves to find out who killed him. But will the local force appreciate him sticking his nose in?

FREE with Kindle Unlimited and available in paperback!

Printed in Great Britain
by Amazon

21596114R00161